A PLUME BOOK

DEEP WINTER

SAMUEL W. GAILEY was rais _____ nnsylva-
nia, which serves as the set _____ r. Before
writing novels, he was an _____ ing and
developing shows for Show _____ es in Los
Angeles with his daughter and his wife, author Ayn Carrillo-Gailey.

To read more about *Deep Winter* and the author's work in progress,
visit his Facebook page or www.samuelwgailey.com

Praise for *Deep Winter*

"Enthralling and suspenseful, like a Michael Connelly novel, but more
elegantly written." —*Esquire*

"Set in rural Pennsylvania, Samuel W. Gailey's *Deep Winter* is a beautiful and brutal debut. Put Steinbeck's *Of Mice and Men* in a blender with
Scott Smith's classic crime novel *A Simple Plan*, then watch as Gailey
hits the switch and everything in this world spins dangerously out of
hand. A wonderful fast-paced read."
—Urban Waite, author of *The Terror of Living*
and *The Carrion Birds*

"This is a harsh, brutal novel, as bleak as its wintertime setting. It's
also so brilliantly done, so artfully underwritten with not a word
wasted, that readers may hate themselves for letting this grim narra-
tive trap them in its coils." —*Booklist*

"A dark, gripping debut novel of literary suspense." —*The Big Thrill*

"*Deep Winter* is a fast-paced thriller tense enough to give you paper cuts from turning the pages so quickly."

—Joe R. Lansdale, author of *The Thicket*

"Gailey writes visually, rendering the characters and action both vivid and alive."

—*Kirkus Reviews*

"The portrait of a distinctive character (think Lennie in *Of Mice and Men*) and of a town hiding nasty secrets."

—*Library Journal*

"A moving picture of a man . . . who becomes a moral compass."

—*Publishers Weekly*

"A quietly told, emotionally wrenching tale of the wickedness a single man can perpetrate with his unchecked actions, and the pain that follows when others set out to put things right . . . This story will engross you, pulling you deeper into its tiny, raw world, filling your heart with alternating pangs of fear and hope."

—BookTrib.com

"Set deep in the heart of rural Pennsylvania, *Deep Winter* hits you with the toxic blast of Frank Bill, combined with the raw emotional intensity of Daniel Woodrell."

—*Raven Crime Reads*

"Gailey's writing is both atmospheric and bone chilling as he tosses the readers knee-deep into the macabre world of Wyalusing and the lies that are entrenched in the town. . . . Gailey's debut novel is the perfect mix of rich, lyrical prose and suspense."

—*Absolute* magazine (UK)

DEEP WINTER

A Novel

SAMUEL W. GAILEY

A PLUME BOOK

PLUME
Published by the Penguin Group
Penguin Group (USA) LLC
375 Hudson Street
New York, New York 10014

USA · Canada · UK · Ireland · Australia
New Zealand · India · South Africa · China
penguin.com
A Penguin Random House Company

First published in the United States of America by Blue Rider Press,
a member of Penguin Group (USA) LLC, 2014
First Plume Printing 2015

P REGISTERED TRADEMARK—MARCA REGISTRADA
THE LIBRARY OF CONGRESS HAS CATALOGED THE BLUE RIDER PRESS
EDITION AS FOLLOWS:

Gailey, Samuel W.
Deep Winter : a novel / Samuel W. Gailey.
p.   cm.
ISBN 978-0-399-16596-2 (hc.)
ISBN 978-0-14-218178-2 (pbk.)
1. Murder—Investigation—Pennsylvania—Fiction.   2. Suspense fiction.
3. Noir fiction.   I. Title.
PS3607.A3594D44   2014   2013036456
813'.6—dc23

Printed in the United States of America
1   3   5   7   9   10   8   6   4   2

ORIGINAL HARDCOVER DESIGN BY AMANDA DEWEY

For Ayn

DEEP
WINTER

1984

Danny had seen Mindy naked once before when they were just eight years old. A long time ago. Just the two of them, back in the cornfield behind Pickett's Bowling Alley. Mindy had stripped off all her clothes and stood shivering in the cold winter night waiting for Danny to do the same. Danny looked at her naked body for a quick, awkward moment, his eyes glimpsing all the places that her cuffed denim pants and flannel cotton shirts usually hid. She had smooth, soft skin dotted with a few bruises and scratches on her knees and shins. He felt curious for sure, but it didn't seem right looking at a girl when she was all naked. It made him feel funny. His stomach grew tight and ached like when he ate too much saltwater taffy. When Mindy told him that it was his turn to get naked, Danny's head felt even fuzzier than it usually did. He knew it was a bad idea. He would get in trouble for sure. If Uncle Brett found out, he would pull out his belt and put a good licking on Danny's backside.

Danny didn't want that to happen, didn't want another beating, so he took off running as fast as he could, through the dead stalks of corn, feet slipping on patches of ice, face and neck getting all scratched up by dried husks, but he didn't go far before he ran into more trouble. Mike Sokowski and Carl Robinson stopped him before he made it back to the bowling alley and beat him up pretty bad. Sokowski was the mean one. Even back then.

This was the second time he had seen Mindy naked. Her body sprawled out on the trailer floor next to Danny like a discarded rag doll. He knelt beside her with his hands folded and clenched together in his lap, like he was praying at his bedside. Blood soaked into the faded carpet from an open wound on the back of her head, and a few pieces of jagged glass were still stuck in her scalp. Mindy's legs were all twisted up unnaturally under her—arms folded over the top of her head as if in midstretch. Danny wanted to brush the blond, knotted hair that partially covered her eyes—still cracked open a half inch—but he was afraid to look at them. Afraid that they might be different from normal. Different from her usual wide-eyed, happy way.

He glanced over her thin, still frame—her legs, her stomach, her arms—but avoided those eyes. Mindy's mouth hung open as if stuck in the middle of a yawn. Both of her pretty white front teeth were chipped in half, making her look like she had vampire fangs.

Danny rocked back and forth, tears and snot running down over his lips, dripping from his chin like water from a slow-leaking faucet. He waited for her to wake up. Waited for her to move even a little bit. Maybe she was just hurt real bad. But Danny knew that she was probably more than hurt. He had never seen a dead person before—except on TV, but he knew that stuff on the television was only make-believe. Both his parents were dead, but he never got to see his folks before they went up to heaven. Never got the chance to say good-bye to them.

"You're gonna be okay, Mindy. All right? You're gonna be okay."

Danny clutched a small, hand-carved wooden robin figurine in his large left hand. His hands were bigger than most—football-player size. But Danny didn't play football or any other games that involved a ball, because he wasn't any good at stuff like that.

You're too goddamn slow and too goddamn clumsy, Uncle Brett always said.

Danny's long fingers wrapped tightly around the wooden bird, and it cut into his soft, sweaty palm hard enough to leave little crescent-moon dimples. He gazed down at the figurine, turned it over a few times, touching the beak, the wings, the tail feathers, then placed it beside Mindy's head, careful not to get any of her blood on the bird.

"Made this special for your birthday. Hope you like it."

Mindy didn't reply. She didn't thank him for the special gift. She didn't do anything but lie there in a growing puddle of her own blood.

Danny pulled an old baby blue crocheted blanket off the couch and draped it over her. He took great care to tuck the blanket around her, under her legs and hips, still trying hard not to look at her big, unblinking eyes.

This was the first time Danny had been in Mindy's home. After all these years, he had finally gotten up the courage to walk the three miles to her trailer and knock on her door—and this is what happened. It wasn't supposed to be like this.

He glanced around the trailer's living room and kitchen—Mindy's home. Everything in it hers. But it wasn't at all what he had imagined. On more occasions than he could remember, Danny had daydreamed about Mindy's home. What it would look like on the inside. What it would smell like. Where she ate her cereal and watched soap operas and brushed her hair. He'd walked past her trailer dozens of times, slowing his stride in the hope that she would pop her head out and invite him in. They could drink a soda together, eat some cookies or crackers, and talk like friends were supposed to talk to each other. But that never happened, because Danny kept to himself, ate all his meals alone, didn't go to the town carnival or Fourth of July parade. He left people alone, because that's the way it was supposed to be. He was different from everyone else in town. He always would be—he'd accepted that now. Most folks just stared at him or crossed the street if they saw him coming down the sidewalk. But Mindy was always nice to him. She didn't laugh at him or make him feel dumb. She treated him like a real person.

Danny thought everything would be pink inside the trailer. Pretty pink walls, pink curtains, pink furniture. Kinda like where a Barbie doll might live. But everything wasn't pink, and it didn't look like a Barbie house at all. There was girl stuff that he didn't have back in his room. Plastic flowers in pots with fake butterflies and ladybugs on plastic leaves. A few bottles of red and purple fingernail polish sat on a TV tray beside a recliner chair. A picture of the ocean and a setting sun hung over the sofa. Stacks of girls' magazines spread out on top of the coffee table and a bookshelf leaned against the wall, crammed with books that were probably about girls and the stuff that they did. Lots of books, mainly paperbacks. Danny didn't have any books in his room.

Danny's knees began to hurt from kneeling for so long, but he couldn't move. Or *wouldn't* move. He wanted to be near Mindy just in case she woke up.

You shouldn't have come here, Danny.

Danny looked up and peered around the trailer for a moment, but he was all alone with Mindy. Nobody else. He didn't expect to see anyone else because he knew where the voice was coming from. He hadn't heard the talking in his head for a long, long time. The talking in his head usually just wanted to help him when he was in trouble or scared and never asked for anything in return. He waited to see if the talking in his head would say anything else. Waited to see if it would tell him what to do or who to go to for help, but it didn't say anything else.

Danny was so distracted by the talking in his head that he let his eyes drift over to Mindy's. It was a mistake, but it was too late. Once he peered into her big blue eyes, he couldn't look away. They held him still and stared back at him, but their sparkle was gone and little beads of blood stuck to her long eyelashes. Mindy wasn't there anymore. She wouldn't be working at the Friedenshutten anymore. She wouldn't be serving him eggs and bacon and hash browns anymore or asking him questions and making him feel special.

A low moan crept out of Danny. Starting from deep in his belly and working its way out his mouth, over dry and cracked lips and into the perfect silence of the trailer. He'd never heard this sound come out of him before. His heart felt funny, as if it might pop like a balloon, and his brain got real fuzzy. He usually tried his best not to cry. Uncle Brett used to say that real men don't cry like little babies. But this noise that came out of him now reminded him of the bawling sound a lost baby calf makes when it can't find its mama. The moan grew louder until his entire body shook with sharp, violent sobs.

Danny cried beside her for a long time, waiting for her to wake up. Waiting for her to get up and smile again.

Eighteen hours earlier . . .

Danny

Danny awoke before the sun rose, like he always did. He wished that he would sleep longer, but he never could. Right before the sun started to climb over the top of the rolling peaks of the Endless Mountains to the north of town, his eyes would open. Try as hard as he might, he could never drift back to sleep. He liked being in his dreams a whole lot better than where he was now. The dreams were always safe and happy, and folks in them treated him like everybody else. He couldn't always remember them so well, but last night's was still real clear and fresh in his head. He was little, maybe around five or six, both of his front teeth missing, and had on a red paper birthday hat with white polka dots. He puffed up his cheeks and got ready to blow out the candles on a big chocolate cake. Chocolate was his favorite. The candles dripped hot wax all over the icing, the wicks burning bright with tiny orange flames. His parents were there, watching him with wide, toothy smiles. A dozen kids he didn't recognize sat around the kitchen table, clapping and laughing and eyeing the triple-layer chocolate cake. Presents were piled up on the long table, wrapped in pretty paper with colorful bows. They were all for him. All from friends he didn't even know. After he blew out all the candles, Danny had woken up.

He'd been lying awake on his thin mattress for a few minutes, his feet hanging over the edge of the cot, wishing he were back in his dream so that he could rip open all those presents and see what kind of toys were inside. Instead he opened his eyes to the dark morning light and watched shadows from the trees outside dance and sway along the ceiling like puppets.

Danny figured he might as well get up out of bed. Today was a big day. He stood and rubbed the sleep from his eyes. Stretched arms and legs, then peeked out of his second-story window. He watched the Susquehanna River churn along outside—dark, slow-moving water rippled over large, moss-covered rocks and lapped along the shore-line. He liked living so close to the river and listening to the sounds it made, but he never went into the water. No, never in the water.

Dawn was almost there. Danny smiled at the pretty pink sky that reflected and glistened off the rolling river water. He'd always had trouble pronouncing "Susquehanna." His papa told him it was an Indian name because Native Americans used to live here before all the Pilgrims took over. His papa said that Wyalusing used to be called M'chwihilusing, which he thought sure sounded funny. His mama and papa used to teach him a lot of stuff, because they were teachers and were real smart. They used to read big books all the time.

Danny felt his way across the room and flicked on the switch. Soft light bathed the small space containing a cot and a secondhand dresser and not much else. The walls were bare and most of the paint missing in fist-size chunks or peeling off in long strips. Danny's head nearly grazed the low-hanging ceiling. Whenever the lightbulb burned out, he didn't need to step on a chair or anything to reach up and change it.

As he pulled on the same pair of green work pants he always wore and a green flannel shirt that fit tight over his belly, he caught his image reflected in the mirror above the dresser. He was thick-necked and bigger than most folks around town, but he didn't have any muscles. He was soft and fat, and most of the kids called him "Michelin Man." His big belly hung over his belt, always making it a chore to lace up his well-worn work boots. At his last visit to Doc Pete's, the nurse told him that he weighed two hundred and sixty pounds. She said that was too much and that he needed to eat more fruit and vegetables and should exercise every day. *An apple a day keeps the doctor away,* she had instructed him. He had nodded and told her he would, but he liked what he ate and didn't like to exercise. He knew that lying was wrong but thought it was less wrong than hurting the nurse's feelings.

After he managed to tie up his boots with double knots, Danny looked at his collection of hand carved wooden animal figures that were proudly displayed on the dresser. Mainly different kinds of birds—blue jays, woodpeckers, horned owls, sparrows—but there were also two squirrels, two snails, three rabbits, and one green turtle. The turtle was Danny's favorite. Its head poked halfway out of its shell like it was checking for any signs of danger. Danny had painted a small smile on the turtle's face, even though he knew turtles didn't smile. The turtle's name was Rudy. All his figurines had names. Besides Mindy, they were his only friends in the world, and he would talk to them and pretend that they would talk right back like friends were supposed to do.

Danny stepped over to the small sink, yellowed and rusty around the drain, and splashed cold water on his face. His strawberry-red hair was cut short. Always had been. Mr. Colgrove would give him a crew cut every few months for three dollars and put in a little Vitalis hair tonic. Danny didn't like the way it smelled, but Mr. Colgrove said that it was good for his hair and made him smell manly. Danny didn't take showers or baths, because he didn't have a bathtub. But that was okay. Being in bathtubs made him feel anxious. He would use a hot washrag every night and give his hair a good washing once a week if he remembered to.

And like he did every morning, Danny lathered shaving soap onto his face with a boar-bristle brush. The boar-bristle brush and straight razor used to be his papa's, and before that his granddaddy's. His granddaddy went up to heaven when Danny was still in diapers. Danny didn't have any photographs of his family, and he couldn't remember what his granddaddy looked like. He did remember what his papa looked like and used to watch him shave in the bathroom early in the morning, painting his face with the bristle brush, tilting his head to the left and right, gliding the straight razor across his skin until it was as soft as a baby's bottom. The boar-bristle brush and straight razor were the only things he had of his papa's. Uncle Brett threw everything else in the trash. Danny put the shaving soap on nice and thick and pretended that he was Santa Claus shaving his beard after Christmas. He picked up the straight razor and guided the blade along his skin, just like how his papa used to do it. He was real careful about shaving his whiskers—didn't like having them at all. They made his face tickle and itch.

He sat back down on the unmade cot and pulled a shoe box out from under it. Opened the lid and took out wood-carving supplies. Two carving knives, different sizes of chisels, and a few well-worn pieces of sandpaper he got down at Farley's hardware store. He laid them out beside him, then took out a block of pine that was in the rough shape of a bird. The head and beak were well formed, but the body and wings needed some more work.

Danny's fingers—nails gnawed and chewed down below the tip of each thick finger—ran over the pine block, skillfully carving and shaving away small slivers of wood. He would blow off the shavings, carefully feeling the texture of its wings. Notched and shaved some more, slowly creating the design of feathers. The small, delicate shape of the bird appeared dwarfed and vulnerable in Danny's giant hands, like he rescued it after it had fallen from its nest.

He always lost track of time when he did his whittling. Would lose himself and forget about who and what he was while crafting his wooden animal friends. The tiny critters didn't make fun of him or laugh at the way he talked. They never called him fat or dumb. They thought he was nice enough and would never say a mean word about him.

The bird he created now would be named Mindy. Mindy the Robin. Danny was making Mindy the person a robin figurine for her birthday because robins were supposed to be smart and a little bossy. Just like Mindy.

His stomach grumbled, but breakfast would have to wait. Danny had other work to do. He put the unfinished wood carving back in the shoe box, stuffed it under his bed, and shuffled out of his small room.

Danny tromped down the narrow steps and flipped on the lights to the Wash 'N Dry Laundromat. The fluorescents overhead flickered on and off a few times before they finally kicked on and shimmered against the linoleum floor. A dozen lime green washers and dryers lined the walls, as well as a soda machine and a boxed-soap dispenser that stood next to the laundromat's small restroom.

Danny grabbed a bucket from the washroom, filled it with steaming-hot water, then poured in a little Spic and Span so that the room would smell real clean and fresh. He mopped down the laundromat floor carefully and slowly just like Mr. Bennett had shown him. Mr. Bennett had to show Danny how to open and close the Wash 'N Dry a few times before Danny had finally gotten the hang of it. After mopping the floors, Danny checked the washers and dryers to make sure no one had left any clothes behind. He had checked the machines the night before, but Danny liked to make double sure he did it right. He wiped all the dust and lint off of the machines, checked to make sure that the soda machine didn't have any "sold-out" lights for any selections, and then inspected the detergent dispenser. Mr. Bennett got awfully sore if Danny let them go and get empty, because he said that was how he made lots of money. Mr. Bennett was the one who filled the machines when they needed filling and took out the coins.

Takin' out the money is a big responsibility, Danny. Best if I do that. Don't want you to lose it or have some youngster stealin' it from you. You just keep her clean for me and lock her up at night. Eleven o'clock sharp. Don't forget, now.

Danny figured Mr. Bennett was right—he was right about almost everything. Mr. Bennett was old and wrinkled like a grandfather and always said, *With age comes wisdom*. Sometimes Danny wondered when he got old and wrinkled if he might get smarter, too. He didn't think that would probably happen but hoped that he wouldn't get any dumber than he already was.

In exchange for keeping the Wash 'N Dry clean and opening and closing it each day, Danny got fifty dollars a week and the room upstairs. Mr. Bennett promised that as long as he did a good job and folks needed someplace to wash their laundry, Danny would have a room to stay in, and a few extra dollars in his pocket for "walking-around money," as Mr. Bennett called it. Danny worked real hard and tried his best to do nothing wrong. Mrs. Bennett would stop by the Wash 'N Dry from time to time to drop off an extra blanket or wool socks when the Pennsylvania winters were especially cold. One time she made him a blue-and-yellow scarf, but Danny had lost it. He lost a bunch of things. Every Monday, when Mr. Bennett collected his coins, he would give Danny a tin of homemade cookies or fudge that the missus had whipped up. They tasted real good, and as hard as Danny tried not to, he would eat them all in one sitting.

The Wash 'N Dry had been Danny's home ever since Uncle Brett passed on. Danny was still a teenager—sixteen, maybe seventeen—when Uncle Brett went up to heaven after being sick for so long. Uncle Brett wasn't an old man when he died like most folks who stopped living—he was about Danny's age now. He had gotten real skinny, vomited most of his meals, and ended up lying in a bed that smelled of pee and number two and talking or crying to himself the last few months. Danny would take him canned tomato soup and saltine crackers and feed him in bed. Sometimes Uncle Brett didn't know who Danny was and would holler at him to get the hell out of his trailer. He'd knock everything off the nightstand and spit chewed up food in Danny's hair. One time he picked up his bowl of soup and threw it all over Danny, scalding Danny's hands and arms real bad. Other times he would accidentally think that Danny was Danny's father. He would call him Hank and cry about not wanting to die. He'd hug Danny with skinny, flour-white arms that used to be strong and tanned. Uncle Brett never hugged Danny before he was sick. The sound of Uncle Brett's cough got worse and worse, the sharp rattle in his chest filling the trailer walls. It was a sound that Danny went to sleep to and woke to in the mornings. Then one morning Uncle Brett stopped coughing.

Mr. Bennett said that Uncle Brett smoked and drank too much and that was why he went away. Danny didn't know why folks would smoke and drink. Cigarettes smelled bad and cost lots of money, and alcohol made folks act real strange. When Uncle Brett got into the drink, he became even meaner than he usually was. Some folks got all happy and silly when they were having beer and whiskey, but not Uncle Brett. If he wasn't yelling or hitting Danny, Uncle Brett would just drink all quiet like and watch hunting and fishing shows on the television set.

Danny took one more pass through the laundromat to make sure everything was in its place and ready for the day. It all looked pretty good, so he unlocked the front doors and headed out to breakfast.

A dusting of fresh snow covered Wyalusing's Main Street, quiet at the early hour. Down the town's quarter-mile main drag, dirty snow was plowed to the curb, caked with cinders, black slush, and cigarette butts. Dark clouds overhead threatened more snow.

Not too many people lived on Main Street itself. Most houses were built back on Front and Church Streets. Big two-story Queen Anne homes with porches that wrapped around the fronts of the houses and had high-pitched roofs with fish-scale shingles. Every lawn had a red maple or a black birch growing on it. Some with a swing hanging from a lower limb. Maybe these houses stood proud at one time, but years of neglect and brutal winters had taken their toll. Roofs and porches sagged, lawns chewed up by trucks parked out front.

There were two churches in town—Methodist and Presbyterian—both of them on Church Street. An old library built back in 1902 stood on Church Street as well. The grade school, high school, and post office were a couple blocks from there.

No red lights in town, only stop signs at busy intersections. More than a few stop signs were peppered and dimpled with shotgun holes. Most folks didn't pay them any attention anyway.

A dozen or so stores and shops lined Main Street itself, most of them in need of a new coat of paint. Donna's Neat Threads, Colgrove's Barbershop, a Shell station, Red's Tavern, First National Bank, Flick's Videos, and a few other stores that weren't in business anymore. Iris's Gifts and More had been gutted by a fire last year and was still boarded up. Plywood had been nailed over the blackened window frames, and some kids had painted graffiti of female private parts onto the wood. Danny knew that the crude artwork was there but tried not to look at the women's private parts, because that was dirty and not very nice.

Danny trudged down the sidewalk with his hands shoved deep in his front pockets. He forgot to wear his jacket and cap again. When he was hungry, he forgot lots of stuff. He figured he would get a cup of hot chocolate this morning if he had enough money with him, but he would have to show Mindy his dollar bills and coins at the diner so she could count it and make sure he could afford it.

A station wagon rumbled down the street with a dead doe strapped down on its roof. Father and son hunters, both wearing orange hunting vests and caps, gawked at Danny as they rolled past. Danny smiled and waved like he always waved to townsfolk, and the boy waved back until his father reached over and yanked his arm down.

Smitty's Gun Shop was opening for the day. Long rows of hunting rifles were lined up and displayed in the front window. Danny slowed a bit and peered at them from a safe distance. He didn't like hunting so much. Didn't want to kill nothing. Uncle Brett took him hunting once when he turned twelve, the age when everybody was given a gun and sent out to the woods. Danny remembered not liking the loud sound of the rifle and the bitter smell of gunpowder. When Uncle Brett asked him if he wanted to fire off the gun, Danny shook his head. Uncle Brett had shot a twelve-point buck and seemed real pleased by the number of antlers on the deer—he counted the points three or four times to make real sure he was adding them up right. He had never seen his uncle so happy before. Uncle Brett was smiling and everything, and he even tried to get Danny to touch the buck's carcass.

Go ahead and give him a feel, boy.

The deer was still warm. Danny remembered staring down at the dead animal and thinking that just a few moments ago the deer was alive and well and walking around in the woods. Dark blood splattered on the white snowbank that the deer had finally fallen into. A pink tongue poked out of its foamy mouth a few inches, and its eyes were wide open and unblinking. Uncle Brett smiled at his trophy as he bent down to field-dress it. He drove his hunting knife into the animal's breastbone and began to cut through the hide to the base of the tail. As the skin split open and a warm tangle of intestines spilled out into the snow, Danny began to cry. Uncle Brett's smile disappeared real fast.

Jesus Christ, Danny. It's just a fucking deer. Don't be such a pussy.

Danny didn't know back then what a pussy was, but he knew he wasn't supposed to be one. That was the last time Uncle Brett had taken him hunting.

Danny forced his eyes away from Smitty's Gun Shop and continued down the sidewalk. He passed by EB's Market. A housewife eager to get a jump on her day hustled inside, still wearing rollers in her hair and wrapped up tight in a long winter jacket. Danny wanted to remember to pick up some pork and beans on his way back home. He could get two big cans for a dollar, and they filled him up fine.

At the corner of Main Street, he went left onto Prospect Street. Up ahead stood the Friedenshutten restaurant, serving breakfast, lunch, and dinner. The sign over the front door promised A GOOD MEAL AT A GOOD PRICE. A half dozen cars, winter-worn and rusted up, and a few tractor-trailers filled the small gravel parking lot. Danny kicked the slush from his boots and stepped inside.

Mindy

The bell over the front door jingled, and the eyes of the regulars all hung on Danny as he entered. Two old farmers, bent and hunched in the first booth, mumbled to each other, coffee mugs pressed to their thin lips. The same two farmers always sat in the same booth every day, and every day that Danny came in, they turned away from him and whispered to each other.

Mindy worked back behind the counter filling the salt shakers and watched the whole thing. She shook her head, irritated with each and every one of the intolerant SOBs.

Oh, Lord, people. You'd think Frankenstein just walked in.

Mindy's blond hair was pulled back in a ponytail, and her eyes sparkled like big blue gemstones. She looked tired but gave customers a wide smile as she replaced their salt shakers with freshly filled ones. Some smoker's lines creased the edges of her mouth and around her eyes, but Mindy didn't try to cover them with makeup. She wore her waitress uniform tight—the way she liked it *and* the way the men customers liked it. The female customers? Not so much. Mindy knew she might be a little too flirty, but it was innocent and all in good fun, and it sure helped with the tip situation.

Mindy watched poor Danny, with his eyes cast to the floor, lumbering his way to his usual spot—the last stool at the end of the long breakfast counter. He plopped down, folded his beefy hands in his lap, and waited.

God bless him. Always so patient, Mindy thought.

Danny didn't move to pick up the laminated menu that stood between a napkin dispenser and a bottle of ketchup. Mindy knew his order by heart—always the same thing. She painted on a big smile and marched straight up to him. "There's the birthday boy!"

Danny smiled at the sweet sound of Mindy's voice and glanced up at her, but his eyes darted right and left, never settling on hers for long.

"How old you gonna be, Danny? And no lying, you hear?"

Danny grinned and shook his head. "Dunno."

"Oh, phooey on that. We got the same birthday, silly." She leaned in close to him and whispered, "But we'll keep our age our little secret. We'll just pretend that we're still thirty-nine, okay?"

"All right. If you say so," Danny answered, still smiling from ear to ear.

Mindy reached under the counter, pulled out a packet of Swiss Miss hot cocoa, and shook it between her fingers. "How 'bout a cup of hot chocolate? My treat."

Danny's round cheeks turned red from all the attention, and he said softly, "You don't have to do that."

"I don't *have* to do nothin'. I want to."

Mindy poured hot water into a mug and slid it in front of Danny. "There you go, hon. Happy birthday."

"Well, ain't this a sweet sight first thing in the morning. A real fucking Kodak moment. Oughta take me a picture and hang it over my dresser at home," Mike Sokowski said, chuckling as he strode up to the counter and plopped onto the stool next to Danny. He took off his deputy hat and ran his fingers through long black hair that dangled down to broad shoulders. A thick tangle of a beard hung from his chin, whiskers creeping up his cheekbones nearly to the eyes. He grinned at Mindy, stroked and tugged on the beard, a few traces of gray hair peppered throughout. Sokowski made no attempt to hide the cauliflower ear on the left side of his head, a small twisted knot of brown flesh. In fact, he seemed to show it off like some kind of trophy.

"You ain't never given me hot chocolate on *my* birthday."

Mindy gave him a sour look, her smile long gone. "That's 'cuz you ain't sweet and don't deserve nothin' nice."

"Shit. Didn't hear you complaining none when we was going out. In fact, if I remember correctly, I always left you with a smile on your face."

Mindy avoided his shit-eating grin and wiped some jelly stains from the counter in front of him. "Yeah, well, I ain't making any more stupid mistakes."

Sokowski chuckled again, clearly enjoying her discomfort. "What do you say to meetin' me at the hotel tonight? I'm buying."

"I'd say 'fat chance.' Besides, I got other plans." She poured Sokowski a cup of coffee without him asking.

"Shit. You're full of piss and vinegar this morning."

"Yeah, well, you seem to have that effect on folks."

"Come on, now. Here I am and everything to wish you happy birthday."

Mindy gave him a look—not quite trusting his sincerity. "You actually remembered my birthday?"

"Hell yes. Got you a present and everything." He took a few sips of coffee.

"Really? A present?" Mindy tried not to, but she felt a twinge of hope. Maybe Sokowski could actually turn over a new leaf.

"You bet. Got it right down here in my pants." He let out a snort, then drank some more coffee.

"Mike. I swear."

"Just kidding with you. Jesus. Like to take you to dinner. Wine, candles, the whole nine yards."

"Said I was busy."

"I bet. Too busy cutting coupons or painting your nails?"

Mindy just shook her head at him. "You eating or what?"

"Shit. I guess I sure ain't here for the company. Pack me a fried-egg sandwich to go. And tell Pat to try not to overcook it this morning. How hard is it to fry a goddamn egg? Bet even Danny here could fry an egg."

As Mindy shook her head again and went off into the kitchen, Sokowski's hazel-green eyes turned on Danny. Danny could feel the deputy's stare but kept his own eyes down while he sipped his hot chocolate. It burned his tongue, but he tried not to let Sokowski notice.

Sokowski lit up a cigarette and played with the Zippo lighter, flicking it on and off, all the while watching Danny. After a minute or two, Sokowski finally spoke up.

"Whatcha know, Danny?"

"Nothing."

"Nothing, huh? Must be nice to know nothing sometimes, Danny. No worries. No problems. Just eat, sleep, and shit. What a goddamned life."

Danny shrugged his heavy shoulders. "Guess so." He watched Mindy working in the kitchen and wished that she would come back over. He didn't like being alone with Deputy Sokowski so much.

"You sweet on her, huh?" Sokowski asked.

Danny stared into his mug of hot chocolate.

"Don't be shy, Danny-Boy. I love women as much as the next guy, but be careful. Women are a tricky bunch. They bitch and moan and run their yap about shit you don't give a goddamn about, but you listen none the same, because you just want to get yourself a little piece. You know what I mean?"

Danny *didn't* know what he meant but nodded because he thought he was supposed to.

"You ever been with a woman, Danny?" Sokowski grinned and stroked his thick tangle of a beard.

Danny didn't say anything.

"Well, shit, we're gonna have to see what we can do about that. Gotta take care of the little man in your pants." Sokowski laughed at the thought and took a sip of his coffee.

Mindy returned, toting a plate of scrambled eggs, bacon, and hash browns and a sack breakfast for Sokowski.

"Leave him be, Mike. He doesn't need your shit filling his head."

"Me and Danny here were just having some guy talk. Isn't that right?"

Danny just plowed into his breakfast.

"Shit. Would you look at this boy pack it away? Fucker can eat."

"Honestly, why do you have to go and be so damned mean?

Danny here is nothing but sweet. Twice the man you are. You know that?" Mindy said while giving Sokowski a cold look.

"Shit o'mighty. He can have you for all I care." Sokowski took another sip of his coffee and put his deputy hat back on. He tossed a five-dollar bill on the counter and gave Mindy a wink.

"Well, I'll be seeing you around, Little Miss Sunshine." Sokowski stood and popped Danny hard on the back. "Remember what I said. Take care of your little man, Danny-Boy."

Sokowski made his way out of the diner, turning on the charm, smiling and nodding to folks as he went. He stopped at the table by the door and clapped one of the farmers on the back.

"Them coons still giving you fits, Merle?" Sokowski asked the older of the two.

Merle shook his head at the thought. "Hell. Caught two of 'em in the chicken coop yesterday morning. Killed three of my hens and ate near a dozen eggs."

Sokowski tugged on his beard for a second, then gave Merle another pat on the back. "Tell you what. I'll stop by in the next day or two with my thirty-aught six and take care of the problem for you. How's that sound?"

Merle chuckled a little. "Sounds like a thirty-aught six is more than enough rifle to take care of them coons. A four-ten would do the trick."

"Four-tens are for women and kids, Merle."

Merle chuckled again. "Appreciate the help, Deputy. My eyes ain't worth a damn no more."

"Happy to do it, Merle. Happy to do it."

Sokowski tipped his hat over at Dotty, one of the other waitresses, and she smiled back at him. He held the door open for an elderly couple coming inside, then slipped out of the diner.

"Some things never change," Mindy said, mostly to herself, before turning back to Danny and noticing how quickly he was scooping the eggs into his mouth. She gave him a little pat on the shoulder. "Don't listen to him. You understand me?"

Danny kept his head pulled between his shoulders and scooped up the rest of the scrambled eggs with a slice of toast.

"He's just mean to some folks. You know? Always has been and always will be." Mindy could tell that Danny wasn't really listening. "Danny." She spoke firmly, like a big sister talking to her little brother who got pushed around on the playground. "Don't let him get to you. Okay? I don't want you to ever change a bit. I like you just the way you are."

Danny finally nodded. "Okay, Mindy."

She smiled wide for him, but it felt more forced than usual. She knew she should take her own advice. Mike always got to *her*.

Sokowski

Sokowski guided his 1981 Chevy C10 pickup down the long driveway, the big twenty-inch tires taking the potholes like it was
nothing. Even though it was barely two years old, Sokowski had
dropped a 383 stroker engine with 450 horsepower, a cast iron crank-
shaft, high-performance pistons, and main bearings into the truck,
and it was worth every penny. Sokowski liked his Chevy truck. It
was his baby and beat the shit out of any Ford or Dodge on the
road—and don't even get him started on any of that foreign crap.
The Chevy's eight cylinders revved high as he pulled beside the
weather-beaten barn that once upon a time used to be a proud shade
of red. His old man—dead twenty-five years now—would shit, then
spin in his grave if he saw the condition of the neglected barn, but
Sokowski had his reasons for keeping it unpainted. He didn't want
to give it any unnecessary attention. A dilapidated piece-of-shit barn

didn't turn any heads. It looked like a barn that was unused and vacant, just the way he wanted it.

Besides, Sokowski didn't really give a rat's ass what his old man would think. The old man had been nothing but soft and weak, and not much of a farmer to boot. His old man sure as hell hadn't cared about Sokowski when he took the coward's way out of life. He'd never be his old man. Never be a gutless piece of shit.

Sokowski tapped a Marlboro Red from its pack and returned the box to his breast pocket. He lit up the smoke and took a deep draw. With the cigarette tucked into the corner of his mouth, he grabbed a pint of Wild Turkey from the glove compartment and then alternated the places of the bottle and the cigarette. He took a long tug on the bottle. The slow burn felt good. So good he decided to follow it with another.

Fucking breakfast of champions.

He looked over at his sacked egg sandwich, and the corners of his mouth turned up at the thought of Mindy. Feisty little bitch. Had a smart mouth, but he'd be goddamned if she didn't have a rocking little body. Nice tits. Her ass might be getting a bit wide, but not bad nonetheless. Helluva lay, too. She got a few drinks in her and all bets were off. She liked being ridden hard, just the way he liked to dish it out. And once she got those fingernails digging in his back, she'd leave some pretty deep scratches.

Mindy had broken off their on-again, off-again relationship yet again, but she would come crawling back like she always did. You satisfy a woman in the sack and she always comes back, begging for more. And he would take her back. Why not? He had fucked a couple dozen women over the years, but she was by far the best, hands down. He would pile on the sweetness for a while, and they would be back in between the sheets in no time.

As he stepped out of the truck, a contented little whistle slipped from his thin lips. "Camptown Races" was a tune that always stuck in his head. Camptown was a piece-of-crap town ten miles outside of Wyalusing. He hated the town and the shitheads that lived there—a bunch of old retired buzzards that thought that they were better than everybody else with their stupid yard gnomes and bird-baths out on the front lawn—but he liked the song. He kept whis-tling as he headed toward the barn with the purposeful stride of a man with life by the tail. Before he opened the barn doors, he noticed the green Pinto parked off to the side of the building.

"Goddamn moron." He flicked his cigarette into the snow, then stepped inside.

All the windows in the barn were tented with thick black plastic tarp, making it nice and warm inside. Probably around seventy degrees or so. A dozen bright fluorescents hung from the ceiling, and in place of a herd of cattle a large crop of marijuana plants basked in the regulated light. Sokowski took off his jacket, dropped it to the floor but kept his deputy hat cocked back on his head.

"Hey, asswipe, I told you to park your piece of shit behind the barn, not in plain view from the road. Jesus. How many times I got to tell you? And what the hell did I say about locking the fucking door? Christ, you're thick as a stump."

A short fireplug of a man, soft and fat, nearly bald, and much younger than he appeared, looked up from watering the marijuana plants at the opposite end of the barn. The man's small face nar-rowed and pinched forward at the nose, two big ears stuck out on either side of his head, and his eyes appeared to be too big for their sockets. He looked like a possum.

"Thought I did. Shit."

"Carl, thinking and doing for you is a wide fucking gap."

Carl smiled and nodded, not sure exactly what Sokowski meant by it. "Get me any breakfast? I'm about near starved."

"Shit, Carl. With all that fat around your waist, it'd take a goddamned month for you to starve to death."

Carl glanced down at his gut and chuckled. His big eyes as red as beets.

"Christ. You been smoking already this morning?" Sokowski asked as he moved through and inspected his crop.

Carl shrugged and kept watering. "Just a hit or two."

Sokowski uncapped the bottle of Wild Turkey and took another tug. He admired a lush plant. Smiled fondly as he caressed one of the large crystalline buds. "Northern Lights are looking mighty fine."

Carl laughed another dumb laugh. "Smokes mighty fine, too."

Sokowski gave him a withering look. "We're supposed to be selling the shit, not smoking it, assfuck."

Carl was stoned and found this very pretty damn funny. "Hell, Mike. It's called quality control. Just wanted to make sure that our stuff is good. We gotta stand by our product." He chuckled at himself a little more.

"My ass, motherfucker."

Carl found this funny, too.

Sokowski went to a long wooden worktable lined with carefully weighed and wrapped plastic bags of pot. A couple dozen of them at least. "We're gonna take a run up to Towanda tonight. Teddie Comstock is buying twenty ounces."

Carl turned off the water and pulled a half-smoked joint from his breast pocket. Fired it up, took a hit, then held it out to Sokowski. Sokowski accepted without hesitation, took a drag, and they passed it back and forth.

"You ain't overwatering, are you?" Sokowski asked as he looked around at his plants.

"Naw. I know what the hell I'm doing."

"Fuck. That'll be the day." Sokowski took another hit.

"Teddie got anything going on tonight?" Carl asked.

Sokowski released a cloud of smoke and nodded. "Having a party, I guess. Might as well stick around. Probably just gonna be a bunch of skanks, but I need to get me some pussy."

"Think DePoto's gonna be there? Man, she's got a nice rack."

"What the fuck is it to you anyways? You got an old lady."

Carl took the last hit from the joint and pinched it out between his fingers. "Tired of fucking that shit. The woman's getting fat."

"You look at *your* fat ass recently? You really think she wants to be crawling on top of that?"

Carl grinned and grabbed his crotch with a dumb sneer. "Not the only thing that's fat."

"Shit," Sokowski muttered.

"What's up with you and Mindy anyways? She not giving you any anymore?"

Sokowski took a sip of Wild Turkey and handed it to Carl. "That, shithead, is none of your fucking business." Carl took the bottle and drank from it. "Besides, I need me some strange." Sokowski smiled, high as shit now. "Mindy's a last resort."

Carl nodded like that made perfect sense, and then something occurred to him. His face grew serious, and he scratched at the top of his head, careful not to disrupt the comb over he had going. He glanced at Sokowski, big bulging eyes darting left to right. "So look, I was wondering. I got some bills piling up to my ass, and my clutch is slipping in the Pinto, and the old lady is riding my case, so I was wondering if I could get a little advance. Nothing much. Just till I get caught up, you know?"

Sokowski lost his smile and glowered at Carl with bloodshot eyes. "Advance?"

Carl still couldn't look Sokowski dead-on. "A few bucks. Nothing major."

Sokowski kept staring at Carl, stroking his beard like he was giving it serious consideration. "I ain't a bank, douchebag. I pay you what I pay you."

Carl nodded and knew better than to argue with him. His shoulders dipped a bit, and he shuffled on his feet like a bashful child. He stuck his hands in his front pockets and let out a small sigh.

It was quiet for a few moments until Sokowski dug his hand into his pocket and pulled out a fat roll of bills. "Christ. Don't go crying like a damn baby." He peeled off a few twenties and held them out in front of Carl's face. "I'm keeping track of all this shit I'm loaning you."

"Thanks," Carl barely mumbled. He reached for the money, but Sokowski held the bills a little higher, right out of his reach.

"Jump for it."

Carl sighed again. "Come on, Mike."

"You want the money? Jump for it, dickhead."

Carl reached higher. Still couldn't grab the money.

"Jump, fat-ass."

Carl finally jumped, his white belly poking out from under his shirt, and grabbed for the money. He missed. Tried again. Missed again.

"Jump, little monkey."

Carl jumped as high as he could manage and finally snapped the money from Sokowski's hand. All the jumping had him out of breath. "Damn, Mike. You don't make nothing easy."

As Carl stuffed the bills into his pocket, Sokowski grabbed him by the back of the neck and squeezed hard. "You're my bitch. You know that, Carl?"

Carl just stared at him with his big possum eyes.

"Say it. Say 'I'm your bitch.'" He applied some more pressure to the folds of fat on Carl's neck.

"I ain't saying that shit." Carl winced in discomfort.

Sokowski kept squeezing. "Say it."

Carl tried to pull away, but Sokowski held him tight.

"You my bitch, Carl?"

"Fine. Jesus. I'm your bitch."

Sokowski broke out into a wide grin and released him. "Shit. I had you going, didn't I? You sorry piece of shit." Sokowski laughed hard. Carl, not so much.

Sokowski kept laughing as he walked toward the front of the barn. "Remember what I said. Don't overwater this shit."

"Where you going?" Carl asked, rubbing at his neck.

Sokowski finished the last of the Wild Turkey and tossed the bottle at Carl, who had to duck to avoid being hit on the side of the head. Sokowski grinned and gave him a salute off his deputy hat. "Protect and serve, motherfucker. Protect and serve."

Carl forced a weak smile as Sokowski slipped out of the barn, then picked up the watering hose and squeezed the nozzle.

Danny

Danny had to keep his eyes nearly closed from the sheer white intensity. He kept his chin tucked against his chest and wore a heavy coat, sweat trickling down his back despite the bitter-cold temperature. He didn't know how far out of town he was, but the road's sharp incline was taking its toll. His frosted breath billowed out in large, colorless clouds, drifting up and into the gray Pennsylvania country sky. Thick, gnarled limbs of birch trees hung low and heavy with snow over the road, creating a blinding white landscape.

A few inches of fresh powder covered most of Turkey Path Road, which wasn't much more than an old dirt path that wound its way up Lime Hill. Other than a few hunting cabins, no one actually lived along the ridge. Rocky terrain ran steep, making it hard to build on. Snowplows didn't get out this way much, so the snow piled up high all around him. A truck passed him earlier, big four-wheel-drive tires covered with chains, clanking up a storm.

Danny's boots squeaked against the snow and ice. It was nice and peaceful. Real quiet. He could hear a hawk cawing from up in the sky. He looked for the bird, but the clouds were too thick. His toes were getting cold, his socks felt wet. Must be a hole in the bottom of his boot. He'd have to save some money before he could go and buy a brand-new pair. He tried not to think about the cold and kept plodding forward.

He heard the sound of children's laughter up ahead of him and over the crest of the hill. He wasn't far now. A few more minutes. His stomach rumbled, complaining of hunger. Danny figured he should have eaten lunch before coming out all this way, but after breakfast his stomach hurt real bad, as if someone punched him in the belly.

He didn't like the deputy one bit. He knew he wasn't supposed to think bad of other folks, but the deputy had always picked on him ever since he was a kid. He still remembered the first time Mike Sokowski had beaten him up. It was over at Pickett's Bowling Alley.

Danny had just turned eight. He was in the arcade with a couple of nickels clutched in his palm, watching the lights blink yellow and red on the Gottlieb Spot Bowler woodrail pinball game. Mr. Pickett had just bought the pinball game and placed it between the Shuffle Alley and the jukebox. Danny played Shuffle Alley a few times but didn't like getting sawdust all over his hands. He stood mesmerized by the newness of the Spot Bowler game. Everything about the pinball game drew him closer, like a kid to a candy counter. The flashing bumpers, the flippers, the miniature bowling pins lit up like candles, and five steel balls about the size of walnuts ready to knock down all the little bowling pins. Danny put one hand on the panel of glass that covered the game and shook the nickels in the other.

"Hey, retard, what are you doing? Laying a turd in your pants?" Danny looked behind him. Two older boys with crew cuts smiled at him with grins that weren't so friendly or kind. One was big-boned, tall for his age, and had a cauliflower ear on the left side of his head. Mike Sokowski, only a few years older than Danny but already the meanest bully in Wyalusing. The other kid was fat and wore clothes a size or two too small for him. Carl's gut hung out from under a stained T-shirt that pulled tight over his belly.

"You deaf, too, retard?" Sokowski asked.

Danny still didn't answer. He looked past the two boys toward Uncle Brett out on bowling lane four. Uncle Brett held a beer in one hand, a cigarette in the other, and talked with a few of his drinking buddies.

Sokowski and Carl stepped a little closer to Danny, boxing him up against the Spot Bowler game.

"Whatcha got in your hand?" Sokowski sneered.

Danny's hand gripped the nickels tighter. "Nothing."

"Doesn't look like nothing," Sokowski said. "Check his hand, Carl."

Carl did as instructed. He grabbed Danny by the wrist and shoved it hard behind his back. Sokowski took Danny's face and shoved it flat against the panel of glass. Danny could smell the licorice on their breath.

"Just give us the nickels, shithead. You're too stupid to play arcade games," Sokowski mocked while Carl twisted Danny's arm up higher behind his back, forcing him onto his tiptoes.

The muscles in Danny's shoulder burned hot, and he could feel them stretched to their limit. A wave of dizziness wrapped around his head like a plastic Halloween mask, causing a feeble moan to escape his lips. The pain was finally too much, and he opened his palm, and the nickels bounced to the linoleum floor. He tried not to, but he started to cry.

Sokowski gave Danny's face a final shove into the panel of glass before letting him go. "Aww, listen to the little pussy cry." Sokowski chuckled.

Carl snorted like a laughing pig and snatched up the coins.

"Leave him alone, assholes," a girl's voice demanded.

The boys looked behind them. Mindy Knolls, pigtails tight on the sides of her head, glared right back at them. She was smaller than the two boys, but that didn't matter to her at all. Her skinny chest swam under a shirt that looked like a hand-me-down, and she crossed her bony arms over her stomach, waiting to see what Sokowski and Carl would do next.

"Why don't you go play with your little peckers somewhere?" Mindy said.

The boys knew that they weren't supposed to beat up girls. Besides, Mindy sported two sets of knuckles nicked up from her fair share of fighting and standing toe-to-toe with two older brothers. She clenched both fists down at the sides of her small hips, ready to use them.

"The retard your boyfriend or somethin'?" Carl sneered.

"Shut up, Carl. You want me to tell my daddy that you're picking on Danny? He'll whup your fat ass."

Carl shut up. They got their nickels. That was enough for him.

But Sokowski wasn't done yet. He pointed to Mindy's chest, snickered a yellow-toothed grin. "Looks like you got two mosquito bites under your shirt. Sure ain't boobs."

If that rattled Mindy, she didn't let it show. "Sure beats your mosquito pecker."

Sokowski's grin slipped right away, and his face brightened red. "Wouldn't you like to know?"

"Bet Carl here already knows."

Sokowski's face burned brighter. He turned his venom back on Danny. "We'll be seeing you around, retard. And next time you won't have any stupid girl to hide behind." Sokowski cocked his fist, made Danny flinch, then left the arcade room and headed toward the soda machine. Carl snorted again and followed right after him like a little duckling.

Danny's breath still hitched in his chest.

"Don't let 'em get to you, Danny. They're just a couple of stupid pudwhackers."

Danny wiped away the tears and snot from his face.

"You know, you're as big as they are, Danny. Why don't you just punch them in the face? That'll shut them up good."

Danny shook his head and rolled his shoulders. "Naw. Couldn't do that."

"You could. Just *won't*," Mindy said.

Danny glanced back at the Spot Bowler pinball game and watched the lights flash for a second.

"Wanna go outside?" Mindy asked him.

Danny looked over her shoulder to where Uncle Brett was high-fiving a fellow bowler. "Can't. Not allowed to go outside."

Mindy followed his gaze. "He's drunk. He ain't gonna notice anything."

Danny didn't resist as Mindy took his hand and led him through all the cigarette smoke, past the clatter of bowling pins, in between a group of men drinking bottles of beer by the bar, and out of the bowling alley.

The moon shone nearly full and the sky was as clear as a tall glass of springwater. Moonlight illuminated the seemingly endless rows of dried cornstalks that surrounded the bowling alley and disappeared into black. A wind gently blew, sweeping through the field, filling the cold night air with the sound of swaying stalks. Dried leaves rustled and brushed against one another, creating a soothing whisper song.

Mindy led Danny through the maze of corn, the dull echo of bowling balls colliding with pins a faint rumble behind them. She stopped in the middle of the field and met Danny's gaze. When she smiled, moonlight displayed the wide gap between her two front teeth, big enough to stick a straw through. "I like coming out here at night I like listening to the corn. Kinda feels like it's talking to me."

Danny listened, but he didn't hear any voices.

Mindy moved a little closer to Danny. He could smell the soft, flowery scent of her shampoo. She smelled real nice. Pretty and clean. Uncle Brett didn't make Danny take many baths. That kind of stuff was up to Danny to do. Washing his own clothes, brushing his teeth, cleaning his ears, and the like. Danny felt dirty all of a sudden. Aware of the grime that covered him and the bad taste in his mouth. His hand went self-consciously to his own hair. If felt greasy and flat and unclean.

"You ain't scared of me, are you, Danny?"

"Naw."

"Good." She picked up a rock and chucked it into the corn. "My daddy says that the accident is what made you slow."

"Guess so." Danny looked around him. He wasn't sure which direction was the way back to the bowling alley.

"You remember the accident and everything?"

"Not really. Some of it, I guess."

She picked up another rock and gave it a toss. "You miss your folks, Danny?"

He nodded and hoped he wouldn't cry in front of Mindy again.

"My grandpa died last year. Grandma says he's up in heaven and it's a better place, but I don't wanna die and be buried in the ground." Mindy shrugged. "Grandma says that's where we all go if we're good, and then we get to be with our families again."

Danny didn't know nothing about heaven. He just knew that his mama and papa were put in the ground and covered up with dirt and he wouldn't see them in Wyalusing anymore.

"How's people supposed to get up to the sky if they're in the ground?" he asked.

Mindy shrugged again. "Guess their body stays down here and another part of them goes up to heaven."

"What part?"

"Beats me." She pulled a dried ear of corn off its stalk and chucked it up into the sky. Danny watched it get swallowed up into the night and land with a thud somewhere in the field.

"Ever seen a girl's boobs, Danny?"

Danny felt his face redden and hoped Mindy couldn't see him blush.

"My mama's got real big ones. Says that mine will get big like hers one day."

Danny looked down at the frozen dirt under his feet and toed a rock. He wished he had just stayed in the bowling alley.

"I'll show you my boobs if you show me your thing."

"Naw. Better not."

"Why?" Mindy smirked at him and didn't wait for an answer. She pulled up her shirt, exposing a flat chest. Danny looked up for a second. Saw her breasts, then looked down again quickly.

"It's okay to look." She pushed her denim pants and underwear down to her ankles.

Danny shook his head.

"Come on. It's cold. I won't tell no one."

He took another quick peek, then tore off running. He ran blindly through the cornstalks. Long, dead leaves smacked against his face. He threw up his hands to deflect the stinging husks of corn from his eyes and searched the rows for the way out. He turned down another endless row, the sound of corn husks whistling past his ears, but it all looked the same.

"Danny!" Mindy yelled from somewhere behind him, but Danny kept on running. His heart thudded in his chest, and he was breathing hard—he didn't run around much like other kids did. Uncle Brett called him a "fat-ass."

The moon slipped behind some clouds, and the ground beneath him darkened. He kept running. Fast as he could. His sneakers smacked against frozen patches of water on the dirt.

He searched desperately for the lights from the bowling alley but found only darkness and more and more rows of corn. His foot caught on a rock, and he toppled forward. Danny tried to catch his fall, but he landed hard on the ground and rolled across frozen dirt and sharp stones.

He jerked upright and clutched at his knee. His pants were torn open, exposing a bloody gash on his leg. The knee began to throb and sting, but he was more worried about his ripped pants—they were his only pair, and Uncle Brett was sure to get good and sore.

When he touched the rip in his jeans, his fingers came back dark red. Danny stared at his fingertips and he felt something warm and thick drip into the corner of his eye. He blinked through the pain and wiped away the stickiness. More blood poured from an ugly cut on his forehead.

"Danny?!" Mindy called again from out in the darkness.

Danny stumbled to his feet, unsteady at first—then began to run again. Ice crunching under his shoes. The crackling sound of the breaking ice filled the night air. He tried running away from the sound, but it just got louder and louder until that was all he could hear. Breaking ice.

"Danny!" But this time it wasn't Mindy calling his name. It was his mama's voice. "Don't go so far out on the ice!" Danny laughed at her. It was all a game to him. The blades of his skates cut across the ice. He glided faster and faster, craving more speed. The cold wind stung at his face, but it was exhilarating. For a moment everything seemed perfect. Blades sliding like butter on a skillet. Blue skies overhead. Birds swooping and chirping. The pond just going on and on. Then Danny's laughter cut short by a thunderous cracking sound. Everything shook, and the world below him gave way, and he was sucked into a cold, wet blackness that shocked the breath from his chest. His arms flailed in the water that wrapped around his body like a heavy blanket. Danny opened his mouth, tried to scream, but water sucked down and into his lungs instead and he sank deeper into the black abyss.

The sound of footsteps poked through the darkness.

"Get your ass up, retard!" a boy's voice barked.

Danny couldn't feel anything. His arms and legs seemed disconnected from the rest of his body. It was like he was still floating in the water.

"I said get up." Something kicked him in the ribs. Pain shot through him, and his eyes flickered open. The nearly full moon and a thousand stars hung above him.

Then he noticed Sokowski and Carl standing over him. They didn't say anything else. They started to kick him hard in the face and stomach with dirty Converse sneakers. Again and again. He remembered hearing Mindy screaming at them to stop before the moon swept down and took him away.

M rs. Bennett said that people were mean sometimes because they didn't like folks that were different from them. She told Danny that he was special and different and that was okay. Danny sure liked Mrs. Bennett a lot—she was kinda the grandma he didn't have—and carved her a bluebird figurine once. She said that bluebirds were independent and didn't take nothing from nobody. Danny wished he was a bluebird sometimes.

The sound of heavy tires chomping and chewing their way through the snow-topped road interrupted the countryside's perfect quiet. Danny wanted to rest for a minute, so he decided to take a break from all the walking and moved off to the side of the road, glancing over his shoulder at an approaching pickup truck on over-size tires. The sides of the truck were eaten up with rust from years of traveling on top of salt- and cinder-covered roads, and the front fender was popped in and dented in a few places.

The truck slowed, and a teenager unrolled the passenger window. Danny recognized the boy from town but forgot his name.

"Duh-duh-duh-duh-Danny the retard does a little dance every time he does the Hershey squirts in his pants!" The driver of the pickup howled with laughter like it was the funniest thing he had ever heard. Egged on by his buddy's cackling, the boy in the passenger seat shoved his middle finger up his nose. "Duh-duh-duh-duh-Danny!" More laughter as the truck crested the hill and slipped away.

Danny wanted to turn and go back home, but he had come this far. Besides, he always came out here on his birthday to be with his mama and papa.

McGee Pond proved to be a popular spot in the wintertime. About the size of a football field, it was frozen solid with a thick layer of ice that had a few logs stuck in place until the spring thaw. On the far opposite side of the pond, a dozen teenagers glided on skates across its smooth surface, pushing and shoving each other and carrying on. Boys taunting girls and the girls giggling and screaming as if they didn't like it. Closer to the shore near Danny, three children were learning to skate with their parents. The two boys were older—eight and ten, maybe—and appeared more adventurous than their sister. The little girl wore a pink jacket and wobbled along the ice with her hands out, ready for a fall. After two near misses, her luck was up—arms spun like mini-windmills and legs went out from under her, and she landed hard on her bottom. Tears promptly followed.

As her parents tended to their daughter with soft, soothing voices that encouraged her improvement, the two boys continued their roughhousing unwatched. They raced each other, teasing with name-calling and hard shoving.

Danny sat on the bank of the pond watching the boys play. He was careful not to sit too close to the ice. His heart raced even though he had been sitting in the same spot for quite a while now. He wouldn't venture out onto the ice anymore. Was too scared.

The two boys skated faster and faster, narrowly avoiding sharp chunks of wood that poked out through the ice, and coasted toward the center of the pond. Puffs of shaved ice kicked out from their skate blades in white little clouds. They threw some elbows at each other, trying to knock the other down. Danny watched them closely, rubbing at his furrowed brow and feeling funny in his belly. He liked it better when the pond was empty so that he could be by himself—watching kids out on the ice just made him too nervous. The two boys raced toward a large round spot in the center of the ice that glistened with a thin layer of water.

Danny pressed his eyes closed—wanting to shut everything out— hoping that when he opened them again, the boys would be skating back toward shore. He could hear them laughing and whooping, not a care in the world. He didn't want to open his eyes yet, but did anyway. And just as he feared, the young boys weren't skating back toward their parents, but instead heading right for the shimmering spot on the ice.

"No." Danny stood, eyes staring toward the soft ice. "It's not safe out there . . ." His hands rolled into fists at his sides, and he looked over to the parents, who held their daughter's hands between them and skated slowly alongside her.

"Tell them to stop." Danny's voice was urgent but not loud enough to get their attention. He gazed back toward the boys, and they got closer and closer to the center of the ice.

The two boys abruptly slowed in their tracks as their blades sank and bogged down in the slushy ice. One of them fell forward and slid face-first into the mush.

"TELL THEM BOYS TO COME BACK!" Danny suddenly shrieked, his voice shrill and full of panic. He waved his arms and screamed again. He sounded like a big, scared, squawking bird that was trying to protect its nest from a circling hawk. The parents finally looked over at him, and he pointed frantically toward the center of the ice. The parents stared at him for a second, taken aback by the large mountain of a man, wearing a red knit hat, screaming and flapping his arms.

"GET YOUR BOYS! GET THEM NOW!"

The father glanced in the direction Danny pointed and saw his two sons. The older one was trying to pick up his younger brother, but he lost his balance and slammed down onto the ice as well.

"Tyler! Jason! Not so far out!" he shouted. But the boys couldn't hear their father. They were too busy grabbing and clawing at each other.

From the shore Danny watched as the older boy struggled to his feet, then abruptly sank up to his waist in the water once the ice gave way. He flailed wildly, desperately grabbing at the edge of the broken ice, but the ice kept breaking off in chunks. Water flung from his mittens in high arcs while the ice continued to crumble and break away as fast as he could grip it in his hands.

Danny saw the panic take hold of the mother's face, and a chilling scream ripped from her mouth. Even the teenagers at the other end of the pond stopped what they were doing and gawked at the scene unfolding. The mother pushed her husband forward, and they both raced toward their boys, slipping and sliding on their skates, leaving the little girl behind them unattended. The little girl reached her hands out toward her mother and father and started to cry, but her sobs went unheard.

The younger boy grasped at his brother, tugged on his arms, but couldn't get his feet planted, then quickly got sucked into the icy water as well. Both boys screamed now. Panicky yells that carried over the ice and filled the countryside.

The little girl began to inch her way toward her parents. Jerky and unbalanced. "Mama!" But her small voice was lost.

Danny watched the girl skate and wobble farther out on the ice—farther from shore and closer to danger. "Little girl, please. Stay where you are," Danny called out to her but her goal was clear—to go after her mama and papa.

Danny moved to step onto the ice but stopped his boot from leaving the safety of shore. He tried, but he couldn't move any farther. The fear grabbed ahold of him like two large fists wrapping around his chest and holding him tight. The screams of the boys seemed to grow louder in Danny's ears. He thought he could hear the sound of cracking ice and the sucking noise of water flowing into their lungs. Even the clatter of their parents' skates cutting into the ice and the little girl's sobs filled Danny's head. He wanted it to stop. He wanted to be back in his room. He wanted to finish painting the robin for Mindy's birthday.

You need to get the little girl, Danny.

The voice spoke to him urgently.

"I'm afraid."

No time for that. Get the little girl.

Danny nodded that he would listen and do what he was told. He pressed his eyes closed and inched forward onto the ice. All he could see was darkness, but he could feel his boot step onto the smooth, hard surface. He felt the rubber soles of his boots glide across the ice, inch by inch, foot by foot. The boys kept screaming from out on the center of the pond, and he stopped and stood for a moment, then opened his eyes. Both feet were planted on the ice, and he was okay. The ice didn't crack or break under him. It was solid. Strong enough to hold him. He saw the little girl gaining momentum toward her parents—getting closer to the soft spot. Danny blocked out all the noise and voices and began to walk-glide across the ice.

Faster now. You're almost there.

His stride easily tripled that of the little girl. It took only a few moments to catch up to her. He slid beside her, and she gazed up at him and stopped skating. Danny towered over her by a good three feet. Like a giant bear looking down on Goldilocks. He forced a smile for her and held his hand out toward hers.

"It's okay. Come with me. Your mama and papa will be right back." His voice was low and gentle. Nothing but kindness.

The little girl hesitated and peered out toward her parents.

"I'm scared of the ice, too. Even a big person like me gets scared. Maybe if we stay together, we won't be afraid anymore."

Tears rolled down her face that shook from cold and fear, but she nodded at Danny. Took his hand and squeezed it tight, and she wasn't about to let it go. Danny slid his boots across the ice and guided them to shore. They walked up the bank a few feet and turned and stared back at the center of the pond. The boys' father sprawled out on the ice, desperately reaching toward his sons. He grasped the younger one first. Pulled him out and slid him on his belly behind him. As the mother collected her younger son, the father reached and grabbed the older son's hand, minus a mitten now, and slowly eased him up and out of the ice-cold water.

Danny sat on the snowy bank, and the little girl stood beside him, pressing her small body onto his for comfort and warmth. She watched her brothers, now howling, one clutched in each parent's tight grasp. The little girl's knees rattled from the cold, and she continued to sob, small tears leaking down chapped red cheeks.

Danny held the little girl's hand tight and whispered softly over her whimpers, "*Shhh.* They're gonna be okay. Your brothers are safe. Nothing to be scared of anymore."

The parents brought Tyler and Jason to the shore, hushed them with comforting words, and stroked their wet heads. The father sat Tyler on the ground with his mother and jogged over to his daughter.

"It's okay, Melissa. Don't cry now." He scooped her up in his arms and she buried her face in his shoulder with renewed cries of relief and fear.

The father looked down at Danny and held his daughter protectively to his chest, wet with water and chunks of ice.

"I didn't want her going out on the ice," Danny said.

The father nodded but said nothing.

Danny gazed out at the pond and shook his head. "This pond is a bad place."

"It's just a pond."

"Kids shouldn't be playing out here."

The father's face shifted and flashed with a sudden burst of anger. "I know who you are, and I sure the hell don't need you tellin' me my business."

Danny looked up at the man, not sure why he would be so mad at him. "I'm sorry. I didn't mean nothing."

The father turned away from Danny and rejoined his family. Over her father's shoulder, the little girl peered back at Danny and waved a small mittened hand. He didn't wave back. He just stared out at the pond.

It was a bad place.

Sokowski

Sokowski and Carl were already shit-faced when they got to Ted-die's. They took turns passing a fifth of Wild Turkey and two fat joints during the thirty-minute drive. They talked about fucking and being wasted and then more about fucking. They discussed who they would fuck, who they wouldn't fuck, and who they had fucked. All the fuck talk had them laughing their asses off. When Sokowski pulled his truck in to the gravel driveway, he nearly back-ended another pickup truck—which happened to be a Toyota, so he didn't really give a shit. As they climbed out of the Chevy, they laughed about that, too.

"You're fucked up," Carl cackled as he stated the obvious.

"Not nearly as much as I plan to be," Sokowski said with a grin he couldn't wipe off his face.

There were over forty men and women drinking and smoking in front of the double-wide trailer. A group of men, most wearing

Harley-Davidson caps and black leather jackets, huddled around the keg on the front porch, taking turns pumping and pouring. The cold didn't seem to bother them a bit.

Sokowski strode up the gravel driveway like a strutting rooster in a henhouse— Carl a few steps behind him. Both of their heads pivoted as they pushed and shoved themselves up onto the crammed porch, gawking at the asses of female partygoers as they went. Sokowski gave a few of them a head tilt—a quick acknowledgment without having to bother saying anything.

A tall, rock-hard man wearing a thick camouflage hunting jacket and a matching camouflage ball cap sipped beer from a red cup and gave Sokowski a sour look. The hunter sported a carefully groomed goatee and had his hand cupped on the ass of an attractive blonde pressed up against his side. Her meticulously feathered hair was bleached to the roots, and she wore an acid-washed denim jacket and tight jeans that appeared to be painted on.

"Look who just stumbled out of the sticks. You busting up the party, *Deputy*?" the hunter mocked.

Sokowski elbowed his way next to the keg and helped himself to some cups. "Kiss my ass, Otis," Sokowski replied coolly. He handed Carl a beer, then poured his own.

"Bet you'd like that, wouldn't you?" Otis grinned at one of his buddies.

Sokowski took in the crowd as if the man's chatter didn't register.

"Heard Mindy dumped your ass again," Otis said over his beer. "Guess she's back on the market."

Sokowski stepped up close to him. His face pressed just a few inches from Otis's. "If you were smart, which you ain't, you dumb fuck, you'd keep your nose out of my shit."

Otis held his ground. "Christ. Your fucking beard stinks."

"Least I'm not growing one of those fucking French goatees."

A few chuckles from around the porch.

"What the fuck ya doing up here anyways?" Otis asked and lit up a cigarette.

Sokowski guzzled his beer, then poured another. He turned to one of the flannel-wearing rednecks. "Teddie inside?" The redneck nodded that he was and motioned toward the door with a jerk of his head.

Sokowski seemed to finally notice the blonde that Otis fondled. Gave her tits a good look and smiled at her. "You got a thing for small peckers, huh? When you're ready for a real man, give me a call." Sokowski flashed Otis a toothy grin and Carl chuckled behind him as they stepped inside the trailer.

A .38 Special song blared on the stereo. *"You see it all around you, / Good lovin' gone bad . . ."*

The party was in full swing. Most of the men sported unkempt beards. Greasy hair shoved under John Deere hats. The women looked like they lived hard lives. Bleached-blond hair pulled back from faces etched with smoker lines. Anyone who wasn't sucking on a Camel or a Marlboro Red was spitting chew into empty beer bottles. They all clutched an alcoholic beverage and drank quickly to get their buzz on. Cigarette smoke hung thick in the air. A group of men sat at the kitchen table playing quarters. Bullshit hunting stories were told. Dirty jokes exchanged. Gossip shared. And through the din of conversation, scattered laughter revealed nicotine-stained teeth and dull yellow tongues.

Sokowski shouted over the music to Carl, "I'll catch you later! Duty calls!" Carl nodded but was more interested in scoping out the party. As Sokowski shoved his way through the crowd, Carl sat down and joined in the game of quarters at the kitchen table.

Sokowski rubbed up intentionally against a stacked redhead, copping a quick feel, and gave her a lecherous grin. "Hey, sweet thing." Sokowski's Wild Turkey breath folded over the redhead, and she rolled her eyes and turned her back to him and continued talking to her friends. Undeterred, he kept pushing and rubbing his way against anyone with breasts as he crossed the living room. He passed by a gun rack mounted onto the wall that proudly displayed three hunting rifles. The victims of the rifles hung around the living-room walls as well, now stuffed and mounted trophy kills. Three buck heads, a black-bear head, and a pheasant repositioned in midflight looked alert with blue marble eyes.

Sokowski pressed on, moving down the narrow trailer hallway toward the back bedroom. The door was closed, but he didn't bother knocking. Just swung the door open and stepped inside the darkened room lit only by a purple mood light that hung from the ceiling.

Two men and two women sat on the water bed, passing around a small mirror lined with cocaine. One of the men, tall and thin with a sharp, hawklike nose, snorted a line and rubbed some of the fine powder on his upper gum. He smiled up at Sokowski, revealing a mouth missing a good number of its teeth.

"Yo, bitch. Where the fuck you been? Want a line?"

"What the fuck do you think, Teddie?" Sokowski took the mirror and snorted two fat lines. Sucked them deep and pinched his nose. Then tilted his head back and savored the drip.

"Fuck yeah."

"Good shit, right? Ol' Teddie's a great fucking host." He clapped a hand on Sokowski's back. "What's new in Wyalusing, Mikey?"

"Nothing. Same shit, different day."

"Yeah. Same shit here. You still fucking that waitress?"

Sokowski shrugged. "Only when I'm desperate."

"I hear that, man. I hear that. You gonna stick around and party a little? I got plenty of blow," Teddie said after doing another line.

"I guess. Maybe. Bunch of skanky bitches out there, though. You get 'em at the dog pound or what?"

Teddie laughed and cupped his hands over his eyes like he was wearing glasses. "Just gotta put on the beer goggles, then, bitch." The two women and the other man laughed at the sight. Sokowski barely cracked a smile and drank his beer.

"Shit, Mike. You're wound up so tight I bet your asshole could slice a diamond right clean in half." The others laughed at this, too, before going back to cutting more lines and passing them around the room.

Teddie put his arm around Sokowski, stinking of beer and tooth rot. "So what do you got for *me*, Deputy?"

Sokowski snorted another line and handed him back the empty mirror. Reached into his deputy jacket and pulled out a thick plastic bag of marijuana. "Some good shit, is what."

"Well, we'll just have to see about that." Teddie eagerly opened the plastic bag and rolled a joint, spilling some of the weed onto the carpet but not really caring. He fired it up, took a hit, and held in the smoke. When he finally blew the cloud of smoke out, he was seized by a coughing attack. His eyes watered as he bent over, coughing hard. He farted twice, then exploded into hysterics.

"My compliments to the chef." The others joined in with snorts of laughter.

Sokowski finally smiled. Took a hit, then passed the joint around.

Out in the living room, Lynyrd Skynyrd's "Sweet Home Alabama" thumped from some speakers.

Teddie grabbed a bottle of Jack Daniel's from his dresser and held it out to the others. "What do you say we get good and fucked up?"

Sokowski felt himself sinking deeper into the couch. The cushions were soft and seemed to be sucking him into the green corduroy material. The music played louder, and the trailer was even more packed with people who were drunk, stoned, or coked up—or all three. Sokowski was seeing double of everybody and everything, and it took real effort to keep his head held straight. It snapped back and forth like a broken puppet head. Beside him a couple groped at each other, oblivious to the party around them. Wet tongues flitted in and out like drunken snakes. The man had his hand up the woman's shirt, squeezing her tits, and her hand was working at his crotch through his jeans.

Sokowski lifted his beer cup to his lips. Half of it sloshed into his mouth, and the other half streamed down through his scraggly beard and onto his jacket. He saw two blurry images of Carl at the quarters table knocking over a bottle of beer, then laughing like a hyena. A fat woman sat on Carl's lap and had her arm wrapped around his shoulders. She drank beer and laughed along drunkenly while Carl's hand was snug between the fat woman's blue-jeaned thighs and worked its way higher.

Sokowski returned his gaze to the couple beside him and watched them suck on each other's face for a second. They were heating up and lost in their inebriated passion—clothes might be coming off pretty quick. Sokowski mumbled something to them, but it came out a thick-tongued, garbled mess. He tried to stand, but his balance was way off. Too fucked up. His beer cup slipped from his hand and spilled onto the floor, and he flopped back onto the couch. The couple squinted over at him and laughed.

"You're messed up, dude," the man offered, half wasted himself.

"Fuck shit," Sokowski slurred in response.

"I want what you're drinking," the man said, laughing, and his girl giggled along with him.

Sokowski's mouth hung open, and he laughed because they were laughing. Then his eyes locked on a nice ass, head level to him, moving past. He squinted up at Otis's blond girlfriend making her way toward the bathroom. Sokowski belched and mumbled something else as she passed in front of him. He leaned forward, snatched her by the wrist, and pulled her down onto his lap.

"Hey, sweet thing." But it came out sounding like *Hey, thweet thang.* The blonde tried to pull away, but Sokowski held her tight. He pressed his face close to hers, rubbing his beard into her neck. "Give up on that faggot boyfriend of yours?"

"Let me go, asshole."

But Sokowski had other ideas. "Don't be that way, baby. Just want to party with you."

The blonde squirmed some more. "The fuck off me."

"Easy, now. How about we go and do some blow?"

She stopped resisting, eyes suddenly interested. "You got coke?"

Sokowski grinned and nodded. "Fuck yeah. All you got to do is suck my fat one."

The blonde finally yanked her wrist free from his grip and stood up. "You're a fucking scumbag."

Sokowski pushed himself forward and stood on unsteady feet. "And you're a stupid fucking whore." He pressed his hand right into the middle of her face and shoved hard— she stumbled through the crowd, knocking loose beers and cigarettes—slamming her against the trailer wall. "How do you like that, bitch?"

Sokowski staggered forward and reached down toward her when a fist collided with the side of his jaw. The punch was delivered hard. Sokowski's head snapped back. He lost his balance and fell onto the make-out couple on the couch. He wiped a trickle of blood from a crack in his lip and squinted up.

Otis stood over him, hard bloodshot eyes glaring at him.

"You just made a big fuckin' mistake," Sokowski slurred.

"Bring it on, you piece of shit."

Sokowski pushed himself off the couple, knocking their beers to the floor in the process, but he didn't give a damn. His momentum drove his two hundred pounds forward fast and out of control. He took a slow, clumsy swing at Otis, but Otis dodged it easily and slammed him against the wall. The wood paneling cracked and splintered, and Sokowski slipped down the wall and slumped to the floor in a heap. He felt all eyes on him—the party grew hushed to watch the night's newest entertainment.

"Why don't you get your drunk ass the fuck out of here?" Otis hissed. The blonde had her hand on his shoulder and huddled safely behind her man.

"Fine." Sokowski pushed himself up the wall and struggled to keep his balance. He closed one eye to stop the double vision.

"That's what I thought. You're nothing but talk."

Sokowski's one open eye stopped on the gun rack beside him. He didn't give it a second thought. He reached over and grabbed the .30-06 and in the same motion swung the butt of the gun and cracked it against the side of Otis's head. The sound of wood against skull popped through the air. Otis's camouflage cap flew off, and he dropped to the floor, clutching at a growing welt on his greasy head.

Screams from the women filled the small space. Someone bumped into the stereo, and the needle scratched off the vinyl and left the trailer in silence. All the partygoers, wide-eyed and not wanting to get caught in the crossfire, backed away from the fight and headed for the door.

Sokowski gripped the rifle and pressed the tip of the cold steel barrel to Otis's temple. "You got anything else to say, motherfucker?" Spittle flew from his lips and clung to thick whiskers.

Otis covered his head with his hands, stared down at the floor, mumbled, "No."

"I can't hear you, bitch." Sokowski clicked off the rifle's safety.

As most of the partiers pushed and shoved their way out the front door, Carl sat at the kitchen table, big eyes barely blinking, watching his friend with a growing sense of dread. The fat woman on his lap had long deserted him. Carl's mouth hung open, and he shook his head back and forth slowly. He started to stand, then dropped down into the chair again.

Sokowski pressed the rifle barrel harder into the soft flesh of Otis's temple and smiled at the man's trembling body. He could see and smell the man's fear and liked the power it gave him.

Teddie appeared in the living room, tucking in his shirt—his pants were half zipped up, and his belt hung open. At the sight of Sokowski wielding the rifle, his face drained of color and he had to lick at his dry lips just so he could talk. "Aww, shit."

The blonde crouched beside Otis and started to cry. Black mascara leaking trails down her cheeks and over trembling red lips.

"You best get the fuck out, bitch. Unless you want to get splattered with this fuck's brain," Sokowski said.

She peered up at him, eyes frozen wide. She stood slow and careful and inched away from Otis, leaving him cowering on the floor by himself.

"Shit, Mike. That thing's loaded, man," Teddie whispered.

Sokowski still squinted through one eye and kept it focused down on Otis. "Good. Blow the fucker's brains out."

Teddie stepped forward. "Come on, man. Put it down. I don't need this shit."

Sokowski ignored him. His lips pulled away from his teeth and gums and he hissed down at Otis. "Next time I pull the trigger, motherfucker. Got it?"

Otis's body jerked and quivered as he managed to nod.

Sokowski spit a mouthful of blood onto the crown of Otis's head before finally lowering the rifle. Then he simply handed the gun to Teddie and walked toward the front door. Those in the crowd who were still sticking their heads inside watching the drama backed off and gave him a wide berth.

Carl quickly jumped to his feet, tripped on the chair, and then rushed to follow Sokowski from the trailer. Out on the porch, Sokowski glared at all the faces staring at him from the front yard. "What are you fucks looking at?"

Folks slipped deeper into the dark or toward waiting trucks.

Sokowski reared his leg back, then gave the keg a hard, violent kick.

"Fuck this shit." The keg wobbled off the porch and crashed to the ground with a thud—its tap snapped off and an explosion of beer foam erupted from it as it rolled wildly across the lawn, spraying the group of drunken men and women.

Sokowski got into his truck and slammed the door hard enough to rattle the window. Carl was only halfway in the cab when

Sokowski fired up the Chevy and gunned it across the gravel driveway. Pebbles showered the side of the trailer and forced the crowd to duck for cover. The truck fishtailed violently, but Carl managed to close the door as his body was flung across the front seat.

The fender clipped the mailbox and sent it flying as the truck hit the street running at forty miles per hour. Carl shot a look over at Sokowski, who clutched the steering wheel with ten white knuckles.

"Fuck," Carl managed.

Sokowski dug his smokes out of his pocket and popped one in between his lips. He punched the cigarette lighter with his fist and waited impatiently for the coils to heat up.

Carl grabbed two beer cans that kicked around on the floor of the truck. Cracked them both and handed one to Sokowski.

"That was some fucked-up shit," Carl muttered as he swigged his beer.

"I should've blown the fucker's head off. Piece of shit."

Carl nodded. "Yeah, well, he ain't worth it."

Sokowski sucked on his beer and pressed his foot harder on the gas pedal.

"You probably did me a favor, though. I would've probably ended up banging that fat bitch and gotten a case of the pecker drips." Carl forced a weak smile and gulped some more beer.

Sokowski looked at him and let out a small, dry laugh. "Your old lady would have chopped off your little friend and fed it to you for breakfast." They both laughed at the thought, which cut the tension a bit.

"That fucker was scared, wasn't he?" Sokowski said.

"I think the dumb bastard shit his pants."

Sokowski nodded and chuckled at the thought.

"So we goin' home?" Carl asked.

The cigarette lighter popped up, and Sokowski pressed the glowing coils to his cigarette, inhaled, and then blew out a cloud of smoke. He shot Carl a sideways look and smiled a smile that gave Carl a chill.

"Hell no. Night's early."

Carl didn't say nothing. Drank his beer and looked out the windshield as the truck weaved down the country road. Trees swept past in a blur. Blackness all around them. He had a bad feeling about where the night would take them, but he knew better than to say anything.

Danny

Danny had put another coat of orange on the robin's breast and now carefully painted tiny white specks on the bird's wings and head. It was shaping up real nice. Looked like a robin Danny saw in the springtime. He felt pleased with himself. Thought it might be the best figurine he had ever made. Of course, he paid special attention to this gift—he wanted it to be perfect.

Danny set the robin on his dresser and blew on it gently. It should be dry pretty quick, so he would be able to deliver it soon. He wasn't sure what time it was. Could never figure out how to tell time. Always got the big hand and little hand mixed up. The moon had been out for a while, and he felt hungry, so he thought it must be seven or eight o'clock. He opened a can of pork and beans and ate them cold because he didn't have anything to heat them up on. After he cleaned out the can of beans, he ate a tin of sardines and then an apple. Doc Pete said that an apple a day kept the doctor away. Doc

Pete was nice enough. Was always real good to him and didn't charge him nothing for his checkups. But Danny didn't like the cold touch of the stethoscope on his skin, and it felt kinda funny to get all naked in front of someone. Doc Pete said that he saw everybody in Wyalusing naked. Called their nude bodies birthday suits. Danny would smile and nod, but he didn't understand that one bit. If he was in the naked, how could he be wearing a suit?

The wind whipped up pretty good outside, rattling all the windowpanes and sending cold air sneaking in under the wood, so Danny put on his jacket and the red wool cap that Mrs. Bennett had made special for him. The cap was made out of wool and felt kinda scratchy, but it covered his ears so he wouldn't catch a cold.

Danny had found the Sunday funny pages someone had thrown away in a trash can down in the laundromat and thought it would make nice wrapping paper. But before he gift-wrapped the robin, he looked at all the drawings of cartoon animals. Those were his favorite. He liked Snoopy the best because Snoopy was smart and didn't ever say nothing. And Snoopy's doghouse reminded Danny of his own room. Small and safe, and nobody ever went inside it except for himself.

He touched the robin to make sure it was dry. No paint got on his fingers, so Danny put the figurine on the funny pages and wrapped it up tight. He didn't have any tape, so he just crumpled the edges together and shoved it deep inside his jacket pocket.

Down in the laundromat, the thump of wet clothes spinning in a dryer filled the quiet space. A woman with a big gut, thick thighs, and loose fat hanging from under her arms sat in front of one of the machines. Greasy, thin hair was plastered to her skull, and her thick ankles were discolored purple with large, bulging veins. She smoked a Salem 100 and sucked on an RC Cola while she stared at her clothes tumbling around and around in the dryer, like she was watching a television set.

She jerked in her chair as Danny stepped into the laundromat from the back stairs. "Hell. You scared the bejesus out of me, Danny."

"Didn't mean to."

She flicked some ash onto the floor. "I know you didn't. Just jumpy, is all. Getting close to closing time? You ain't gonna kick me out yet, are you, Danny?"

"Naw."

She turned back to the dryer to watch her clothes spin some more.

Danny looked at the other washers and dryers to see if anyone else would be coming back. They were all empty—she was the only one left.

"You got an extra quarter, Danny? Wanna get me another RC."

Danny dug in his pocket and took out three quarters. It was all the money he had until Mr. Bennett paid him for the week. He stared at his quarters for a second before he handed her one.

"You're okay, Danny. You're A-okay."

She struggled to her feet, let out a few hoarse grunts, then waddled over to the soda machine.

"Where you goin' anyways? It's late, ain't it?"

"I suppose. Just wanted to give Mindy a birthday present."

Phlegm rattled in her chest as she chuckled. She dropped the quarter into the slot, heard the can thump into the opening, then grabbed her ice-cold soda. "You've always taken a shine to that girl, ain't that the truth?" She cracked open her RC and plopped back into her seat, her breath rasping like she'd just finished a hundred-yard dash.

"Don't know nothing about that. She's just nice to me, is all."

"You're a good boy, Danny. Maybe not the sharpest knife in the kitchen drawer, but a nice boy like you should have a nice girl by his side." She smiled and blew out a cloud of smoke.

"Maybe so." Danny wanted to get going. He gripped the robin figurine in his pocket and shifted his feet back and forth. It was a good long walk to Mindy's, but the heavyset woman seemed lonely and clearly wanted some company.

"You still livin' upstairs?"

"Yes, ma'am."

"Shoot. Such a small room for a big fellow like you. How long you been livin' in that room anyways?"

"Ever since Uncle Brett went up to heaven."

She chuckled again, but there was no humor in her voice this time.

"Don't think that boy ever made it into heaven, Danny. Probably got turned right around at the Pearly Gates and sent downstairs with a one-way ticket. Mean son of a bitch. Always angry about something." Her cigarette hung from her lips, and a few ashes fell onto her lap as she talked.

Danny looked to the front door of the laundromat. "Yeah, well, he was just real sad most of the time and had a lot of bad things happen to him."

"Him? Ha. He was just born mean as a snake, is all."

"Maybe so."

The heavyset woman spit a piece of tobacco off her tongue and shifted in her seat. "Weren't really your fault about what happened to your folks."

Danny nodded.

"God knows you suffered enough from the whole thing." She shook her head at the thought. Slurped some more from the cola can. "Your poor mama and papa would be brokenhearted knowing how you ended up. Can't imagine one of my young'uns turning out like you did. Mercy me."

Danny stared down at the linoleum floor and noticed how dirty it was. A big wad of pink gum was stuck to the floor. He wanted to remember to scrape it up with a razor in the morning. Mr. Bennett said that folks only respected places that took pride in themselves.

"What time you locking up tonight?"

"When I get back, I suppose."

"That's a long walk, and it's colder than the dickens out there. You sure you don't want to just go in the morning?"

He shook his head. "Wouldn't be her birthday then."

Fat rolls on her belly shook from a spasm of laughter. "You're right about that, boy. Too sweet for your own good." She dropped her cigarette to the floor and squashed it out with her heel.

"Well, my clothes are near done. Won't be here when you get back, I suppose."

Danny smiled with relief. "Okay, then. S'long."

He made his way toward the front door. As he slipped into the cold night air, the heavyset woman called out after him, "Thanks for the RC, Danny!"

Sokowski

They drove in dead silence. The truck's wheels occasionally drifted and veered off the road and rode hard on the berm. The Chevy shook and rattled everything inside the cab. Sokowski was in a fucked-up mood and didn't feel like talking. He glanced at Carl out of the corner of his eye. The guy was a dumb-ass, but he knew better than to try to talk Sokowski out of anything. Carl didn't say anything, just sat there like a big, stupid bump. Quiet as a god-damned church mouse. He had Carl trained right. Just like a dog. If they shit in your house, you've got to keep shoving their nose in the mess and give them a good whupping until they get it. Carl was his dog, and Sokowski had him trained pretty well.

"Man's best friend," Sokowski mumbled under his breath, and chuckled a little.

Carl gave him a sideways look. "Huh?"

"Nothing. Just thinking about my dog."

Sokowski didn't have a dog, but Carl didn't question it.

As they flew through a stop sign, the way back to town zipped past them. They weren't far now. Sokowski spotted a white-tailed doe up ahead along the side of the road. The animal's eyes glowed white from the headlights, and it stood frozen at the sight of the approaching truck, then bounded the wrong way and into the path of the vehicle. Sokowski didn't slow down one bit. He kept his foot jammed to the pedal, fed it a little more gas, not giving a shit about the deer or his truck.

"Fuck, man . . ." Carl held on tight to his beer and pressed his free hand onto the dashboard and prepared for the collision that was about to happen. The left front fender of the truck clipped the hindquarters of the bounding animal and sent it flying into the ditch. The Chevy shuddered for a moment, swerved from the jarring impact, but didn't slow down. Carl whipped his head around and peered out the back window. The deer flailed in a flurry of hooves alongside the bank of snow before the truck turned the corner of the road.

"Fuck it. Roadkill now," Sokowski muttered under his breath. His bloodshot eyes stayed focused on the road. His destination was up ahead a quarter mile.

The truck finally slowed and pulled up a gravel driveway and skidded to an abrupt stop behind a blue Volkswagen Rabbit. The VW Rabbit had a few stickers of flowers and peace signs on the back window. Sokowski cut the ignition, and the truck's engine ticked angrily. He swung his door open, then turned and looked at Carl over his shoulder.

"You coming?"

"Shit, Mike—I don't think this is such a good idea."

"Didn't ask you if it was a good idea. You can stay out here and freeze your ass off or come in and drink a beer while I give Mindy a good fucking."

Carl swished his near-empty beer can. "Why don't we just head to my house? I got half a case of Schlitz."

"Fuck that. Mindy's got beer."

"You really think she wants to see you? It's late, and you're pretty messed up."

"Don't really care if the bitch wants to see me or not." Sokowski stepped out of the truck and slammed the door hard. Carl watched him weave his way toward the front porch. The path was icy, and Sokowski lost his footing and landed hard on his ass. Carl heard Sokowski cuss to himself and stand back up again. Sokowski took the steps two at a time and started to pound on the front door like there was a fire.

"Shit." Carl shook the last few drops of beer into his mouth, tossed the empty can to the floor, and stepped out of the truck.

Danny

Storm clouds choked out the moon and stars, leaving the countryside in a cover of darkness, black as a cup of coffee. The woods pressed close to the sides of Tokach Road, maple and pine trees moaning and swaying, limbs bare of any leaves. A creek—not yet frozen—ran along the side of the road, ice-cold water racing past rocks the size of garbage cans and over trees that finally toppled after their roots turned to rot. Turkeys, deer, raccoon, possums—all animals of the forest—kept hidden away, nestled somewhere warm, out of the wind and snow.

No signs of life except for the hunched lone figure tromping through the snow, leaning into the biting wind. Danny plodded forward, slow and steady. The wind suddenly changed direction and swept across the road, carrying with it large flakes of snow. They stuck to Danny's face like pieces of wet newspaper. His cheeks and nose were numb, but the cold didn't bother him none. He always liked wintertime and the cold it brought with it. The cold always made him feel a little different—not like the heat and humidity summer invited. He could think better and thought that the cold made him a bit smarter somehow. It probably didn't, but he liked to think that maybe it did. Being smart would sure be nice.

Since he'd been hiking up Tokach Road, not a single car had passed him by. It was pretty late, and most folks were probably already in bed. There were only a handful of houses out this way. Most were dark. Porch lights off. He passed by a house where two miniature snowmen stood in the front yard with carrot noses and knit caps perched on top of their heads. One of the snowmen was missing a coal eye.

Danny smiled with the memory of building his first snowman with his mama and papa. He was probably around five. Before the accident. He could remember a lot of things before the accident. The snow had been powdery dry and too light. It wouldn't pack right, and the snow fell apart in Danny's little mittened hands every time he tried to make a snowball. Frustrated tears ran down his small, chubby cheeks, and his papa had smiled down at him.

"Now, Danny-Boy, tears aren't going to help us none. We're not going to let a snowman get the best of us, are we?" Danny shook his head up at his father. "Your old man's got a few tricks up his sleeve."

He watched his father unspool the garden hose and spray down an area of snow on the driveway. His father winked at him. "Your tears won't be near enough. Need a little H_2O magic." He turned off the hose and bent down in the wet snow. He scooped a pile of snow into his lap and began to pack and shape a large ball. Tears slowed as Danny sat beside his father and watched his snowman start to take form. His father handed him a snowball about the size of a basketball. "There. We got us one snowman's head. Got to start somewhere."

Snow spit into Danny's eyes and shook him out of the memory of his first snowman. Up ahead, fifty yards or so, he saw Mindy's trailer. The porch light burned bright, so maybe she was still awake. A rusted blue Volkswagen Rabbit was parked out front of the trailer with a few inches of snow on the hood and roof. Parked behind it, blocking in the VW, a black pickup truck seemed to stand guard.

Danny noticed that there wasn't any snow on top of the big black truck. The truck looked like a lot of trucks around this area, but Danny knew whose it was. He kept walking anyway.

Mindy

It had been another long day on her feet—twelve hours that crawled by and seemed like days—and the shower felt invigorating. Hot water ran over her smooth body until her white skin had started to turn a light salmon pink. Mindy knew she wouldn't get out of the shower until the water heater ran cold. The shower seemed to be the only place she could escape everything for a while. All the disappointments, all the second-guessing, all the hopelessness she felt every day. She looked down at her paunch and pinched the extra flesh between her fingers. Could definitely pinch more than an inch. She made a promise to herself to start exercising again. Jogging, maybe. It was too cold right now, but maybe in the spring when the weather warmed up. When she turned thirty-five, she had made the same promise to take better care of herself. Exercise, better diet, better choice in men, the whole nine yards. That lasted a few days before she was back to the same old bad habits. The cigarettes, the drinking, the crap fried food, even assholes like Mike. Maybe this year would be different. Birthdays were always a good place to try to start. At the very least, she knew she should quit drinking so much beer. Stick to wine for a while.

Forty years old. I'm officially an old maid.

Mindy hated spending birthdays alone. She had a few girlfriends who offered to take her out, but she wasn't really in the mood. Shelly and Rhonda had invited her to go with them to the Cork and Bottle up in Towanda, but she'd declined. Too far to drive and she had to work in the morning, she told them. She enjoyed the company of men better than women anyway—Shelly and Rhonda usually ended up talking about their kids or their lousy marriages or the jobs that they hated. *Bitch, bitch, bitch.* Mindy just wanted to have a little fun and forget about her troubles and not worry about all that was missing in her life. Men were just more fun to hang with. Funnier and laid back and didn't get all petty when they went out drinking. But she wasn't in the mood to hang out with men tonight either. She'd had about enough of Wyalusing men for a while.

Mindy's mother had invited her over for dinner, but she knew that it would only lead to her mother's favorite—and Mindy's least favorite—conversation topic. Settling down and getting married. It's not that she didn't want to find someone to spend her life with, but it was slim pickings in Wyalusing. Mike definitely wasn't the answer. It had been fun at the beginning. The partying, the sex. He was wild and unpredictable. That might be fine in your twenties, but she wasn't getting younger, and what did she have to show for herself? A trailer her folks had bought her, a car that broke down more often than not, and a job slinging eggs and hash browns.

Great. Sounding like my girlfriends now.

Part of her couldn't deny that she was still drawn to Mike, but the smarter and more sensible part of her was scared of him. He had a short fuse and drank too much. Besides that, he didn't respect women. That much was clear.

God, I hate this town. Should've moved out of here after high school, when I had the chance. Maybe when Mom's gone.

She squeezed some cream rinse into her palm and ran it through her long hair. Maybe she should cut her hair real short. A little change would do her good. Any kind of change would do her good.

Mindy knew that she'd probably never leave Wyalusing. Where would she go anyway? And what would she do to make ends meet? All she knew how to do was wait tables. Been doing it ever since graduating high school. She had given the Friedenshutten twenty years of her life and would probably end up giving it twenty more. She thought about poor old Dotty—almost sixty now—hustling plates of food for maybe twenty dollars in tips on a good day. Dotty would probably be waiting tables at the diner until her hips gave out. Mindy shaved one of her legs and wondered if that was what she had to look forward to.

Maybe Prince Charming would roll into town one day and sweep her off her feet.

And maybe pigs will fly.

She started to shave the other leg and thought about putting in an application over at Taylor's. Half the town punched the clock over there, but the thought of working the kill floor, shooting a steel rod through the heads of beef cattle, or working the processing line for eight-hour shifts and coming home smelling like blood and cow shit didn't really seem like something she wanted to do. Mindy figured that waiting tables beat that kind of nonsense. Besides, with all the kids in town graduating high school and willing to work for minimum wage, Mindy knew she'd be hard-pressed to even get a job.

The water started to run cold, so Mindy turned off the shower and stepped onto the thinning bathroom mat that she'd had since forever. She wrapped herself in her favorite lavender robe and began drying her hair when the pounding on the door nearly made her jump out of her skin.

"Jesus Christ. Who the hell?"

She tightened her robe belt and walked out into the living room. She peeked through the curtain and saw Sokowski and Carl standing outside. Mindy could tell that they were both shit-faced.

"Goddamn it, Mike." She stomped over to the front door and swung it open. She was about sick and tired of this bullshit.

Sokowski

W hat the hell are you doing here? Said I didn't want to see you tonight." Mindy's hands were propped on the sides of her hips.

Sokowski grinned up at her, eyes gawking at her clean pink skin visible under the robe. "Good. You're all showered." He pushed past her, stinking of booze, weed, and a few days of not bathing. His eyes were glazed over, and his face had that slack effect he got when he was wasted—an expression Mindy had seen too many times to count.

"Jesus. You smell like hell. Your hot water not working?"

Sokowski chuckled a little. "Thought you liked the smell of a real man."

"Just what the hell you want?"

"Well, shit. We were just in the neighborhood and in the mood for a little nightcap." He helped himself to the refrigerator and grabbed a couple bottles of beer.

"Christ. Löwenbräu? This all the shit you got?" He popped the caps off on the edge of the kitchen counter and sucked one half empty.

Mindy turned to Carl, who was still standing in the doorframe, and shook her head. "Take his ass home, Carl."

Carl shook his head as well. "Tried to. He's in a mood." He stepped inside and stomped the snow from his boots onto the doormat.

"Well, I ain't in the mood for this shit tonight." A cold breeze blew into the trailer and sent a chill up Mindy's robe. She closed the front door and wrapped her arms around her chest.

Sokowski smirked over his bottle of beer. "You ain't gonna turn away an old friend, are you?"

Dirty, snowy footprints started melting onto her linoleum kitchen floor.

"You're tracking a mess in. I just cleaned. Jesus. What the hell do you want?" She grabbed a handful of paper towels and mopped up the slush on her floor.

Sokowski bent over and took her by the wrist. Pulled her up toward him. "Come on, baby. Want to wish you a happy birthday."

She pushed him away. Grimaced from the stench of his breath. "You're drunk."

"Yeah? So what of it?"

"I'm tired and want to go to bed."

"So who's stopping you? I'll join you."

She shook her head again, opened the refrigerator, and took out a cold beer. Sokowski removed it from her hands, popped off the cap, and returned the bottle to her. She took a sip of beer, then another. She had forgotten to eat dinner, and the beer sure tasted good.

Sokowski put his hand on her cheek, but she swatted it away. "I miss you. Lonely without you."

"Yeah? Got a funny way of showing it. Go on home, and we'll talk when you ain't so wasted."

He shrugged his shoulders. "Got a little buzz, is all."

Behind them Carl searched the kitchen cabinets for something to eat. Mainly cans of soup and instant noodles. He kept searching until he found a loaf of white bread and a jar of peanut butter. "You got any jelly? Strawberry or something?"

"No, Carl, I don't have any damn jelly. You two are unbelievable. I swear." Mindy bent down and resumed wiping up the floor, revealing a full view of her heavy breasts. Sokowski smiled and put a few dirty fingers between the lapels of her robe.

"Whatcha got hiding in there for me?"

She stood upright and gave him a good shove. "I ain't doing this anymore, Mike. It ain't worth it. You're sweet for a while, then you go back to your same old bullshit. We're through this time. I mean it."

"Says who?"

"Says me. I want no part of you anymore. You got to get your shit together."

"I got my shit together."

"Jesus, Mike."

"What? You fucking somebody?"

She laughed. "Yeah. I'm fucking somebody."

Sokowski's shit-eating grin melted away, and his eyes narrowed into tiny slits. He sucked down the rest of his beer and gripped the bottle in his fist good and tight.

"Who is it? You fucking Pat?"

"Pat?"

"Yeah. Pat from the fucking diner."

Mindy glared right back at him. "You're pathetic, you know that?"

She turned away from him, and he grabbed her wrist again. Harder this time. His fingers dug into her soft skin and pulled her up against him. He kissed her on the mouth as she tried to push him away.

"Stop it."

He kept on, kissing her cheek and neck. His beard scratched at her skin as she tried to wriggle free.

"Said to stop. Your beard. It's disgusting. Like a damn Brillo pad."

He didn't stop. Held her tighter and shoved his whiskers harder against her skin, rubbing and scraping at it like sandpaper.

Mindy shoved at him, then finally brought up her knee and popped him a good one right in the balls.

An explosion of wind dislodged from his lungs. He bent over, cupped his balls, and tried to catch his breath.

"Told you to stop, Mike. Wouldn't listen, would you?"

He wiped the tears from his eyes and gave her a deadly look. "If you're fucking someone else, I'll find out who it is and cut their fucking throat."

"Jesus, Mike. You're the one that fucks anything that moves."

"And just who am I fucking?"

"Who ain't you fucking?"

"Watch your mouth now, bitch."

"Come on, Mike. Let's go on home," Carl managed. He had some peanut butter smeared on his weak chin, and he gnawed on the sandwich like a rat.

"Shut it, Carl. I'm talking to the little whore here." He snatched Mindy by the arms and gave her a shake hard enough to snap her head back. "Gonna set her straight before we leave here tonight."

"I fuck whoever I like. Now, get the hell out." She snapped her arm free and slapped him hard across the face. The sound bounced off the trailer walls, and the smack left an angry red welt by his eye. "Fuck you, okay? Just fuck you."

Sokowski glared at her. "Fine. Ain't worth fucking anyway. You're nothing but white trash."

Mindy slapped him again and then spit right in his face. "You ain't no kind of man, Mike. You think you're all hot shit, but the truth is, folks think you're a joke. You walk around all tough. Mr. Big-Time Deputy. But you're nothing, Mike. Nothing."

"You best stop, bitch."

"I'm just getting started. You're just a mean, nasty little man, and nobody likes you. Why should they? You're a fucking waste."

Sokowski's whole body tensed and trembled. Rage growing. Feeding itself. "Shut up, woman."

Mindy laughed. Pointed a finger right into his face. "And you want to know something else? You're a shit lover."

"Not one more word. Or I swear to God."

"You can't fuck worth a damn. Not with that little pecker of yours." She watched him wipe the spittle from his cheek, then turned and walked toward the front door.

"Told you not to fuck with me." He raised the empty Löwenbräu bottle over his head and threw it hard. It zipped through the air and collided against the back of her skull. The bottle exploded into a dozen razor-sharp shards of green glass and rained down onto the floor.

Mindy slammed against the front door, and then her legs collapsed from under her. She didn't even bring her arms up as she fell face forward onto the hard linoleum floor with a sickening thump. Her front upper teeth shattered from the impact, and fragments shot into the back of her mouth. She took a quick reflexive inhale, swallowing jagged bits of teeth until they lodged deep down her throat. Her arms and legs jerked a few times, quick at first, then slowing until she grew completely still. Foamy white bubbles dribbled from the corners of her mouth and leaked onto the floor around her head.

"You fucking bitch. How do you like that?" Sokowski breathed heavy, his lungs whistling and his heart pounding rapid-fire in his chest.

Carl stood frozen in the kitchen, mouth full of peanut-butter mush. "Christ o'mighty." His tongue was thick and sticky. "What the fuck did you do, Mike?"

Sokowski stepped over the top of Mindy, staring down at her motionless form. A thick vein pulsated in the middle of his forehead. His head hurt, pulsating with rage. "Get up, bitch."

Mindy didn't move. Didn't twitch.

Sokowski tapped the tip of his boot into her side, but still nothing. He bent down and rolled her over onto her back. Her robe fell open, exposing her breasts and the brown patch between her legs. Blood flowed from the gash in the back of her head and spread across the floor around her.

Behind him Carl paced like a cat at a dog pound, all the while staring at Mindy and the growing puddle of blood. "*Ahh,* Jesus. You killed her, Mike. She's dead. She's fucking dead."

Sokowski whipped around and snarled, "Shut the fuck up. She ain't dead."

When he looked back down at Mindy, her eye flickered open, pupils fully dilated. A blast of adrenaline shot through her, and she swung her hands at his face. Slapping and clawing, yanking on his beard. She was stronger than she looked.

Sokowski grabbed at her hands, but she got one loose, and he took a violent smack to the face. Then she got fingers to each side of his head and ripped at his cauliflower ear. Her fingernails dug deep, leaving a trail of broken skin behind them.

"Knock it the fuck off!" he screamed down at her.

Her mouth opened, revealing bloodied gums, and gargled something. Her eyes bulged in their sockets, wide with fear. She kept fighting him as he pressed his weight down on her chest.

"Christ. Grab hold of her hands!" he barked at Carl. But Carl stood still, unable to move his leaden feet.

Mindy screamed, but it came out sounding like a thick hacking cough as she choked on the shattered teeth that stuck in the back of her throat. She spit up blood, and some more white foam bubbled from the corners of her mouth.

"Goddamn it, Carl!" Sokowski yelled.

This finally jerked Carl out of his trance. He dropped to his knees behind Mindy's head and grabbed at her hands. His palms were slick with sweat, and it took a few tries before he managed to get a good grip on her.

"What you gonna do?" he whined as Mindy bucked and flailed under Sokowski's mass.

Mindy's eyes bulged out even further, face turning redder and redder, but she managed to choke out a few ragged words. "You bastard . . . gonna go to jail . . ."

"Shut up."

"Fuck you, Mike. Fuck—"

"I said SHUT UP!" Sokowski wrapped both hands around her throat and started to squeeze. He didn't want to hear any more. Not one more word. He wanted to stop Mindy from saying anything more about him being nasty and mean. He squeezed harder, making sure that she couldn't spew more lies about him.

Mindy continued to fight him, gasping desperately for air as her windpipe was slowly crushed together. Her throat whistled and clicked. Her arms jerked, fingers trying to pry herself loose from Carl's grip, and her feet kicked against the linoleum floor, slipping in her own blood.

Sokowski's face twisted, darker and darker, as he used all his strength to squeeze the last of the air from her lungs. The fight in Mindy slowed a bit. Her jerky motions lost their strength until she finally stopped moving at all.

The trailer got quiet except for the labored gasps of both Sokowski and Carl. Their breaths catching in their throats. Chests rising and falling.

Carl stumbled backward and fell against the front door. He grabbed at his face, squeezed and pinched it together, then started to sob like a baby. He stared at Mindy and shook his head back and forth, crying and moaning. His blue jeans darkened at the crotch as his bladder vacated.

Sokowski finally loosened his grip on Mindy's neck, and her head lolled to the side. There was blood everywhere now. Smeared on the linoleum floor and soaking into the living-room carpet.

Blood from an open wound on his messed-up ear dripped down Sokowski's neck. He winced as he touched his cauliflower ear and took a look at the blood on his fingertips. Rage had sobered him up a little.

"Damn bitch." He stood and went to the kitchen sink and washed his hands real good. Ran a paper towel over his face and neck and shoved it into his pocket.

Carl was still crying, his knees pulled up and into his chest. He stared over at Mindy, snot running from his nose and leaking all over.

"Get up." The calm in Sokowski's voice wasn't natural.

Carl looked up at him like he didn't quite understand what he was saying.

Sokowski grabbed ahold of Carl's jacket collar and yanked him to his feet. "Stop your fucking crying, Carl. Christ."

"What do we do?" Carl blubbered.

"We get the fuck out of here. What the hell you think?"

Carl watched as Sokowski grabbed a handful of paper towels and wiped down the refrigerator door handle and the cabinet knobs that Carl had touched. Sokowski noticed the jagged beer neck on the floor and wiped that down, too. Carl's unfinished beer stood on the kitchen table. Sokowski drank it down in a few gulps and shoved the empty bottle into his jacket pocket.

He took a look around the trailer, making sure he took all traces of himself and Carl with him. Calm eyes stopped on the jar of peanut butter with a knife next to it. "Grab that shit and take it with you."

Carl nodded and picked up the jar and knife and held them awkwardly in his hands.

When Sokowski swung the front door open, Danny stood out in the driveway, still as a statue. Carl moaned at the sight of the big man, but Sokowski stood in the doorframe and maintained his composure.

Danny

Snow came down harder, a wall of white behind Danny, sticking to his cap and jacket in clumps. He could feel the heat from inside the trailer and thought it sure would be nice to warm up for a minute or so, but if the deputy was visiting Mindy, he didn't think he wanted to go inside.

"Whatcha doing out there, Danny?" Sokowski asked.

Danny looked up at him and put his hand protectively to his pocket, making sure Mindy's birthday present was still safe.

"Got something for Mindy, is all."

Sokowski stepped out onto the porch.

"Yeah? Well, kinda late, ain't it?"

Danny dug the toe of his boot into the snow. "Suppose so. Got her birthday present."

"Uh-huh." Sokowski ran his hand over his beard. "Well, we got a little problem in here. Mindy had an accident, Danny."

Danny looked at Sokowski, trying to figure out what that meant. Then he looked past him to Carl, who looked away real quick and wiped at his nose.

Sokowski went down the porch steps and stopped right in front of Danny. He never took his eyes off him. His movements were carefully measured as he put a hand on Danny's shoulder.

"Here's the thing, Danny. I need you to do me a favor. She's hurt kinda bad."

Danny swallowed hard. Nodded.

"Me and Carl are gonna go get help. I want you to go inside and stay there. That's real important. You gotta stay here with Mindy."

"Okay," Danny said.

Sokowski kept his hand on Danny's shoulder. "Someone hurt Mindy, Danny. We got here, and somebody did something real bad to her. You need to stay here just in case they come back."

All this scared Danny. He couldn't figure out who would want to hurt Mindy. She never hurt no one. She was nice and kind and for sure wouldn't hurt anyone.

"Can I count on you, Danny?"

"Yeah. I'll stay right here."

"Good boy, Danny. We'll be back as soon as we can."

Sokowski looked over his shoulder toward Carl, who stood very small behind him. "Let's go."

Carl didn't say anything. Just walked down the steps still holding the jar of peanut butter and headed to the truck. He made sure he didn't look at Danny—wasn't able to look him straight in the eyes.

Sokowski found his keys and climbed behind the wheel. Gave Danny a final glance. "Counting on you, Danny." He slammed the door shut and fired up the truck. The tires spun on the ice, finally got some traction, and then the big black truck backed up and pulled onto the snow-covered road and roared off.

Danny watched the taillights disappear into the night and turned back to Mindy's trailer. Some snow blew in through the front door and settled on the floor, making a real mess. He felt scared, but Mindy needed him. Besides, the deputy was counting on him. Said so himself.

Danny walked up the steps slowly, peeked inside, and slipped into the trailer.

Lester

Lester thought he heard the phone ring. It brought him out of a deep, solid sleep. Went to bed early these days. Lucky if he made it past nine P.M.

The phone kept ringing. God, how he hated that thing.

The wife nudged him with a solid elbow to his back and pulled a pillow over her head. "Phone," her muffled voice said from under the pillow.

"They can call back in the morning," Lester said as he glanced at the clock. It was a few minutes after midnight.

The phone didn't stop its awful clanging. Whoever it was, they weren't giving up, and since Lester didn't have one of those new answering machines, the phone would just keep on ringing.

Lester's wife gave him another shove. She wasn't going to let him sleep through this. She never let him sleep through phone calls in the middle of the night. She said that he signed up for the job and by God he had to hold up his end of the bargain.

"Might be important," she mumbled through half sleep.

"Hell." Lester sat up and rubbed at tired eyes that had heavy bags under them, bags the size of mandarin-orange slices. He had short-cropped hair. Simple and neat. Gray had replaced the black, and his bald spot kept expanding. The unfortunate by-product of his thinning hair was to make his already big ears look even bigger. He'd heard it all: Dumbo, Alfalfa, Howdy Doody, and Gomer Pyle. Gomer Pyle was the worst. He really hated that one.

The phone kept clanging. An old-fashioned phone he got back before his hair turned gray, the ringer nothing more than a brass bell with a small brass hammer that kept tapping as fast as a hummingbird's wings, annoying as hell.

Lester grumbled to himself and swung his arthritic legs out of the warm security of the blankets. His knees were a mess, all the cartilage nearly gone. Bone rubbing on bone in the joints. Winter was the worst on his old body. The cold made his legs so stiff that it took over an hour every morning to get him walking without looking like Frankenstein lurching about.

Eyes half closed, he stumbled out into the hallway and jammed his toe on one of the damned porcelain cats that Bonnie had placed all over the house. Her obsession with all things cat drove him nearly out of his mind. Cat calendars, cat figurines, cat bookends, cat-embroidered sweaters. She even wore cat pajamas to bed every night. Lester hated goddamn cats.

They had two slinking around here somewhere. Sneaky little critters. Probably clawing at his favorite reading chair or taking a crap in the litter box that stank up the whole damn house. Early on, after years of trying to start a family, Lester and Bonnie had to accept that kids weren't in the cards. Bonnie's body just wasn't built for it. Heck of a thing for a woman to endure. To make matters worse, Bonnie came from a big family. Six brothers and sisters. All of them had kids. Lots of them. Bonnie was the only one who couldn't produce. And now all of Bonnie's nieces and nephews had kids. Going to a family reunion was like attending a preschool with all the young'uns running around. So in came the cats. Thirty years of goddamned cats and Lester was ready to take a gun to either them or himself.

He fumbled for the phone that hung on the wall and answered it more to shut the damn thing up than to find out who might be calling. "Sheriff."

Lester listened for a second, and then his eyes opened a little wider. It was his deputy. Sokowski was usually such a hard-ass, but his voice sounded a little shaky. Unchecked.

"Danny Bedford? You sure?"

Lester kept listening. His hand went automatically for his shirt breast pocket—searching for his pack of smokes—then realized that he was wearing a pajama shirt.

"Slow down and back up a little bit, son. How long ago did Mindy call you?" Lester rubbed the gray stubble on his head as was his habit when he was taking in troublesome information. "I'll be damned. It's after midnight. What the hell is that boy doing out there so late?"

Lester walked into the kitchen. The telephone cord uncoiled and stretched to its limit as he kept listening to the deputy. Sokowski might be a little hotheaded, and a bit hair-triggered at times, but the man took his job seriously enough to keep folks in line. He usually played the bad cop to Lester's good cop. Sokowski tended to be rough around the edges and rubbed some people wrong, but he was still young enough and would hopefully mellow over time. The fact was, Lester knew he'd been growing soft over the years—hell, he'd always been pretty soft—and sometimes folks in town needed someone to keep them in line, or otherwise those same folks would just walk all over you. If you gave them an inch, they'd take a damn mile. Walk quietly and carry a big stick, that's what Lester always thought made for a good law-enforcement officer. Between himself and Sokowski, Lester walked quietly and his deputy carried the big stick. Besides, it wasn't like folks were exactly lining up to get the job of sheriff or deputy.

He grabbed his smokes from the kitchen counter and lit up a Camel and sucked in deep—he kept promising the missus that he would quit the habit, but it sure wasn't going to be tonight. Bonnie would throw out his packs of cigarettes when she didn't think he was looking, but he always kept a carton hidden around somewhere. Bad habits proved hard to break, especially when you'd been doing them for nearly fifty years. He would try to cut back a little. More for Bonnie than anything else. Maybe to half a pack a day. If he couldn't do that, maybe he'd try some Camel Lights. Baby steps, he told himself. Baby steps.

Lester nodded as Sokowski finished up what he was saying. "All right, then. Let me throw on some clothes. Meet you out there in ten minutes or so."

He put the phone back on its cradle and looked over to Bonnie, who was standing there now, wrapping herself up in a big, thick terry-cloth robe.

"Everything okay?"

"I don't know. Probably nothing."

Lester moved past her and turned on the hallway light. He kept working the cigarette in the corner of his mouth as he grabbed his uniform pants off the hook and hiked them up and over his pajama bottoms.

"The Knolls girl called Mike. Got herself all worked up because Danny Bedford showed up at her doorstep tonight."

"At this hour? What in the world for?"

He threw on his heavy sheriff's jacket and zipped it up to the neck. Didn't want to be catching a cold. That's all he needed right now. His immune system wasn't worth a damn these days. "Don't know. But according to Mike, Mindy was scared. Living alone and all, and Danny's a big drink of water."

"Oh, for heaven's sake. That boy wouldn't harm a hair on her head."

Lester nodded. Stabbed his cigarette out in an ashtray. "Maybe so. But she's got it in her mind that she needs us to get Danny out of there."

Bonnie nodded. "Well, be careful. The roads are likely to be pretty slick."

Lester plopped on his sheriff's hat, which had seen better days and could use a good washing. "You know me. Always careful." He grabbed an old leather gun holster worn smooth from years of riding on his right hip, strapped it around his waist, and cinched it up tight.

"You really think you need your gun belt?"

"Nope." He gave her a quick peck on the cheek. "And don't let them goddamned cats into bed."

She smiled at him. "You know me."

"Yeah. I do." He grinned right back at her.

"Want me to make you a cup of coffee?"

"Would love one, but I better get. Should be home in an hour or so." He headed for the door when he heard a jingling sound behind him.

"You might be needing these." Bonnie held out a set of truck keys between her fingers.

He smiled, took the keys from her, gave her another peck, and shuffled out the door.

Sokowski

Sokowski could smell the piss in Carl's pants. The idiot was stewing in his own urine and stinking up his whole damn truck.

"Jesus, Carl. You smell like hell. Shoulda changed into a pair of my pants."

"Huh? Naw. Your pants wouldn't fit me."

"Better than swishing around in your own juices. Shit."

Carl didn't answer. Just chewed on his thumbnail.

They had stopped by Sokowski's house to make the call to the sheriff. After Sokowski took care of that business, he made sure to grab a bottle of Wild Turkey—he had a few to spare in his liquor cabinet.

Now they were parked back in Mindy's driveway again, idling in the cold. Sokowski kept his eyes locked on the rearview mirror, watching and waiting. He wanted to suck dry the bottle of Wild Turkey nestled between his knees but thought better of it. He didn't want to stink of whiskey when Lester showed up. Miserable prick was always silently judging him. Sokowski lit up a cigarette instead.

Beside him Carl kept rocking in his seat, twitching and jerking like a chicken at feeding time. "Christ, Carl. Don't be going and *shitting* your goddamned pants, too."

"This is wrong, Mike. We're in a lot of trouble. Jesus. A lot of damn trouble."

A set of headlights appeared down the road a ways. Sokowski turned to Carl and gave him a cold stare. "Just keep your pie hole shut. I'll take care of it. I don't want you saying shit."

"But Danny's gonna say that we were here. That Mindy was already dead when he got here."

"Goddamn it, Carl. I got it covered. Don't say nothing or you'll just fuck everything up."

Carl nodded. He shoved his hands in his pockets, then took them back out again and resumed gnawing on his already gnawed-down thumbnail.

Snow crunched beneath the sheriff's truck tires as it pulled alongside them, white plumes of exhaust getting swept up in the unrelenting wind. Sokowski shoved the bottle of Wild Turkey under the seat, stepped out of the truck, and met Lester in the middle of the driveway.

"Well?" Lester worked a fresh cigarette in the corner of his mouth.

"Just got here. Haven't been in yet."

"Seen Danny?"

"Nope. Not out here anyways," Sokowski said.

Lester noticed Carl sitting in the truck. "What've you boys been up to?"

"Just doing a little drinking. Party up in Towanda."

Lester noticed a few tiny specks of dried blood on the side of Sokowski's neck and on his mangled-up ear. "What happened to your face, son?"

Sokowski rubbed at the side of his head. Shrugged. "Got into a little tussle at this party. Somebody mouthing off. Stupid shit."

Lester nodded and stepped up to the trailer door. Gave it a hard knock. No answer or sound from inside. He knocked again, harder this time.

"Mindy? It's Lester and Mike. You in there, missy?"

Again no response.

"Maybe Danny went on home," Lester thought out loud.

"Maybe so, but I didn't see him walking on the road or anything on the way out here," Sokowski offered.

Lester nodded. Better check and make sure. "Well." He tried the doorknob and found that it was unlocked. He pushed the door open and stepped on inside. He stopped short as his boot slipped in something slick. He looked down at all the blood, and the color drained from his smoke-lined face at the sight before him.

Mindy's corpse lay sprawled on the floor in front of him, half covered with the crocheted blanket. Blood and chunks of glass everywhere. The back of her head looked smashed in. Her throat discolored, black and swollen. And there was Danny, kneeling beside her, rocking back and forth on his knees.

"Jesus, Danny . . . what have you done, son?"

Danny heard his name and looked up to Lester. His eyes were red and puffy from crying. His head quivered a little. "She won't wake up, Sheriff."

"Son of a bitch!" Sokowski barked from behind Lester, spit flying from his lips. He shoved past Lester and threw himself right on top of Danny. Swinging wild fists that connected with the side

of Danny's face a few times, and Danny offered no resistance. He
kept his hands at his sides and took the beating.

Lester reacted, but too slow. Before Lester could get to him,
Sokowski hovered over Danny and delivered a violent steel-toed-
boot tip into his gaping mouth. A loud popping sound echoed off the
trailer walls as Danny's jaw cracked and shattered. Blood exploded
over his gums, and Danny's deadweight fell on top of Mindy's body,
snapping two of her ribs from the impact.

"Hell, Mike!" Lester grabbed Sokowski by the arm and tried to
throw him backward, but the deputy outweighed him by at least
fifty pounds. Even so, it was enough to knock Sokowski off balance.
Lester staggered back, slipped on a patch of congealed blood, and
fell into the kitchen table.

"Back off this now, Mike!" Lester's heart hammered in his
chest—hammered too damn fast. His face turned a bright shade of
crimson, and his eyes bulged in their sockets near to the point of
popping right out of his skull. He plopped down on a kitchen chair
to catch his breath and watched as Danny rolled off of Mindy.

Danny whimpered like a puppy pulled off its mama's teats. He
grabbed at his jaw and moaned again. He didn't even try to get up.
He just lay there on the carpet and stared up at the trailer ceiling.
His eyes flickered a few times before they rolled into the back of his
head and he shut down. His arms went limp and folded at his sides,
and blackness enveloped him and swallowed him whole.

Danny

D anny had the same dream again. It seemed to visit him when he was scared or confused or missed his folks a whole bunch. The dream always started in the middle of the pond. Wind snapped across the hard surface of frozen water, flurries of snow whizzing past. He stared down at his skates with two different-colored laces and watched them slice over the ice that blurred under them. He was laughing even though his nose stung and his ears throbbed from the cold. Then everything changed. The ice groaned and shifted under his ice skates, followed by the sound of snow crunching under his feet, and then the crackling of breaking ice filled the air. Above him the sky drifted clear as a bell jar. He tried running from the sound, but the crackling just got louder and louder no matter how fast his legs took him, until that was all he could hear. *Breaking ice.*

The world below him gave way, and he got sucked into cold

darkness. The cold touched every part of him, water soaking through his winter clothes. His arms flailed in the ice water as it wrapped around his body like a wet sleeping bag. Screams were cut short as water was sucked down into his lungs, and he kicked and thrashed, but he sank deeper and deeper into the black abyss. Above him he could make out the shadows of his desperate parents, reaching down for him and yelling for help. They were surrounded by a cone of light. The same sunlight penetrated the dark water's surface, creating a hazy shaft of brightness that stopped short of reaching Danny. He kicked desperately to try to reach it. His hands stretched up toward the two shadowy forms that seemed to lean through the light. Under the water Danny could hear another cracking sound. It was louder than the one that had sucked him in. It sounded like hard claps of thunder. Loud and thick, and he could feel it in his bones. Ice collapsed all around the cone of light, and the shadowy figures plunged into the water over him. Their bodies twisted and swirled above him, creating clouds made up of thousands of tiny white bubbles of air. More water filled Danny's lungs, and he sank deeper. He let it take him and stopped fighting. Just gave up. The image of the sun above him grew smaller and smaller until it was a tiny point of light.

Then voices broke through his dream. Men's voices. They sounded familiar, but he had never heard them before in this dream.

"His jaw is broken in a few places. That much is for sure. Probably needs to be wired. Possibly surgery, but he's gonna have to go to the hospital for X-rays to determine all that." The man sighed with a hint of a dry chuckle. "I'll be damned. Your deputy gave him a good walloping for sure."

"Hell." It sounded like the sheriff's voice.

Danny's eyes slowly flickered open. He stared up at the ceiling, where a bright exam light shone down on him. He tried to lift his head up, but a shock of searing, red-hot pain ripped through his body from crown to toe. It kinda felt like when he was playing with that yellow jackets' nest behind the house when he was just a kid, but even worse. A few dozen angry wasps took after him and stuck their stingers in his face and neck and back. Danny had never felt pain like it again. Not until now.

Doc Pete put a warm hand to his chest. "Easy, boy." Doc Pete always had a smile for Danny, but he wasn't smiling now. His pock-marked face and smudged-up glasses stared down at him, real sad like.

Doc Pete looked over to Lester. "You going to run him up to the hospital?"

Lester shook his head. "This situation's a little bigger than me right now. A homicide makes for state business. Fixing to put a call in to the Towanda state police office. Guess I need to call for an ambulance, too. Hell."

"You want me to run over and take a look at Mindy?"

Lester shook his head again. "No need. She's gone. No way around that."

Danny turned to look at Lester and tried to speak. He wanted to know where Mindy had gone to. Maybe she was okay after all. He opened his mouth, but his tongue stuck thick in his throat and another shot of pain made his skull flinch with a flare of white light.

"Never thought this boy could hurt a fly. Can hardly believe he would do such a thing." Doc Pete spoke to Lester like Danny wasn't even there.

"Yup. Missus said the same sort of thing. But he was never the same after the accident. Losing his folks and all. Who knew what was ticking inside that brain of his?" The sheriff reached into his shirt pocket and grabbed his smokes. Tapped one out and offered one to Doc Pete. The doctor accepted and both men lit up and sucked on their cigarettes.

"Well. Mind if I use your phone? Need to make a couple of calls."

"Help yourself. Might just as well brew us a pot of hot coffee. Figures to be a long night. A long night."

Lester sighed again and followed Doc Pete out of the exam room, neither one of them turning around to look at Danny.

Carl

Carl slouched in a waiting-room chair that had seen better days, chewing at his fingers and his eyes twitching as if someone had just kicked a bunch of sand into his face. He never much cared for Doc Pete's office, because it was too quiet, and all the plants were made of plastic, and the pictures hanging on the walls were paintings of fields of flowers, and all the magazines were boring and out of date. The last time he'd visited Doc Pete's office had to be twenty years ago when he busted his head open after turning over his dirt bike. Doc Pete put more than a dozen stitches in his skull and told him to come back in a few weeks to have them removed. Carl never came back. He ended up taking the stitches out himself.

Carl had to help load Danny into Lester's truck and then drive over to Doc Pete's with him. Sokowski stayed behind at Mindy's, and when Carl left the trailer, Sokowski gave him a look that said it all: *Don't say a fucking word.*

Carl jumped an inch off his seat as the door to the exam room opened and Doc Pete and Lester stepped out into the hallway. He saw Danny sprawled out on the exam table for a second before they closed the door behind them. Carl tried to read their expressions. Tried to figure out if they knew what he and Sokowski had done. Danny probably told them everything. Probably told them that Mindy was dead when he got there.

Oh, Jesus, they know what I've done.

Carl's heart pounded like a jackhammer. He could hear the thudding in his chest and thought that Lester and Doc Pete would be able to hear it, too. He kept his gaze on the two men at the end of the hallway, whispering to each other and looking his way every few seconds.

Maybe I should run. Just run out the goddamn door.

But it was too late for that. Lester and Doc Pete came down the hallway and stopped in front of his chair.

Lester sighed, searched his pockets for his pack of smokes, and lit a fresh one off the one that was still burning. "Carl."

Just a single word, but it scared the hell out of Carl. He stood up with a bolt, barely able to contain the twitching in his arms and legs. He wanted to confess. Wanted to blurt out his guilt and be done with it.

Lester pressed his index finger and thumb into the corners of his eyes and rubbed at them hard. "Do me a favor and stay here and make sure Danny doesn't go nowhere. He's a mess and probably can't stand on his own two feet, but you never know. I'll meet up with the staties over at the trailer and send them back to pick him up in a little bit. Doc Pete will be here, but just in case."

"What did Danny say? He talking?" Carl asked, a little too quickly.

Lester stopped working at his eyes and gave Carl a curious look. "You okay there, son?"

Carl found himself taking a step away from the sheriff. He forced his head to nod up and down. "Yeah. Just kinda in shock, I guess. Thought maybe Danny might've said what happened."

"What's to say? Pretty clear what he did. Besides, his jaw is so messed up, I don't imagine Danny will be talking for a while."

Carl glanced over at the door to the exam room. "You sure you want me to stay here? With Danny."

"Don't have much of a choice here at the moment. Once I get back to the trailer, I'll send Mike on over. Shouldn't be but a half hour or so."

Carl's big possum eyes blinked rapid-fire for a second. "But I ain't a deputy or anything."

"Well, I guess for the next few hours you'll be an unofficial one. I don't believe Danny will be doing anything else, but just in case it might be better to have someone here with the doc."

Carl kept staring toward the exam room, opened his mouth to say something else, then just nodded instead.

Doc Pete showed Lester into his office and shut the door behind them, and Carl went back to gnawing at his fingernails again. Chewing at them until his fingers started to bleed a little. He kept glancing toward the door of the exam room, knowing he should just stay put, but finally started to move toward it. He got a few feet, stopped halfway down the hall, and checked back over his shoulder.

What the hell am I doing?

He was having trouble thinking—his brain doing flip-flops. He rubbed at the thinning hair on his head and noticed how badly his hands were shaking. Everything had happened so fast. He knew that Sokowski had a hair-trigger temper but never thought he was capable of what Carl saw him do to Mindy. This thing was bad. Part of him knew he should tell the sheriff what had happened before things went any further, but it wasn't just Sokowski that was in trouble. Carl had held her goddamned hands and watched as Sokowski had choked the life right out of her.

He helped. He helped Sokowski kill her for no good reason. He'd be going to jail for what he did. Rotting away in some cell all because of Sokowski.

Carl got to thinking about his kids, little Betty still tromping around the house in diapers. She went through about six or eight of them a day, and he wished he would have changed them once in a while instead of making the wife do all that kind of stuff. Baths, supper, bedtime—all that fell to Kelly to do. And Ben was an awful handful, always skinning up his knees, breaking everything he touched, and picking on his sister until she bawled louder than a coyote. Carl would sit right there in the living room chair, drinking beer and watching it all unfold and never lift a damn finger to help out his old lady.

Maybe he always bitched to Sokowski about Kelly, but she was a good woman—married *his* sorry ass. She was a good mama, too. Raising the kids the best she could. And what did she get in return? All he did was bitch and bellyache about having to always eat chicken-fried steak, that the trailer was a pigsty, that all she did was sit around and watch that stupid *Wheel of Fortune*. Maybe she'd gained a little weight since having the kids, but Carl knew he wasn't any prize. Losing hair and gaining weight around the belly by the day.

Carl regretted everything he didn't do for Kelly. Never took her to a nice dinner at the Salty Cow. Hardly ever remembered her birthday, and even if he did, he never got her anything. Never bought her a new dress or fancy shoes for Christmas or their anniversary. He never did shit but bitch.

It was now only because he faced a whole mountain of trouble that Carl got to thinking about all this stuff—taking his wife and kids for granted and treating them like shit. If he somehow got out of this whole mess, he promised himself all that would change. He'd help around the trailer, take some time for the kids, and treat Kelly like something other than a royal pain in the ass. If he got away with what he'd done tonight, he'd stop hanging out with Sokowski and get a real job over at Taylor Beef or up at Sylvania in Towanda. Hell, he would even be willing to give up the pot and slow down his drinking to just the weekends. Whatever it took.

Damn Mike.

Carl licked at his dry lips and reached for the door to the exam room.

Taggart

State Trooper Bill Taggart sat in the rec room that was the gathering place for officers reporting to duty and for those who were wrapping up their shift for the day. He nursed a lukewarm cup of awful coffee, rereading a dog-eared copy of Charles Bukowski's *Post Office* for the fourth or fifth time. He liked all Bukowski's books, but *Post Office* had to be his favorite. The crazy bastard drank too much and chased too much tail, but his observations of all the little things in life—sad, pathetic people and the lives they led—cracked him up. Taggart always kept some kind of book handy. He'd rather read a book than talk to the mental midgets he worked with.

A half dozen officers shot the breeze at other tables, talking about their night and making plans of where to go after they clocked out for the day. Taggart was at least twice as old as every one of them and looked twice as old as well. In their mid-twenties, single, and horny, and they partied as if every day was a Friday night. The rec room was like a frat house around the station, and Taggart was the dinosaur that didn't fit into their clique. The odd man out. Story of his life. He knew they talked about him and laughed their asses off at him behind his back. Taggart's fondness for books earned him the nickname of "Professor" in the Towanda office, and that was fine with him—let them laugh.

He glanced at his watch. One-forty A.M. Twenty more minutes, and then he would pack it up for the night. His shift had been pretty uneventful. Dealt with a few snow-related automobile accidents in the area and assisted in a holdup at a doughnut shop downtown. A junkie needing to get some fast cash for his fix had walked into a Dunkin' Donuts with nothing but a baseball bat and a bad jonesing for heroin. The dirtbag had smashed a few windows and broken the arm of the teenage clerk, then made the mistake of using the john to relieve himself. Happened all the time—a felon so wired and jacked up by committing his little crime of theft or rape or murder that the urge to defecate becomes too overwhelming. When Taggart arrived, the junkie still sat in the men's-room stall, heeding the call of nature. Taggart enjoyed shoving the punk's head into the unflushed toilet. Served the bottom-feeder right.

Worthless street scum. It's just getting worse.

From the corner of his eye, Taggart watched the new guy approach. Tall and gangly, a big pointy nose over thin lips, and barely any facial hair to speak of. At the table behind the new guy, three other officers looked on with big, stupid grins.

"Hey, Bill. A few of us are heading over to the Cork and Bottle after our shift if you want to join us," the new guy offered.

The other officers cracked up at the table, loving every second of it. Taggart picked up his coffee, stood, and spoke loud enough so that the others could hear him.

"Tripper, right? I appreciate the offer, but I don't drink. Five years sober now."

Tripper turned a bright shade of red and backed away from Taggart like he might be contagious. "Shit. Sorry. I didn't know. I was just talking with the other guys. I'm sorry. Really."

Taggart gathered up his book and newspaper and spoke slow. "I know you didn't. You're just getting initiated, is all. Have a good time, and drive safely." After Taggart stepped out of the rec room, he heard the eruption of laughter behind him.

Assholes. Self-righteous assholes.

He walked down the long hallway, fluorescent lights glimmering off the spick-and-span linoleum floor, and stepped into the men's room. His blood pressure was soaring.

Bullshit at work. Bullshit at home. Can't get away from the bullshit.

He stepped into the last stall and locked the door behind him. He listened to make sure that no one else was in the restroom, then removed the lid to the toilet basin.

They can kiss my ass.

Taggart reached into the water basin and pulled out a pint of Smirnoff vodka. It was half empty. He spun the cap off and tilted back the bottle. He drank deep twice, then washed it down with the cup of coffee he was still carrying.

Taggart recapped the bottle, then looked at his watch again. One forty-five A.M.

Hell with it. Almost quitting time.

Before he could talk himself out of it, Taggart spun the cap back off and drained the rest of the clear liquid down his throat. He wrapped the empty bottle in the sports page and stuck it in his back pocket. And, as was his routine, Taggart took the ever-present box of peppermint Tic Tacs from his breast pocket and popped three mints into his mouth and crunched them up.

Taggart stepped to the sink and washed his face a few times with soap and hot water until he thought he could pass the sniff test. He dried his face off and then made the mistake of glancing in the mirror—he looked like hell. His face was red, splotchy, and bloated. His head looked enormous, too big for his body, like the Pillsbury Doughboy minus the cheery smile. He had a pronounced brow that stood guard over deep-set, kelly green eyes. Blond hair turning white. Big, thick shoulders supported a thick neck. He had always been barrel-chested, but now his gut kept getting larger, heavier, and lower. He leaned a little closer to the mirror and inspected a few tiny red spider veins on the tip of his nose.

How does everybody not know? It's written all over you, you piece of garbage.

He turned away from his reflection. Couldn't stand looking anymore at the man he had become. Once upon a time, some twenty years ago, Taggart used to look good in a uniform. He turned quite a few heads in his day. But not recently. The booze had seen to that.

He shook a few more Tic Tacs into his mouth and stepped out of the restroom. He headed in the direction of the locker room to put another day to an end, tired feet barely lifting off the floor.

"Bill?"

Taggart stopped at the sound of his name. He turned too quickly and almost lost his balance. The half pint was hitting him pretty fast and hard. A female desk sergeant walked down the hall toward him holding a blue slip of paper.

Shit. You got to be kidding me.

The female officer stopped in front of him and held out the blue slip of paper. "We got a call from the sheriff's office in Wyalusing over in Bradford County. Homicide. Female victim. The local sheriff says that they have the suspect in custody."

Taggart listened to her but still didn't take the blue slip of paper from her hand. She extended it out a little further. "Ferguson wants you to take this."

"Christ. Just great." Taggart reluctantly took the slip of paper. "I was just getting ready to head home."

She shrugged her shoulders. "Guess you'll get the OT."

Taggart looked at the slip of paper like it was written in Latin. "Wyalusing? Sounds like the sticks. Where the hell is it?"

"About thirty miles southeast of here. You know where Wysox is?"

"Yeah. I know the place."

"Well, Wysox is the last town with streetlights before you get to Wyalusing."

"Christ," he said again.

The female officer offered him a half smile. "Drive safe." She turned and went back down the hallway.

Taggart stared at the blue slip of paper for what seemed like an eternity, then sighed and made his way toward the locker room. He needed to get something for his drive.

Sokowski

The trailer reeked something awful. Mindy's body had released a bunch of shit and piss, and the place smelled like a goddamn outhouse. A garbage can propped the front door wide open, but it didn't help matters much.

Sokowski sat at the kitchen table smoking another cigarette. He had found a bottle of Jack in the cabinet and was in the midst of putting a pretty big dent in it. He didn't give a shit. Who would blame him for taking a drink after he found a murdered girlfriend in her trailer? Everybody in town knew that they dated off and on over the years. He planned on playing the victim card and soaking up all the sympathy that it would bring with it. Most folks would be glad that he kicked the shit out of Danny—served the retard right. If he played this thing the correct way, he could come out looking like a goddamned hero.

Sokowski smiled to himself. He knew exactly what he would say.

The son of a bitch killed my girl. Murdered her for no good reason. I knew something was bound to happen. Goddamn retard showed up at the diner nearly every day. Always staring at her, gawking at her. He probably planned this thing for years. If he couldn't have her, he didn't want anybody else having her either.

Sokowski thought he'd even be able to work up a few tears when he delivered his sad-ass speech. Folks around here would eat that shit up. By kicking Danny's ass, he'd provided a little street justice and done a service for every father out there that had lost a daughter at the hands of some murderer. Every man in town would be lining up to thank him and admiring his self-control in not killing the stupid moron.

Carl, on the other hand, needed to keep his big fat yap shut. Sokowski knew that Carl wasn't that bright, and if he got asked too many questions and got too nervous, he would slip up about something. Sokowski wished that he'd had the chance to talk to him before he left with the sheriff, but Lester needed help unloading Danny's fat ass over at Doc Pete's.

Sokowski also wished that Lester would have just brought Danny's ass down to the station and tossed him in the lockup, but the old buzzard wanted Doc Pete to take a look at the retard's jaw. Doc Pete's was closer, Lester said. Besides that, Lester thought Danny wouldn't try anything else. Goddamned Lester. Treated everybody with kid gloves. The old bastard was more worried about how people would feel and what they would think of him than just doing his job right. He wouldn't even let Sokowski cuff Danny, for Christ's sake.

Fucker needs to go and retire already.

He poured another drink and drank it down. His head was buzzing pretty good now. The numbness gave him a sense of calm. It was all gonna work out. Danny was so fucking dumb that he wouldn't say nothing, and even if he did, who was gonna believe a goddamned retard?

He looked over at Mindy's corpse.

Her and her big fucking mouth. If she weren't such a smart-ass bitch and just gave me a little, this whole thing wouldn't have happened.

She knew about his temper. Wasn't nothing new. She should've known better than to pop off at the mouth. He would have probably ended up getting married to the woman someday and having kids and all that happy shit. He made good money selling weed, and once Lester dropped dead or hung up his hat, Sokowski would step into the sheriff's shoes and make even more money off the county.

It's her own damn fault that she's dead.

Sokowski had witnessed death up close—it wasn't anything he hadn't seen before. Not long after he put on the deputy hat for the first time, he found his own father with his head split open like a smashed watermelon. Found him in the same barn where Sokowski currently grew his weed. The old man hadn't been dead long. Blood hadn't dried, still trickling down the walls, and the shotgun still leaned against the bastard's chest. The ten-gauge had removed the better part of his skull and splattered his pathetic brain across the barn. It was up to Sokowski to clean up the mess after they hauled away his old man's sorry ass. The old bastard was always weak. He was soft. Never had a backbone. Then he got even weaker after his whore of a wife ran off for the last time when Sokowski was sixteen. The old man became a walking shell. Many a night Sokowski could hear him crying like a goddamn baby in his bedroom. Pissing and moaning about losing his wife. Love made the old bastard weak. Sokowski could never understand it—he didn't even love his own goddamned mother. She slept around, drank like a damn fish, and treated the two men in her life like an inconvenience. Then, on Sokowski's twentieth birthday, the old man couldn't take it anymore. Couldn't take the loneliness and knew that his whore wife wasn't ever coming back. He stuck a ten-gauge shotgun in his mouth—the same ten-gauge he gave Sokowski one Christmas—and blew his troubles away.

Sokowski wasn't weak like his old man. No sir. He'd never let some stupid bitch ruin his life.

The bottle of Jack called his name, and he answered. Poured another drink and looked over the glass at Mindy as the burn went down. Blood still worked its way out of the back of her head, soaking into the carpet. Sokowski snorted a laugh at the thought of Mindy and his old man having something in common after all—the backs of their heads split open at the end of their sorry lives.

Sokowski looked over at Mindy's phone and had a thought. Maybe he needed to stir the pot a little more. Make sure this thing looked like what he wanted it to look like.

He drank some more, then stood and dropped his cigarette into the sink. He searched through her kitchen drawers and finally found what he was looking for—a thin Yellow Pages book, dog-eared and dirty. Mindy had doodled a few flowers on the cover and written down a couple of phone numbers.

Probably some guys she's been fucking.

Sokowski considered calling their sorry asses and finding out who the hell they were, but he wanted to stay focused on the task at hand. He'd deal with them later. He thumbed through the phone book and squinted at the names and numbers that were blurry spots of ink from the whiskey. He found the number he was searching for and reached for the old rotary phone and dialed a number. After a few rings, someone on the other end picked up.

"Red's."

"Hey, Bobby. It's Mike. Is Johnny Knolls drinking tonight?"

"We're closed, Mike."

"Hell. I know that. But I figured that you hadn't kicked Johnny out yet. So is he there or not?"

Bobby didn't answer. Just banged the phone down on the bar and Sokowski waited and could hear the din of drinking and laughing on the other end of the line. After a long minute, a man got on the phone.

"Hey, Mike. What's up?"

"Johnny. 'Fraid I got some bad news. Been an accident out here at Mindy's. Might want to head out this way."

Johnny asked a few questions, irritation in his voice. Sokowski said yes to a few things and reached for the bottle of whiskey.

"Best you come out and see for yourself. Gotta go. Sheriff will be here any second."

He returned the phone to its cradle and decided to skip the glass and drink straight from the bottle. It bubbled a few times before he set it back on the counter.

Damn. Bladder's full. Have to piss like a racehorse.

He stepped over Mindy's body like she was a piece of furniture and made his way toward the bathroom.

Lester

Lester's truck rumbled and bounced on Tokach Road back toward Mindy's trailer. He had the wipers going on high as a heavy layer of snow started coming down pretty good. Big, wet flakes pelted against the windshield from the hard wind, covering the road and making it a bitch to see. Now, with the dropping temperature, he'd have to worry about the dirt roads icing over. When they did that, they were going to be slicker than bacon grease. Like the missus always said, *When it rains it pours.*

Lester had called up to the state troopers' office in Towanda from Doc Pete's office. Told dispatch about the situation he had on his hands so that they'd send a cruiser down his way. They had asked him if he had a suspect, and he told them that he did. He didn't tell them about Danny's broken jaw. He figured that could wait. *Put out one fire at a time,* as Lester's grandfather used to say. The Towanda dispatch told him to hold tight and help would be on the way.

This whole thing was a damn mess. He knew he'd be the one to have to make the call to Mindy's folks. Probably best to do something like that in person, but he didn't know if he was up to that. How exactly do you tell two parents that their daughter was beaten and strangled and killed in cold blood? Johnny Knolls was a big son of a bitch, too. Temper like a hound with ticks. Mindy was his baby girl, and Lester knew what he'd want to do in Johnny's situation: hang Danny up by his bootstraps and gut him like a deer. And, to make matters worse, Mindy had a pair of older, overprotective brothers. Nothing like their old man. Not mean and unpredictable like Johnny, but two no-nonsense kind of men who would want an eye for an eye.

"Hell."

Murder wasn't something he signed up for. He'd grown used to dragging drunks out of bars on payday. Breaking up fights. Domestic stuff. Housewives taking a bottle or a frying pan to the side of a drunk or cheating husband's head. But at the end of the day, it was usually just a broken nose or a few stitches. Not anything like this nonsense.

And the cherry on Lester's turd sundae was that his deputy lost his cool and went apeshit and broke a man's jaw. Danny probably deserved it, but it wasn't their job to give payback. Lester knew that Sokowski had dated Mindy off and on for a while now. He didn't even try to keep track if they were currently an item or not. The fact was that Sokowski stuck his weasel in near everything that moved in Wyalusing, and everyone knew it.

Lester had been wanting to take the wife up to Niagara Falls for a few days in a week or so. Their forty-fifth wedding anniversary was approaching, and Niagara was where they had spent their honeymoon. It was only a four-hour drive up that way, and he figured that the missus would like that pretty well. Bonnie deserved a special weekend. The woman earned it. She was a damn good wife who had lived a life full of disappointments; not being able to bear any children was definitely the biggest. Still to this day, he could see her inner longing for kids and grandbabies every time they were out at a restaurant watching other families together. Eating and laughing and enjoying themselves. At least Lester had had his job over the years to fill the emptiness. All Bonnie had were the cats and sewing and tending to her garden. Yet she never complained none. God bless her.

A nicotine craving started to crawl all over him, so he found his cigarettes and lit one up. Unrolled the window despite the freezing cold outside. The breeze felt mighty good on his face.

"Hell," Lester muttered again as he blew out a cloud of smoke. Up ahead he saw Mindy's trailer and took another, deeper draw on his cigarette.

Danny

The exam room was in sore need of a patch-and-paint job. The ceiling peeled in a few spots from years of rain damage, and the walls weren't in much better shape. A long counter with a stainless-steel washbasin was lined with jars of cotton swabs, wooden tongue depressors, bandages, ear- and eye-exam lights, and the like.

Carl fidgeted in a small chair and looked around the room at everything except Danny, who now sat upright and on the edge of the exam table. Flecks of dried blood stuck to Danny's face and neck, and his jaw had swollen up and hung open, slack and to the right. The inside of his mouth wasn't much better—a mess of loose teeth and torn-up gums. Danny looked down at his hands and said nothing to Carl.

Outside the exam room, they could hear Doc Pete moving around and probably fixing himself a pot of coffee.

Carl kicked some mud off his boots and cleared his throat. "It was an accident, you know?" His voice came out sounding small and uncertain.

Danny picked at a rip in his work pants and was quiet for a second before responding. "Where's Mindy now?" Saying just these three words caused Danny a world of hurt, and they came out sounding like he was talking with a mouthful of marbles. *Wharths Mindee na?*

Carl looked over at him, then turned away and shook his head. "She's gone, Danny."

Danny finally looked up at him. Tears welling in his eyes. "What do you mean she's gone? What happened to her? She's really *dead?*" The words came out sounding like, *Wha ya meen sheez gon? Wha hapin to har? Sheez reelly ded?*

Carl fidgeted in the seat and ran his hands over his bald spot, near tears himself. "We'd been drinking, and Mike wanted to see her." He bit at his fingers again. "Shit o'mighty."

Everything was moving fast in Danny's head. The notion of Mindy really being dead and gone didn't quite seem real. He could still see her smashed-in head and her swollen throat and all that blood. *What kind of accident could make all that happen?* He wanted to understand.

"How . . . ?" was all he could manage.

The question made Carl stand up like he'd just sat on a piece of glass. He crossed to the window that looked out from the back wall of the exam room. He peered outside, seeing a cornfield covered in snow that led to a tangle of thick trees and brush. Beyond that, the trees faded into the blackness of the Endless Mountain range that surrounded the entire town.

A phone rang from somewhere in the doctor's office. A set of heavy footsteps walked quickly toward the source of the ringing, and Doc Pete's muffled voice could be heard talking on the phone.

Carl turned around and finally faced Danny.

"Look, Danny, I know I ain't never done shit for you, and I was like everybody else in high school, picking on you and making fun of the way you talk and act and shit. I guess I never cared about how all that stuff made you feel, but I was just a kid, you know?" Carl stopped and thought for a moment before continuing. "The fact was, I didn't think you and I were that different." He wiped his nose on his sleeve, leaving behind it a snail trail of wet snot. "Every class has to have a kid to pick on and get their balls busted. I didn't want it to be me, so I joined right in with the other kids and made you the butt of the joke."

Doc Pete stopped talking, and the office outside the exam room went quiet.

Carl noticed this and kept on talking. "And I'm sorry about what happened to you and your folks back then and all, but that wasn't my fault." He ventured another step closer to Danny. "This shit that happened at the trailer between Mindy and Mike, there's nothing we can do to bring her back. It's done. She's gone. You understand?"

Danny usually had a hard time looking at folks when they spoke to him. He always looked at his hands or his feet or up into the sky, but right now he kept his eyes on Carl, listening to everything he said real careful.

"I got a little boy and a little girl at home, and they're all I really care about. They're just youngsters, and they need their old man. I feed 'em and keep a roof over their heads. If they go and put me in jail for this thing, my kids won't have nothing. You know? They won't have no one to take care of them."

Tears rolled down Carl's rutted face. He wiped them away, but they kept flowing, and he never took his eyes off Danny. He waited to see what Danny would have to say.

Danny felt real thirsty all of a sudden. His throat was dry, and when he swallowed, it hurt his jaw something terrible. He looked away from Carl—other than Uncle Brett when he was getting ready to go up to heaven, Danny had never seen another grown-up man cry. Sometimes when Danny got to thinking about his folks, he would cry a little even though he knew he wasn't supposed to.

"They're gonna blame you for killing Mindy, and I know it ain't right or fair, but I don't want to get locked up." Carl was really crying hard now. His hands hung at his sides, and he just let the tears and snot run over his lips and chin.

"I'm sorry, Danny. I really am. Shit."

Danny didn't know what to do. If he didn't hurt Mindy, why would he get blamed for doing such a bad thing? He would never do anything to Mindy. Nothing at all. She was his friend.

"They're gonna come for you, Danny, and take you away from here." Carl turned and walked back to the window again. Snow was picking up steam and blowing horizontally outside.

"Goddamn it all," Carl muttered softly. He peered outside for another minute, then turned and slinked out of the room. He didn't look at Danny. Didn't say another word.

The door closed, and Danny kept sitting on the exam table. He heard Carl say something to Doc Pete out in the office. His throat clicked from the dryness again. He had never been so thirsty. He stood up, wincing at the pain that even standing made his jaw feel. Stepped over to the small sink and turned on the water. Cupped his trembling hands under the stream of water and put the cold liquid to his lips. He sucked in a little of the water and let it run down his throat. He did this a few more times, then turned off the water.

He caught his reflection in the mirror above the sink and stared at what he looked like now. Face swollen and splattered with dried blood. His jaw flopped open like a dog panting in summertime. Even his eyes were different—red and glassy. He looked like a monster—the kind that hides under your bed at night and waits for you to stand up so that it can grab you by the ankles. Danny brought his fingers to his cheek just to make sure that it was him looking back from the mirror—it was. His hand. His face. It was what he had become.

He stepped over to the window and stared at the falling snow slapping against the glass in layers, getting thicker and thicker until the view of outside grew hazier and hazier, the world going white. The snow was pretty. Calming to him—made him forget about turning into a monster. Lots of times Danny would stand outside in a heavy snowstorm with his head turned up and let the frozen flakes land on his face and tongue. He liked rain, too, but snow was his favorite. Looking up into the sky and watching the snow fall around him made him forget what might be troubling him.

He put his hand on the pane of glass and watched the condensation form around his fingers. He wanted to forget about what had happened to Mindy. Wanted to forget about the blood and her dead eyes. He wanted to be in the snow again.

Lester

Lester sat on Mindy's porch step and glanced at his watch. Two-forty A.M.

Lord, this night is crawling by.

He figured that a statie should be arriving any minute. He felt dog-tired and wanted to climb back into bed beside Bonnie. He wanted to press up against her, feel her warmth, and listen to her breathe. Hell, he'd even let the cats up on the bed at this point.

He flicked his cigarette into the snow and lit up another. He only had two more smokes left. Just one more thing to be miserable about. He wished he had grabbed another pack on his way out.

The tips of his fingers, his ears, and his nose were freezing out there, but he'd be goddamned if he was going to wait inside. Couldn't bear to see that poor girl all twisted up and lying there.

He kinda regretted that he had to send the deputy off to Doc Pete's. He could use the company even if Sokowski was a prickly son of a bitch. A nasty little boy who grew up to be a nasty man. Back in high school, Sokowski was always getting in trouble, picking fights, and stealing things left and right. Lester thought the kid would mellow out, but he still carried a chip on his shoulder that wouldn't or couldn't get knocked off. Maybe it all started because of his messed-up ear. Kids could be cruel, so Sokowski probably just wanted to be the one to throw the first insult or punch.

When Sokowski's old man pushed hard for Lester to take him on as his deputy, Lester didn't like the notion much. But Sokowski's old man, Pepper, God rest his soul, was a stand-up guy and a good friend. Hell, they had known each other since fifth grade and had been hunting and fishing buddies for three decades after that. He knew that Pepper wanted his only son to turn over a new leaf, and old Pepper thought that Lester, with his evenhanded nature, was the best person to rub off on his hell-raising son. Lester told Pepper that he would owe him big, and boy, had he hit the nail on the head with that one. Lester's way was to earn respect, not force it down folks' throats. But against his better judgment, he gave the boy the badge and that was that.

Then, after Pepper took his own life when Sokowski was still growing whiskers on his chin, he got even worse. Sokowski was two years out of high school and was one year wearing the deputy badge, and whammo—his old pappy couldn't take the hand he was dealt no more and left his only child alone and responsible for the farm. Poor kid was barely a man, but he grew up quick. Turning bitter, angry, and even nastier.

Lester knew that Sokowski bullied folks too much, but by and large he did his job and was younger and more fearless when walking into a bar fight. It only took one hard look or the occasional five-knuckle surprise from the deputy to keep drunks in line. Lester still held out some hope that Sokowski would change. That he would turn all that anger into something good. He believed that a tiger could change its stripes. Might not be easy, but it could be done.

When he had come back to Mindy's trailer, Lester could tell that Sokowski had been into the drink again. He didn't want the state trooper to see his deputy liquored up. That would be one more unwanted problem to add to the night's growing list. Besides, Sokowski was better off keeping an eye on the Bedford boy. Carl had about as much sense as a jug of water and appeared to be barely holding it together. Lester made Sokowski promise to keep his mitts off Danny. A broken jaw and a few loose teeth were bad enough. Sokowski gave his word—for whatever that was worth.

Lester took a final drag on his cigarette and looked back into the pack, hoping by some miracle that he had miscounted. Nope. Still only two. He decided to hold off for a few more minutes before he lit up again.

A pair of headlights appeared down the road and headed his way. He sighed out loud, more than ready to pass this mess off to someone else. His knees popped and complained of the cold as he stood and watched the headlights approach. The vehicle was driving fast and erratic. Lester heard the engine chewing up the cold night air and could tell it had eight hardworking cylinders—he had a good ear for engines and guns. Could tell by the pop of a shotgun if it was a ten-gauge, a twelve-gauge, or a single-shot .410. Bonnie always gave him grief that he couldn't hear her ask him to take out the trash but could hear a pickup truck a half mile away and know if it was a six- or eight-cylinder.

The driver of the approaching car punched the accelerator, and Lester noticed that the vehicle didn't have any emergency lights on its roof. Definitely not a state police vehicle. His stomach dropped when he finally recognized the ride.

"Hell," he whispered to himself. He blew on his fingers in a futile attempt to warm them and prepared for the worst.

The Lincoln Continental veered off the road and skidded to a stop on the icy driveway. The driver's-side door swung open, and Johnny Knolls pulled his large mass out from behind the steering wheel. He appeared about as tall as he was wide and kind of wobbled as he walked. Johnny reached into the backseat, pulled out a rifle that Lester knew would be loaded, and clutched it in his thick hands.

Lester stepped off the porch. "Goddamn. What're you doing out here, Johnny?"

Johnny strode up and got right in Lester's face. His eyes were small black circles, and his nose was piglike—pink and round and turned up at the tip. He was breathing hard, beer and whiskey on his breath.

"Where the fuck she at?"

Lester stood his ground and tried to sound calm. "Now, hold on here a second, Johnny . . ."

"Either tell me where she's at or get the hell out of my way, Lester. God as my witness, I will take you down."

Lester nodded and kept his voice nice and even. "I don't want you going in there, Johnny. It's bad. Real bad."

Johnny hung on those words. His eyes went past Lester and looked toward the front door. Tiny specks of spittle clung to the man's beard, and his breath billowed out in rapid white plumes.

"It ain't something a father should see." Lester immediately regretted uttering those words when he watched Johnny's eyes glaze over. All reason, if Johnny were ever capable of any, got swept away by a blinding rage.

He put a beefy hand on Lester's shoulder and shoved him aside like a bowling pin. Lester's feet went out from under him, and he slipped on the icy walkway. Tried to break his fall but failed miserably. The side of his head smashed up against the edge of a cinderblock wall that ran along the sides of the driveway. He rolled onto his back, grabbed at his temple as blood seeped from an open wound and stained his fingers a crimson red.

Lester could only watch helplessly as Johnny marched past him and squeezed inside the trailer. He struggled to his feet, seeing white stars flash and dance in front of him. It got quiet for a second, and then a deafening scream erupted from deep within Johnny.

"JESUS! MY BABY! MY BABY! JESUS CHRIST!" The big man's howls were replaced by a smashing sound, and then it went dark inside as a lamp was thrown against a wall. Johnny flipped over furniture, punched at walls, and screamed and cried at the same time. It was a disturbing sound that Lester wouldn't be able to get out of his head for a long, long time. He held himself back from going inside after Johnny. It was already done. There was no taking it back now—the man had come face-to-face with a father's worst nightmare.

After a minute of silence, Johnny filled the doorway—his head nearly touching the top of the frame. He gripped his rifle to his chest in both hands as if he were ready to storm a beach. Lester looked up at a man who had slipped over the edge.

"Who was it? Who did this to my baby, Lester?"

"We got him, Johnny. Don't you—"

"WHO THE FUCK KILLED MY BABY!?" Johnny's voice boomed, bouncing off the mountains around them, kicking off rocks and trees, then returning to the two men with a soft, echoed response.

"I ain't gonna tell you that right now, Johnny. Not right now. We got him, and the state police are on their way here as we speak."

Johnny yanked back the rifle's bolt handle and snapped off the safety. "I ain't gonna ask you again, Lester. You tell me who did this to my baby." Johnny shouldered the rifle and aimed the barrel at Lester point-blank.

Lester took a step back. He could count on one thumb the number of times he'd stared down the barrel of a rifle. Old Tom Dickerson suffered from Alzheimer's and had gotten into the whiskey a couple of summers ago. Tom's wife phoned up Lester because she was scared that old Tom was gonna blow his own head off. When Lester got out there, old Tom was standing in the garage with nothing on but a pair of dirty boxers, soiled with piss and shit. He'd scream one minute, cry the next, the whole time waving his gun around like a baton. Lester had finally managed to calm him down, but only after Tom's rifle was pressed into Lester's chest.

This time the man on the other side of the gun wasn't suffering from Alzheimer's and was being fueled by drunken fury instead.

"I'm gonna put a bullet into you, Sheriff."

Neither man saw or heard the state trooper's patrol car rumble down Tokach Road from the north. The vehicle pulled off the road behind a row of hedges and eased to a stop twenty yards from the trailer. The cruiser killed its lights, and a large man stepped out of the car.

"Don't do anything stupid now, Johnny." Lester raised both of his arms and held his hands high. "Shooting me isn't gonna help matters none."

"Goddamn you, Lester . . ."

A shot rang out. The sharp report of a handgun.

Lester's heart seized up as Johnny snapped back and a bullet ripped through his chest and exited between the shoulder blades. Johnny's knees buckled, and his two hundred and fifty pounds of deadweight fell back into the trailer and thudded to the floor. His legs jerked a few times, a gargling sound slipped out of his lips, and then he became completely still. Johnny's dirty work boots hung over the doorstep, and blood and tiny pieces of flesh were splattered against the trailer's aluminum paneling, running down slow before freezing.

Lester's head was still ringing from the gunshot when he turned and searched behind him. He reached for his gun out of reflex, but his hand stopped on the holster. A state trooper stood at the end of the driveway, crouched in a shooting stance, his pistol resting on the trunk of Johnny's Lincoln. As the state trooper lowered his firearm, Lester felt his legs give out, and he couldn't stop himself from falling to the frozen ground.

And the snow continued to fall. Falling heavier. No letup in sight.

Danny

Danny ran because he didn't know what else to do.

The cornfield behind Doc Pete's didn't look so long from the window, maybe about as long as a football field, but Danny had been running for what seemed like a few minutes and he wasn't even halfway across it yet. He was afraid of stopping because the crop of corn had been cut down to the bases of their stalks, and he didn't have nothing to hide behind. He didn't want Doc Pete to see him running away.

Danny couldn't remember everything Carl had said to him, but he knew that Carl seemed scared and upset and didn't want to go to jail. He had seen Carl's kids around town, and they always smiled at him when Carl wasn't looking. He didn't want Carl to be put in jail because of him and leave them kids all alone with just their mama. Danny knew how hard it was to be without his own papa.

Danny didn't care so much about the deputy. If he went to jail, that is where he probably belonged, but if the deputy got in trouble, so would Carl. Danny couldn't do that to Carl and his kids.

Still, it didn't make sense why he'd be blamed for what happened to Mindy. Didn't make any sense at all.

His heavy boots clomped over the thick layer of snow that covered the cornfield, crunching it right down to the hard dirt beneath it. The snow went up past his ankles and made it difficult for him to lift his feet out and keep them moving forward. His lungs burned from the cold, and he could feel his heart pounding hard in his chest.

He wanted to stop, but the forest was up ahead a little ways more. Once he got there, he figured he would rest for a bit. Catch his breath and think about where he should go.

His boot laces got tangled up in a cornstalk, and he fell forward onto the snow. He put his hands out to catch his fall, but he hit the ground hard, and it sent a shock of pain through his jaw that made him cry out into the night air.

Danny rolled over onto his back between the rows of corn and could feel the tears leaking from his eyes. The snow underneath him felt real soft, like a fluffy feather pillow. The moon shone down at him through a falling blanket of snow, and he didn't want to get up. He just wanted to stay put and rest for a minute.

Get up, Danny.

Even with the wind howling all around him, Danny heard the talking in his head clear as day, like it was right there next to him. This was the third time in the last few hours that the talking in his head had said something to him. Months, sometimes years went by and he didn't hear the talking in his head. He was in an awful lot of trouble, and that's probably why it was back again so soon.

Just a little further. Then you can rest.

The very first time he heard the talking in his head was when he was a little kid. Around six or seven. After the accident. He had been looking for Donald Duck Cola bottles along old Route 6, and it was real hot. August was always the hottest month in Pennsylvania. The sun burned the back of his neck, and sweat rolled into his eyes, stinging them and making it hard for him to see. He kept wiping the sweat onto the shoulders of his T-shirt and kept his eyes searching for bottles hidden in the brush. Back then Donald Duck Cola came in all sorts of flavors—lemon-lime, grape, black cherry, and his favorite, strawberry. All the bottles had a picture of Donald Duck on the front, and Danny liked Donald Duck better than Mickey Mouse because his voice sure sounded funny. He had a pretty good collection going. Almost twenty bottles.

Danny had been searching in the bushes when Mr. Dempsey's car pulled alongside of him—the car was a brand-new Chrysler Imperial, and Mr. Dempsey was one of the first people in town to drive around in a fancy car like that. Because it was so hot outside, Mr. Dempsey had all his windows rolled down. Mr. Dempsey was a short little man with thick-framed glasses, and his head barely peeked over the big steering wheel. He smiled a toothy grin and called out to Danny.

"Hey, Danny. Whatcha doing?" Mr. Dempsey had a funny smile on his face. Danny remembered how small Mr. Dempsey's teeth had looked. Danny thought maybe he still had his baby teeth, but that didn't make sense. Grown-up people didn't have baby teeth. The Tooth Fairy took them away when you were little. But Mr. Dempsey's were small. That was for sure. Maybe the Tooth Fairy didn't visit him at night.

"Looking for Donald Duck bottles, is all," Danny replied.

"Oh, yeah? You know, if I'm not mistaken, I got a half dozen bottles or so in my refrigerator back home. Nice and cold. Why don't you hop in, and we'll both go and have us a soda?" Mr. Dempsey lived all alone up on Terrytown Mountain Road. A lot of the men-folk in town didn't like him so much. They said he was "funny," but he didn't ever make Danny laugh.

"Whadaya say, Danny? It's hotter than heck out there. How about we go for a little ride?" He leaned across the seat and pushed the passenger door open. "Think I might have a fresh batch of cookies in the jar, too."

Danny sure was thirsty, and a cookie sure sounded good right about then.

Don't get in the car, Danny-Boy, the talking in his head warned him.

Mr. Dempsey patted the car seat and gave him a wink. "Come on, Danny. Hop on inside." Danny had his hand on the door handle.

Go home now, Danny. Run!

Danny did as the talking in his head told him to. He took off running and went straight home but didn't tell Uncle Brett about anything. Uncle Brett always said real bad words about Mr. Dempsey. Words that Danny didn't know. Mr. Dempsey moved out of town a few years later. His garage had burned down one night, and the next thing Danny knew, he had up and moved away. One day he was there, and the next he was gone, and Mr. Dempsey's leaving sure seemed to make a lot of the men in town pretty happy. Uncle Brett told him that he probably moved to San Francisco to go live with all the other fruits.

The talking in Danny's head was back again tonight, but he felt sleepy and his jaw hurt and he didn't want to move anymore.

Get up, Danny-Boy. Not safe out here. Keep walking.

Danny did as he was told. The talking in his head was always looking out for him. It never told him to do something wrong or anything that got him in trouble. He struggled to his feet—his jaw

throbbing and complaining with each jarring movement—and
started tromping through the snow again. He dug his hands in his
pockets and put his head down to block his eyes from the hard-
falling snow.

He plodded forward until he stepped into the forest—pitch-
black—and immediately felt better. The woods were quiet and
peaceful, and the snow wasn't falling as hard down under all the
trees.

Danny liked that the talking was back again. He had missed
hearing from it. He wished it would visit him more, not just when
he seemed to be in trouble or scared. He wondered if the talking in
his head was a little angel or something else he couldn't see. Maybe
this time it would stay with him for a while so he wouldn't be so
lonely. And maybe it would help him figure out what he should do
next.

Taggart

Trooper Taggart had finished his call to dispatch a few minutes ago—made the request for a detective and the coroner's office to report to the scene down here—but he kept the radio mike clenched in his hand and pressed it to his lips. He knew that the sheriff was watching. Waiting to talk to him again. He needed a minute to think. Needed a minute to have another drink.

After he'd gotten the order to head down to Wyalusing, he had grabbed his flasks from his locker. He called them Starsky and Hutch. It was a long trek down here to the sticks, and he thought another drink or two would make the drive a little more bearable. He didn't usually start drinking until the end of his shift, but he figured why the hell not? He was supposed to be home right now. Not out here in the middle of nowhere.

Who are you kidding, Bill? You always manage to find an excuse to drink. Any excuse is a good excuse.

He kept the flasks hidden in his locker or the trunk of his cruiser. He could fit a fifth into both flasks real nicely. He'd rather have too much than not enough. *Be prepared* was always his motto. What a great God-fearing Boy Scout he turned out to be.

Taggart looked down at his hands. A wedding band was wedged over the knuckle of his fat left ring finger. Both hands trembled. He wasn't sure if it was because he had just shot and killed an innocent man or if he needed a drink. Probably both. He pulled one of the oft-used flasks from his bag, Starsky this time, and topped off his cold coffee. Mixed it with his finger and took a long drink.

The hayseed sheriff wouldn't give him space. He gazed out the windshield at Lester, who paced the driveway, staring at Taggart the whole time. Taggart pressed the mike to his lips and pretended to say something official to buy him some more time from the sheriff.

"Give me one stinking minute here, Sheriff. Christ," he muttered into the mike instead.

He poured another shot into his coffee and drank it down. He told himself the drinks were calming his nerves and helping clear his head. Why should he feel any regrets about firing his service revolver? The hell with that. Another law-enforcement officer stood at the receiving end of an armed suspect at the scene of the crime. Textbook stuff. If he couldn't trust his instincts, then it was high time to turn in his badge. He didn't give a damn if he had a little buzz or not. He would have done the same thing if he were stone-cold sober. He finished his coffee cocktail and put his hat back on. Shook a few Tic Tacs into his mouth, took a breath, and stepped out of the patrol car.

Lester

Lester was waiting anxiously. Taggart stepped in front of him, towering over him by a good eight inches.

"All right, Sheriff, they're going to send the coroner down straightaway. Detectives should be here in a few hours as well."

Lester shook his head. "What a goddamned mess. Sweet Christ."

"Yeah. It is what it is," Taggart replied coolly. He looked over to Johnny Knolls's fallen body in the trailer doorway. "The father of the victim, did you know him well?"

"Yeah. Hell, everybody knows everybody around here."

Taggart nodded. "He always carry a firearm?"

"Son, everybody around here always carries a firearm. Got one in our truck and a half dozen others back home. Way of life."

Taggart grunted. "That may be, but this man's dead because of it." Taggart's tone was flat and matter-of-fact. The way he intended it.

Lester let this roll off him. He needed help, and there was no good that could come from getting defensive.

"So you said you got the suspect in custody?" Taggart wasn't wearing a jacket. If he was cold, he wasn't letting on about it.

"Yep. Local boy. Big fella. Always thought he was more of a gentle giant," Lester offered.

"Seems like that's always the case."

Lester played with the stubble on his head. "Yeah. Danny Bedford. Might be big as an ox, but he's a few cards short of a full deck."

Taggart gave him a look. "How so?"

Lester didn't keep his gaze. Something about the trooper made him uneasy. "Had him an accident on a frozen pond when he was a boy. Five or six, if I remember correctly. The winter of '49. The damn kid was underwater for near ten minutes. Suffered pretty severe brain damage as a result of it."

"Guess he should have stayed off the ice or learned how to swim."

Lester finally gave him a look. This state trooper fella seemed to be a bull in a china shop. Like a lot of city cops and state law officials, men like Taggart elbowed their way around life. "Lost both his folks in the same accident. Helluva thing."

"You got him in lockup?" Taggart asked, ignoring Lester's last statement.

"He's laid up at the doc's office right now." Lester stopped himself. Thought about what he would say next. Wanted to be real careful. "Danny suffered a broken jaw when we brought him down."

Taggart almost smiled. "I'm sure he did."

Lester didn't let the other man bait him. He continued on, also matter-of-fact. "Like I said, he's the size of two of me, so it took all that my deputy and I could do to restrain him." Lester hated lying, but he figured it was better not to raise any eyebrows when it came to Sokowski's actions.

"I take it your deputy is with the suspect now? Has him under careful watch?"

Lester nodded and took out a pack of cigarettes. Tucked one in the corner of his mouth and cupped the match from the wind. He only had one cigarette left now. The state trooper looked at the pack, and even though Lester didn't want to, he offered the man the last smoke. Common decency had it that you never took a man's last cigarette.

Taggart accepted the smoke.

"Deputy Sokowski is there with him now. Just waiting to turn him over to the state. He's in good hands."

"I would hope so." Taggart took Lester's pack of matches and lit up. He gazed around the countryside. It was pitch-black, and beyond the trees there wasn't much to see for miles. "You born and raised around here?"

"Yep. This has always been home. Never seen a reason to leave."

Taggart looked at all the trees and rolling countryside around him with a bemused expression. "Never cared for the country myself. Too damn quiet. I'm a city boy. Would drive me nuts living out here with nothing to do."

Lester kept smoking. "Guess it's not for everybody."

"Living out here would be a prison sentence for someone like me." Taggart laughed at the thought.

"Suppose that's true for some." Lester was going to stop there but couldn't help himself. "Then again, I think life in the city tends to suck a man dry of what's important."

Taggart gave the sheriff a look. "And how's that?"

Lester knew he shouldn't go on, but he did anyway. Something about Trooper Taggart provoked Lester and didn't bring out the wisest part of himself. "Seems like city folks are always so busy rushing around with places to go and things to do that they forget what it's like to take one day at a time and enjoy the small things in life."

"That right? You sound like a Hallmark card."

Lester shrugged. "Used to get bent out of shape when city dwellers rolled into town looking down their noses and laughing at our ways, all the while wondering how anyone would actually choose this life, but now I just feel sorry for them."

Taggart seemed to consider the sheriff's words for a moment. "I see what you're saying. And I hope I'm not coming off that way. Not my intention." The man exhaled, shook his head. "Guess you're right, though. City life can be a grind, but it's all I've ever known. For better or worse."

Lester finally grinned at the man—part of the state trooper's wall came down just a bit. "Life here grows on you. Hell, you spend another few hours out here in the fresh air, you might just be coming back for more."

Taggart grinned a little himself. "Don't know about that." He flicked his cigarette to the snow and gazed over at Lester. "What I do know is that we'll be needing another pack of cigarettes."

Lester flicked his cigarette to the ground as well. "Hell. Ain't that the truth."

Carl

All the fucked-up shit that had happened in the last few hours had sobered him up but left him as jittery as hell. He sure could use a drink or a hit from a joint. Or both would be even better. He needed to get a buzz.

The front door opened, and a blast of cold night air rushed inside, carrying with it a wave of powdery snow. Carl looked up at Sokowski, whose face was flushed red, and his hard eyes were even more bloodshot than the last time Carl had seen him.

"Where's Doc Pete at?"

Carl shrugged. "In his office, I suppose."

Sokowski glanced over at the office door, then turned back toward Carl. "You didn't say nothing, did you?"

"Naw. Didn't say nothing."

Sokowski was all tensed up. A bundle of nerves. His shoulders were tight around his neck, and his fists clenched and unclenched at his side. "Where'd they put Danny?"

Carl pointed down the hall, then returned his fingers into his mouth. Tore off a piece of nail and spit it out. "Sheriff ask you anything? Doesn't suspect anything, does he?" Carl asked, and immediately recoiled from Sokowski's cold, dead expression.

"Nothing to suspect. Unless you went running your mouth."

"I ain't stupid, Mike. Kept my mouth shut like you told me to."

Sokowski muttered at him and strode down the hall toward the exam room, and Carl could tell by the way he walked that he'd been drinking again.

"What are you doing?" Carl asked.

Sokowski put his hand on the doorknob and gave him a look. "Gonna have a little talk with the retard, is what." He swung open the exam-room door and stepped in.

It was cold inside the room. Felt like a walk-in cooler. The window on the back wall stood wide open, and snow was spitting inside. Most of the snow melted as soon as it hit the floor and left behind puddles of water covering the linoleum tiles. Sokowski looked around the empty room, eyes stopping on the paper covering the exam table that was dotted with dried blood.

Sokowski glanced back to Carl. "Fucker's gone."

Carl walked behind him but didn't say anything. He just stood there, looking guilty as he continued picking at his fingers.

Sokowski walked to the back of the exam room, peered out the window, took off his hat, and ran his fingers through his hair. He was almost smiling.

"This is good. Hell yes. This is real good."

"But Danny's gone."

Sokowski glared at Carl like he had shit all over his face. "Think about it, Carl. Christ. A guilty man runs."

"Shit. What do we do?" Carl asked.

"That, dumb-ass, is obvious. We go and tell the sheriff the truth. Prisoner got loose, and a killer is on the run. Danny did us a big fucking favor."

Carl looked around the exam room. "Wasn't my fault. I don't want to get blamed for nothing."

Sokowski glanced at Carl, and his eyes narrowed a bit as an idea took form. "You're right about that. It wasn't. You put up much of a fight?"

"Huh?"

"Danny outweighs you by a hundred or so pounds." Sokowski took a yellowed handkerchief that got plenty of use from his back pocket and wrapped it around his knuckles. "You did all you could, but the son of a bitch was strong and scared out of his mind, and he put a hurting on anything in his path."

Carl watched Sokowski tighten the handkerchief around his fist and hold it down at his side. Carl stopped picking at his fingers. "We really gotta do it like this?"

"Yeah, we really do. Gotta make this look believable." Sokowski was really grinning now. "The sheriff didn't have Danny cuffed, so he sucker-punched you and escaped out the window. It was over before you knew it. When I got here, you were still scraping yourself off the floor. That's the story. Short and sweet. You got any questions?"

Carl shook his head that he didn't, eyes down on the floor, and waited for the punch that was coming. He didn't have to look at Sokowski to know that part of him was enjoying this.

Danny

Filtered moonlight peeked through the dense cover of trees, coming down in soft shafts of light. The limbs of centuries-old maple, oak, and birch trees stopped most of the snow from falling to the frozen ground, but the flakes that did manage to get through floated slow and easy, creating an almost dreamlike setting.

Danny had given up running a few minutes ago. The jarring motion from the thudding of his boots on the hard ground was too much. Too painful.

His jaw hung open like a broken mailbox door—hurt too much to close it. And his tongue, thick and swollen now, filled his mouth like a bloated breakfast sausage. He felt a few teeth rattle around with each step he took. The wind still blew pretty hard in the woods, so his shoulders hunched forward as he plodded through the snow, frozen leaves and dried twigs snapping beneath his feet.

Finally he stopped walking altogether. It was all too much. His head pounded and felt as if someone were kicking it every few seconds with a steel-toed boot—Sokowski's steel-toed boot. He couldn't feel his fingers or toes, and he didn't know where he was or where he was going. Everything was so dark around him, and Danny hated the darkness almost more than anything else.

Maybe it was his fault that Mindy was gone. Maybe if he had finished the bird carving in the morning like he planned, he would have gotten to her trailer earlier. Maybe he could have stopped the deputy and Carl from hurting her. Maybe she wouldn't be dead.

Danny dropped to his knees, crunching the snow under him, and began to cry. His wide shoulders shook and built to a violent shudder as he let it all out. He cried for the ache he was feeling in his jaw. Cried for Mindy being gone forever. Cried for being slow and dumb and different from everybody else. He didn't want to be here anymore. Not just here in Wyalusing but here in this world, where so many bad things happened. He wished he could be with his folks again. Up in heaven where it was supposed to be safe and happy, with all the other angels.

He lowered his head and let out a slow howl. Maybe he should talk to God, but he had never talked to him before and didn't know what he should say or what he should ask of him. If God were looking down on him right now, sitting on his throne with his white beard and robe, maybe he would see that Danny was in a pinch and could use some help.

The snap of a dry twig echoed softly through the woods somewhere around him. Danny looked up, peered around at all the trees, but didn't see anything. Another snap, followed by a rustling sound. He kept listening, and every few seconds there would be another soft crunch of snow.

"That you, Carl?"

The movement stopped at the sound of his voice.

Snow started to soak through Danny's trousers at the knees, and the cold began to numb the skin. He tried to stand back up on his feet when a dark shape slipped across the forest floor in front of him. Slow and careful.

Danny's cries hitched and caught in his chest as he watched the shadowy figure move behind a clump of brush.

Get up, Danny-Boy.

It was the voice again, but it sounded a little different now, and even though it seemed different, the voice itself was familiar.

Listen to me, Danny-Boy.

Danny's papa used to call him Danny-Boy. Danny wiped the tears from his eyes so that he could get a better look at whatever was out there.

Come on, Danny.

Danny stood up, and his knees cracked a bit. "Pop?"

The shape moved a little deeper into the woods, away from Danny. "I'm scared."

No time for that.

The voice—it kinda *did* sound like his papa's—made Danny cry again. Tears rolled down his checks and froze like tiny stones around the corners of his mouth.

"What am I supposed to do?" All this talking made his jaw feel even worse. A lot of his words were slurred and muffled, and this made him cry even harder.

Follow me.

The shape disappeared into a wall of darkness. Danny didn't want it to go away, so he put his right boot forward, and the other one followed. It was slow going, but at least he was moving.

"I'm cold."

I know.

"I want to see you."

Soon. Soon.

"Is Mama with you?"

The voice didn't answer. There were no more sounds of break-ing twigs or crunching snow. The woods were quiet again except for the sound of wind rattling leaves on the tips of tree limbs. Danny forced himself to walk faster, hoping to catch up with whatever or whoever was leading him deeper into the forest.

He climbed over a fallen tree covered with a thick layer of ice and snow and kept walking. He squinted into the night air and tried real hard to hear any more sounds in the woods around him.

He started getting scared that he might be walking the wrong way—if there was a wrong way. He was tired. So tired. Just when he felt like stopping and lying down, he saw a flicker of movement ahead of him. Could have been a grouse or a clump of snow falling from the tree branches, but he kept moving.

Danny wasn't sure how long he walked. It sure felt like a long time. His legs burned, and his muscles screamed out for rest, but he kept his feet moving at a steady pace. The snow was up past his knees now.

The wind intensified and started whipping against his face. It felt like it was turning into sleet. The soft snowflakes had become hard and small and stung his cheeks as they pelted against his skin.

"How much further?"

We're almost there.

The voice didn't really sound like his papa's now. Truth be told, his papa had died so long ago that he couldn't say for sure what his voice sounded like. Maybe it wasn't his papa's, but even if it wasn't, Danny wanted to think it was somehow.

The wind started really howling, like someone had flipped a switch. His pants flapped hard against his legs, making his skin tingle a little. Danny stopped for a second to scoop up a handful of snow and pressed the clump of frozen crystals to his lips. He tried to lick at it, but it hurt his tongue too much. He leaned his head back and dropped in a few chunks of snow and let it melt down the back of his throat.

He started walking again, but his arms and legs were growing heavier, making it harder to trudge through the snow. He let his eyes flicker closed, and he walked blind. With his hands held out in front of him, he felt his way deeper into the woods. A low-hanging branch tore at his face, leaving a thin red welt on his cheek, but he kept walking, waiting for the voice to tell him what to do next.

Okay. We're here, Danny. Time to rest.

Danny forced his eyes open but saw nothing except darkness and more trees.

"I don't see nothing."

The wind blew in response.

"All I see is the woods."

The voice wasn't there anymore. It must have left him again. He turned in a complete circle and searched all around him without knowing what he was looking for.

"Why am I stopping here?" His answer came to him when he leaned against a tree and felt something hard and smooth press into his lower back. He reached behind him and ran his hands over the trunk of the tree until they came into contact with a wooden plank nailed into the bark. A foot above it was another plank. He peered up at the tree and saw that the planks continued upward and disappeared into the darkness above him.

He gripped a plank at chest level and pulled himself up the tree.

His fingertips reached up and found the next piece of wood, and he pulled himself up the side of the tree, plank by plank. One felt kinda loose, so he balanced himself as carefully as he could and continued on.

The boards were frozen solid and real slippery. Halfway up the tree, he glanced down but couldn't see the ground through the darkness. He looked above him and saw darkness up there, too. He kept climbing the ladder and was glad it was nighttime, because he didn't like high places. They scared him. He had always been afraid of heights and never climbed trees like all the other kids did.

When Danny reached up again, his knuckles knocked against a piece of wood that was too big to be a climbing plank. Working in the dark, he let his fingers feel around the edges of a wooden platform, soft with rot, which had been built on top of a few thick branches. He pulled himself onto the wooden stand, which couldn't be more than a few feet wide and a few feet long. Danny thought for a second that maybe kids had built a tree fort way out here in the forest but then remembered that Uncle Brett used to climb trees to hunt for deer sometimes. Uncle Brett had built three or four deer stands out in the woods and would hide up in the branches and wait for a deer to pass under him before he shot it with a gun.

On his hands and knees now, Danny felt along the platform to check for the edges. Four pieces of two-by-four had been nailed to the tree limbs a few feet above the platform and served as a railing. He touched one of the two-by-fours, and the piece of wood jiggled with rot. He scooted himself to the middle of the planks and rested. Something rattled and flapped beside him. When he reached over, he felt a piece of plastic tarp whipping in the wind.

Danny squatted and pulled the small piece of plastic over him. It didn't help much. He could still feel the wind and snow smacking against his makeshift blanket, but it would have to do.

After he put his head down on the rough wood, he gathered a clump of damp leaves for a pillow. He thought about his room above the laundromat and how warm it always was. The dryers always made it nice and cozy in the wintertime.

As his eyes flickered closed, he remembered that he hadn't locked the laundromat up for the night. He hoped that Mr. Bennett wouldn't be too sore with him. He was never supposed to leave it unlocked at night. Kids might come in and mess around with the washers and dryers. And Mr. Bennett didn't like folks using the toilet. Said folks don't treat public bathrooms as well as the ones in their homes.

Right before sleep took him away, Danny wished that he would get the chance to see Mr. and Mrs. Bennett again. They sure were nice to him.

Lester

Lester told Taggart that he wanted to take another look at Mindy's body. See if he noticed anything unusual. Taggart told him not to tamper with anything until the forensics team and the detectives arrived. Lester nodded, bit his tongue, and said he wasn't gonna touch anything.

The snow had been coming down harder, the wind stronger, so they had to keep the front door closed up, since Mindy's place was still considered a crime scene. It might preserve the condition of the room itself, but the unfortunate end result was that it kept in the smell of death. Lester shut the trailer door behind him and still couldn't believe what surrounded him. Mindy and Johnny Knolls. Dead. Worse yet, murdered.

Lester gave the kitchen a quick search for a pack of cigarettes. He knew that Mindy smoked. Hell, who didn't? He felt a pang of guilt for only coming in here to look for cigarettes, but his craving for a smoke was greater than the guilt. Good old nicotine. The kitchen stood neat and tidy except for a bottle of whiskey his deputy must have gotten into, but no sign of cigarettes.

He glanced over at the living room and spotted an ashtray and a carton of Salems on a TV tray beside the recliner. Lester avoided looking directly down at Mindy as he walked over and pulled a pack out of the carton. He smacked the pack against his palm a few times and tore off the foil. Lit up and took a deep draw.

Lester didn't particularly care for menthol, but this would have to do the trick. He was moving toward the front door when his eyes finally fell on Mindy's corpse. Her face and head weren't covered, just everything else from the neck down. He knelt to pull the blanket over her but stopped himself.

Funny. Didn't notice that before.

He inspected a few abrasions on the side of her cheek and neck. The skin looked red and irritated. Probably happened when she fell down. Maybe Danny dragged her across the carpet and it scuffed up her face.

Lester touched her cheek gently. Her skin cold now, and growing stiff.

I'm real sorry, little lady. You were a good kid.

As Lester pulled the blanket over her face, his eyes went to the robin figurine that was still lying beside Mindy's head. He knew immediately that it was Danny's handiwork. He had seen the boy playing with blocks of wood, whittling away outside the Wash 'N Dry, lost in his own little world. The boy had a knack for carving—that much was for sure.

Lester picked up the wooden bird and turned it over in his hands a few times. Specks of blood dotted the robin's feathers, staining them red on the orange belly of the bird. It was evidence that the detectives would probably want to take a look at, but something about it troubled him a little. Why in the hell would Danny go through all the trouble of carving this figurine, hike all the way out here three miles in the freezing cold, then beat the poor girl to death? Just didn't make sense. Maybe Mindy didn't react so well to him showing up in the middle of the night unannounced. Rejection was a damn strong emotion, especially if the boy had held a torch for the girl for so many years. Maybe she was a bit too nice to him over the years, and that gave him false hope. Hope could be a double-edged sword. Once hope got turned away and crushed, it could make a person do things he wouldn't normally do.

A truck pulled up outside and killed its engine. He heard voices talking to each other, making their way toward the front door. Lester hoped that it was the coroner's office. He wanted to get the bodies out of here before anybody else showed up. He still couldn't figure out why in the hell Johnny showed up. Maybe Mindy had phoned him before making a call to the deputy.

He couldn't give it much more thought, because the front door swung open and Taggart stepped inside with Sokowski and Carl in tow. Lester did a double take at Carl's face—his lip was busted open, and his cheek had swollen up to the size of a peach.

"Christ. What in the hell, Carl?" Lester managed.

Carl didn't answer. Just looked down at the floor, wide-eyed. He and Sokowski were both staring down at Johnny's Knolls's body.

"Let's take this outside," Lester said, and motioned toward the door.

Sokowski and Carl remained frozen in their spots, trying to piece together exactly what they were seeing. Sokowski saw Johnny's rifle on the floor beside him and glanced over at Lester.

"Johnny showed up a bit ago. Madder than hell, and for good

reason. He had his gun drawn on me, and Officer Taggart here did what he had to do."

Carl could only stare at Johnny's body while Sokowski gave Taggart a look. Taggart stood stone-faced but kept Sokowski's gaze.

Lester moved forward and finally managed to guide them out onto the porch. He shut the door behind them and sucked his cigarette down to the filter. He flicked it into the snow and went back to the business at hand.

"Tell me what happened here, Carl."

"Danny is what happened. Fucker attacked him," Sokowski responded instead.

"Hell. You okay, son?" Lester asked Carl, who kept his head down and nodded.

"Ain't the worst of it. He got out the back window of Doc Pete's and took off running. I knew we should have cuffed him. Christ."

Lester felt Taggart's eyes on him. Judging him and their small-town ways.

"When exactly did this happen, Carl?" Lester asked.

Sokowski didn't give Carl a chance to answer. "Dunno. Probably thirty, forty minutes ago."

Lester looked past them and up into the night sky. The snow was still coming down pretty good.

"You know what direction he was heading in?"

"Up toward Spring Hill, I think," Carl muttered softly.

Lester looked down at his old Timex. It was a little after three in the morning.

"Well, we ain't gonna find him tonight. That much is for sure. Deputy, why don't you take Carl and go on home and try to get a few hours' sleep? We'll meet up at the office before six and go see if we can't track him down. He ain't gonna get far tonight."

Taggart finally spoke up. "You really think that's such a good idea, Sheriff?"

Lester felt his stomach tighten up and his blood pressure soar. "Yeah, I do. It's hard terrain around this way. We ain't gonna find him in the dark, and I think we're better served having fresh legs."

"I think we might be 'better served' going after the suspect while we might still have a trail," Taggart stated matter-of-factly. "Snow might be covering some of his tracks at the moment, but by morning there'll be no sign of them."

Lester ignored Taggart's suggestion and instead nodded at Sokowski. "I'll see you in a few hours."

Lester watched and waited for Sokowski and Carl to get into their truck and back out of the driveway before he turned to Taggart again. "Look, son, I appreciate your help in this situation, and I fully expect to cooperate with your office, but there are a few things in play here that I need to better inform you on."

Taggart's expression remained unchanged.

"Danny Bedford has a bunch of limitations. He ain't very bright, and he doesn't spend much time in these woods. That much I do know. It's true that we don't see our share of homicides out here, but I think it's best if me and my deputy get our heads screwed on straight so that we can properly assist in the tracking of him. We know these woods better than anyone. A few hours ain't gonna hurt nothing."

Taggart let out a small breath. "Fine. Have it your way, Sheriff. I just hope your boy doesn't hurt or kill anyone else before you find him."

The strobe of emergency lights pricked through the dark countryside and wound their way toward the trailer. Another set of emergency lights wasn't far behind the first vehicle. Lester and Taggart watched the ambulances as they got closer.

"Well. I suppose I should head over to Sarah Knolls's house and let her know what happened out here. She'll be wondering where the hell Johnny is, and I don't want her hearing the news from anyone else."

"You do that, Sheriff. I'll handle the situation here." Taggart walked to the end of the driveway and waited for the two approaching ambulances.

Lester found his new pack of menthol cigarettes and lit one up. He climbed into his truck and pulled away from the trailer, glad to put some distance between himself and it. In his rearview mirror, he watched Taggart greet the ambulance technicians as they hauled two gurneys from the back of their vehicles.

Lester returned his attention to the road and tried to figure out the best way to let Sarah Knolls know that both her husband and daughter were dead.

Carl

The first thing Sokowski did when they got back to his house was head straight to the liquor cabinet and haul out a half bottle of Wild Turkey. It was the same house that Sokowski grew up in, a big, two-story home with four bedrooms. The furniture remained unchanged, a worn sofa with the springs poking out of the fabric, chair cushions held together with duct tape, a kitchen table buried under boxes of cereal and stacks of unread newspapers, and a gun cabinet lined with various shotguns and rifles.

Carl watched Sokowski pour two drinks into dirty glasses and hand one to him. Carl accepted the glass but didn't feel much like drinking.

Sokowski drank his down with one swallow and poured another.

"You got any ice for my lip? It's throbbing like a bitch," Carl asked.

Sokowski chuckled and pointed toward the freezer. He watched as Carl took a few ice cubes from a tray and wrapped them in a paper towel.

"Shit. Danny whupped your ass pretty good, huh?" Sokowski laughed again.

Carl didn't say nothing back. He just held the ice cubes to his throbbing lip and cheek. He couldn't figure out how Sokowski could be so damn happy. Two people were dead because of them.

"Christ. Don't be such a fucking baby," Sokowski said as he took another sip of his whiskey.

"Why didn't you just take me on home?"

Sokowski flashed a smile over his drink, but there was no humor in it. His eyes were dead and vacant-looking. "'Cuz we ain't done yet."

Carl wasn't sure what that meant. His lips were getting numb, but he kept the ice right where it was.

Sokowski shook his head at Carl and jabbed a dirty fingernail toward him. "You and me ain't done, chief. Not by a long shot. We gotta track the fucker down."

Carl sighed out loud. "Shit, Mike. I ain't a deputy. I'm done. I didn't even do nothing. Besides, you were the one that killed her." It slipped out just like that.

Sokowski slammed his drink onto the kitchen table, walked up close to Carl, and glared down at him. The whiskey was strong on his breath, stinging Carl's eyes and making them water up. "Let's get one thing real straight here, asshole. We're in this thing together. From start to finish. And from what I remember, I didn't see you trying to stop anything."

"Yeah, but I . ..." Carl didn't even bother to finish. He knew that Sokowski wasn't going to go down by himself. Carl was tied to him, and there wasn't a damn thing he could do about it.

"Look, this whole business is gonna go away once we track

Danny down. I plan on us finding him first, and when we do find him, he's gonna resist arrest, which means we'll have to put a fucking bullet in his thick head. Then this whole fucking thing ends right there. That's our only option. You got a problem with that?"

Carl looked down into his drink and decided to have a sip after all. In one motion he drank every drop of it, then held the empty glass out to Sokowski.

"Hell, fucking yeah." Sokowski grinned as he took the glass and filled it back up, sloshing some over the top of it. "This shit is almost over, Carl. We'll be back to selling weed, getting high, and making money in no time."

Carl sipped his whiskey and watched Sokowski for a minute. "Ain't you sorry none?"

Sokowski glanced at Carl. Thought about the question for a second. "Sure I'm sorry. I loved that bitch. I didn't show up at the trailer planning on killing her, but what's done is done."

Carl kept staring at him, and Sokowski let his guard down a little more. "It was an accident. You heard her. She said a bunch of shit to provoke me. I got pissed, lost my cool, and it just happened. I ain't a killer, Carl."

Carl knew that part of Sokowski actually believed it. He figured that kind of thinking would help Sokowski sleep at night. Carl, on the other hand, knew what Sokowski was. And somehow he had become the very same thing.

"I don't want to be the one to do it," Carl muttered.

Sokowski lit a cigarette and gazed at Carl through the haze of gray smoke.

"Killing Danny. I ain't gonna be able to do it," Carl continued.

Sokowski put his hand on Carl's shoulder and squeezed it a little too hard. "All right, Carl. I get it. You're a regular Mother Teresa."

Sokowski pinched his fingers tighter into the flesh of Carl's shoulder, making him wince. "I'll take care of it." He released Carl with a wink and the bare hint of a smile.

Carl rubbed at his shoulder and took a step back from Sokowski. "I should call my old lady. She's probably shitting bricks 'cuz I ain't home yet. Can I use your phone?"

"No. Fuck, no. You ain't doing nothing. You can call her after we finish what we started. Now, drink up." Sokowski didn't wait for Carl to drink with him. He slurped down some more whiskey, then went to the refrigerator and looked for something to eat.

Sarah Knolls

Sarah Knolls slumped on the couch, dressed in a shabby night-gown worn thin from years of use. Her long and graying hair was pinned tight to her skull with a handful of bobby pins. Liver spots dotted her scalp like a leopard's skin. Only sixty-eight years old, but she looked and felt seventy-eight. She clutched a Kleenex in her hand and stared at the front door. Her expression was dull and flat, and she didn't seem to notice the cold that hung over the quiet house like plastic tarp.

She heard Lester's truck pull out of the driveway and was glad to have him finally gone. He had asked her if she wanted him to stay for a while. Asked her if she wanted him to take her over to Scott or Skeeter's house. Asked her if she wanted a drink. Asked her about a bunch of stuff that she didn't want or care about. She shook her head to all of that. She wanted him to leave. To get out of her house and leave her alone.

Right before he stepped outside, Lester had asked her if she was going to be okay. She thought she nodded yes, but what kind of question was that? Her daughter and husband were murdered in cold blood. Dead. It just didn't seem real. She wished that this were all a horrible nightmare, but it wasn't. It was really happening.

How am I gonna go on? How?

She bit at her lower lip hard enough to draw blood.

Why would God let this happen to my baby? What did she do to deserve this?

The house had never felt so quiet. The furnace was set to sixty, and the dogs were still sleeping upstairs, so only the occasional creak of the house settling interrupted the absence of noise. After all the kids had moved out, she complained to Johnny that it was too quiet. No quarreling. No tattling on one another. No whining about homework or chores. None of the squawking she thought she would never miss until it was gone.

When Johnny was at work, the whole house sank into a horrible silence except for the sound of the wind and the ticking of clocks. Sarah didn't know what to do with herself. Didn't know what to do with all her free time. Johnny wasn't so good about expressing his feelings or comforting her when she was feeling out of sorts. He told her not to get so worked up—all their kids still lived in town. Then he told her that maybe she would be able to keep the house a little cleaner with all her spare time. Son of a bitch only cared about himself. The love had slipped out of their marriage some thirty years ago.

Sarah felt numb. She didn't remember everything Lester had told her. She was fast asleep when he'd banged on the door. The dogs yapped a few times before burrowing back under the covers and dozing off again—guard dogs they were not. She figured Johnny was drunk again, couldn't find his house key, and was pissed off about something. The nights of him coming home drunk and horny and wanting to crawl on top of her were long gone. Now he was always breaking something or punching walls or swearing to himself when he got all liquored up. He had hit her a few times when they were first married, so she was careful to stay clear of him when he was in a mood.

She knew Danny Bedford. Everybody in town knew everybody. Sarah always felt sorry for the boy. Big and dumb and all on his own. First his parents had their accident, then his uncle passed young. No loss with Brett, though. Johnny used to drink with Brett and bring him into the house from time to time after working second shift over at Taylor Beef. When Johnny would get up to fetch a few more beers, Brett would sit on her couch with his dirty boots kicked up on the coffee table, staring at her with those eyes. Eyes crawling all over her backside, and she could tell what he was thinking. She didn't like to be in the room alone with him if she could help it. And she noticed the bruises on Danny's arms when she saw him around town. When she went to Johnny about what she suspected with Danny, he told her to keep her big nose out of Brett's business.

Got to be hard enough raising that retard. No harm in using the belt when the occasion calls.

So it had made Sarah feel good that Mindy was so nice to Danny when everyone else laughed and picked on him. Even her boys, Scott and Skeeter, taunted him awful in school back in the day.

The urge to get up and off the couch hit her, but when she tried to stand, her knees buckled and gave out and she flopped back onto the cushions. Her little girl was gone? Just like that she was no more. Mindy hadn't even given her any grandbabies yet.

Mindy had wanted to leave Wyalusing right after high school. She was young and wanted to spread her wings and explore the world, but Sarah encouraged her to stay put. She told Mindy that there would be plenty of time to go out on her own. She convinced Mindy that she belonged here with her family. Sarah knew that was selfish. She just didn't want her daughter to leave. Didn't want Mindy to leave her here all alone with Johnny since the boys were married and leading their own lives.

Oh, God, this is all my fault. I made her stay, and look what happened to her.

She held back her tears. Not yet.

Lester didn't want to say who had done it, but she wouldn't let him leave until she knew the truth. When he finally told her, she informed Lester that she wanted to see Danny. She wanted to ask him why. Why would he do that to her poor Mindy? How could he have murdered her baby? Lester wasn't able to keep her eye when he said that Danny had run up into the woods around Spring Hill, but he promised her that they would catch him after sunrise and lock him up.

"We'll find him, Sarah. You've got my word on that. We'll get him and lock him up so he can't hurt anyone again," Lester had promised. Sarah heard herself laugh at him.

"That gonna bring Mindy back?" she had asked.

Johnny was dead because he was drunk and stupid. Sarah knew that he probably would have shot Lester if the state trooper hadn't shown up and killed him. She wasn't so sad about Johnny. Not really. She hadn't loved him in a long time. In fact, she had grown to hate the man. He hadn't used his hands on her in the last few years, but he didn't hold back on using his words on her. They were mean words—hateful, ugly words. She would have left him twenty years ago—after the kids were all gone—if she thought she could live on her own. As drunk as he always was, he still collected a paycheck.

He paid the bills and put food on the table. She didn't know a thing about working a job and taking care of finances.

She felt herself stand up on legs that were cooperating now and snatch the car keys from the hook by the door. Some part of her brain was telling her body what to do, and that was fine by her. She went outside without grabbing a jacket. It was cold and snowing, but she didn't care.

Oh, God, my baby girl is dead.

She got into the station wagon and felt the cold vinyl seats through her paper-thin nightgown. There was a layer of ice and snow on the windshield, but she didn't have it in her to scrape it off. The engine turned over after a few tries, and she pulled out of the driveway. She clicked on the windshield wipers, and they slowly pushed off the top layer of snow, but the ice stuck fast no matter how many times the wipers ran over it. Heck with it—she would drive anyway.

As she pulled the car out onto the road, she felt like she had tunnel vision. Like she was staring through a telescope. Dark on both sides of her. Through patches of ice on the windshield, all she could see was the road directly in front of the station wagon. Her hands clutched at the steering wheel, and her body began to tremble, but not from the cold—shock was creeping its way in. Closing her throat and making it dry as paper. Her tongue clicked on the roof of her mouth, and she had a hard time swallowing. The darkness on both sides of her narrowed even tighter—the road just a speck of light before her—but she needed to keep going before she completely shut down.

Please, Jesus, let them be on time . . . just let them be there.

Her mind felt foggy, as if she was dreaming or ready to pass out. She cranked open the window and let the bitter cold whip against her face. Her feet felt so cold. She looked down and noticed that she wasn't wearing slippers or socks. She could feel the rubber pad of the gas pedal against her bare skin.

She drove through town, never stopping or slowing at stop signs. If there were other cars out this early, she didn't see any.

She passed the feed shop and turned right at the bottom of the hill. Her bare foot pressed harder on the gas pedal, and the station wagon started to slide on a patch of ice and drift toward the ditch, but she didn't slow down any. Her reactions were sluggish. She didn't jerk the wheel or let up on the gas. She let the car slide—she didn't care if she ended up in the ditch. If she crashed and was slung through the windshield and died, that would be fine by her. She could be with Mindy again. That thought made the lump in her throat get that much bigger. The car fishtailed two or three more times before it finally straightened out and she managed to stay in the middle of the road.

She saw the sign up ahead for Reliable Auto Repair. The boys had painted the sign themselves. Instead of slowing, she gunned the car faster. It took the dip into the parking lot and skidded to a halt in front of the glass office door. Just a few more inches and she would have run the car right through the panel of glass. She put the station wagon into park and sat there. She wasn't sure for how long. Her body shook, rattling the dentures in her mouth, and she couldn't feel her numb feet and toes, which felt like they were a mile away from the rest of her.

Sarah gazed down at her hands and saw that she was still clutch ing the piece of tissue. A dot of liquid dropped onto the lap of her nightgown. Then another. A warm trickle of tears flowed from her eyes and rolled off her tired cheeks. She shoved her knuckles into her mouth and bit down hard enough to give her body a jerk.

Just hold it together for a few more minutes. Just keep it together.

She didn't hear them turn in to the lot. Scott's red pickup truck pulled up beside her, and he beeped the horn. Skeeter sat in the passenger seat smoking a cigarette. She looked over and saw them exchange a look and say something to each other.

Sarah fumbled for the handle and tried to open the station wagon's door, but it wouldn't budge. She put her shoulder against the door panel and gave it a shove—the damn thing still didn't give. She slammed harder and harder, feeling trapped and panicked. Then she noticed that the lock was down. She yanked it up, shoved once again, and the door swung open easily. Sarah toppled out of the car and landed on her hands and knees in a few inches of frozen slush on the parking lot pavement. When the boys climbed out of the truck, she began to cry—loud, gut-wrenching sobs.

Sarah tried to stand but slipped onto her back in a frozen puddle of water. She didn't try to get up again. She just lay in the icy water feeling the cold soak through her nightgown as her two sons swooped down on her, grabbed her by the arms, and tried to get her back on her feet.

Taggart

As the sun peeked over the tip of the mountain, casting an orange glow off all the snow, Taggart excused himself and made his way to the cruiser while the two detectives from Towanda walked through the crime scene with the sheriff. He closed the door behind him, placed his hat on the passenger seat, and ran his hands through short blond hair—tight on the sides and top as stipulated by the Pennsylvania State Police handbook.

He watched as the paramedics laid Johnny Knolls in a black body bag and zipped up the plastic. He glimpsed the dead man's hand. His left hand. A wedding band gleamed in the morning sunlight.

Taggart peered down at his own wedding ring and thought about his wife and two girls. They were growing up fast. Emily was eleven. Jackie had just turned thirteen. Both girls were beautiful like their mother, but the lights of his life had become increasingly more and more of a drunken blur. He'd been stuck in second shift for years now and never got to see the girls. He left the house for work when they were still at school, and by the time he woke up in the morning, they were back in class.

How in the hell did I get to this?

A beer or two at home after work soon became four or five beers with the boys at Moriarty's Pub. But after his drinking crew started to settle down with wives and kids, Taggart soon found himself drinking alone on a barstool with enough Jack and Cokes to make him so numb he couldn't feel his feet. After getting drunk and belligerent one too many times, he found himself banned from Moriarty's, then Fergie's, then a few more neighborhood bars, until he ended up drinking alone in his car with a bottle nestled between his legs, listening to a Phillies or Eagles game. Another place he liked drinking was at the movie theater, hunched down in the dark, sipping his vodka uninterrupted for a two-hour stretch. He didn't care what movie was being projected onto the screen—all the action and dialogue served as a diversion.

He could barely remember how and why exactly the hard drinking had started. Chalk it up to his genes—his father and mother, both raging alcoholics. Growing up, he swore it would never happen to him, the everyday drinking. But it did, just like it did with his two older brothers, two hard-drinking Philly cops. For him and his brothers, all three apples didn't fall far from the tree—they landed right down by the trunk, as a matter of fact.

Drinking wasn't fun anymore. It was just drinking. Most mornings he couldn't remember coming home the night before. Birthdays, holidays, and special occasions were even worse. Most were vague memories, because the better parts of them were spent sneaking off to the bedroom or the den to dig into his secret stashes—water bottles filled with vodka. When he looked at pictures that were snapped on Christmas mornings or during Thanksgiving dinners, Taggart wouldn't remember a thing about that day. He hated looking at his glassy-eyed expression in photographs. He would have a half smile on his fat, bloated face, sneering at the camera like some kind of playground pervert. Those pictures made him sick to his stomach, so he tried his best to avoid family photo ops if he could help it.

The wife didn't know the extent of his drinking. She wasn't dumb but had never been able to see all the signs. Or if she did, she suppressed the awareness deep down inside her. Taggart was a stoic, stone-faced drunk. He was a hands-off dad. Always had been. That's the way he'd been raised. He felt like an outsider most of the time around the three girls. They did everything together. Always laughing and carrying on. Doing art projects or cooking together. They were a close-knit little group, and he hated that about them. He would just sit in his chair watching baseball and drinking beer. The wife would keep an eye on the number of beers he would consume, so his little trick was to fill the can half full of vodka from one of the bottles he kept hidden around the house—he could have two cans of a beer/vodka cocktail and get good and blasted. Taggart didn't go to the park with the girls or shop at the mall with them or do whatever else they were doing. When he wasn't working, he stayed to himself and stewed. The joke around the house was that he was moodier than a girl. *Ha fucking ha.*

The shit hit the fan five years ago when he got drunk on the job and popped a supervisor in the mouth. Miserable prick deserved it, but it had cost Taggart his badge in Philly. Taggart got lucky—they didn't press any charges and dismissed him from the department instead. He came clean to his wife about the drinking and vowed to change his ways. He gave her all the empty promises she wanted to hear and even threw in the token tears of regret and sincerity. Taggart entered into a treatment program and stayed sober for six months. He went to his AA meetings, held the hands of other addicts, and recited the same garbage along with them, week after week. Then he moved the family to Towanda to get a fresh start and joined the state troopers' office on a probationary status. Taggart had felt clarity for the first time in twenty years, but that didn't last long. The stress of a job he hated and a marriage that wasn't working—or at least one he wasn't working on—made it too easy to turn back to the bottle and crawl inside.

Taggart dug into his pocket and felt the chip he carried everywhere with him. He took it out and rolled the bronze-colored coin between his fingers. He read the inscription on the front: TO THINE OWN SELF BE TRUE. UNITY. SERVICE. RECOVERY. Taggart looked at the six-month chip probably a dozen times a day. It was a reminder, all right.

Living a goddamn lie.

He flipped the chip over and examined the engraving on the other side: EXPECT MIRACLES.

Still waiting for mine. Christ. A headful of AA and a bellyful of booze.

Taggart had managed to hide his drinking from his fellow officers and supervisors pretty well over the years. If they suspected anything, they didn't let on about it. He kept to his own business and did his job. But tonight he'd crossed the line. He shot a man dead while under the influence. He was pretty sure that his life, which was pretty much crap anyway, wasn't going to survive this particular fuckup. He had put his career, his family, and his home at stake. The fact was that this mess was probably going to take him down. Part of him always expected that something like this would happen—surprised it didn't happen sooner. When you cross the line so many times, eventually you're going to find yourself looking back at some great regret. And lo and behold, here it was.

All these thoughts racing through his head had his heart thudding in his chest, making it difficult to breathe, and sweat rolled down his back by the buckets. He felt the panic setting in.

Hold yourself together, Bill. Maybe you can walk away from this. Just stay the course.

Taggart reached under his seat and found one of his old friends. Hutch this time. The flask felt half full. That was good. His coffee was gone, though. Nothing to mix it with.

The hell with it. Just need to stabilize.

He poured a straight shot into a Styrofoam cup and drank it down before he could talk himself out of it. The familiar slow burn in his stomach felt good. The sweet numbing in his head would soon follow.

Taggart was pouring a second round when the passenger door opened and the cold wrapped around him. The sheriff stood there staring down at him. A gust of wind brought a sprinkling of snowflakes into the cruiser that settled on the dashboard and seats.

Taggart capped the flask and held the cup to his lips.

"You don't want to do that, son," Lester said softly.

Taggart stared out his windshield. "You're wrong about that."

Lester removed Taggart's hat from the passenger seat and sat down. He closed the door, cleared his throat, and joined Taggart's gaze out the windshield. They sat in silence for a few moments. The steady strobe of the ambulance lights rolled across their faces every other second.

The drink stayed in Taggart's hand.

"The bottle is a tough son of a bitch. Known many a man that found themselves in the bottom of one. It can grab you by the throat, squeeze like hell, and not let go. Quitting is hard, but it can be done, son," Lester offered—no judgment in his voice.

Taggart lowered the cup to his lap. "Maybe. Tried that once and failed, though."

"Not many get it right the first time. Can always try it again."

"I wish it was that easy."

"Not a single part of me believes that it's easy, son. I feel blessed that I don't have that kind of thing hanging over my head."

Taggart nodded and sighed out loud. "I've been a public servant for almost twenty-five years. Right out of high school," he said. "Growing up, I never wanted to get into law. I wanted to go to college. Do something with my brain. Always fancied myself being an architect. Loved buildings and design." He glanced over at the sheriff to see if the man was smirking at his story—he wasn't.

"But I come from a family of cops. Father, older brothers, uncles, cousins. Everybody. A bunch of blue bloods. The old man didn't want to spring for college, and I didn't have it in me to follow my heart, so I did what everybody expected of me. Guess I always take the easy way out."

"Being a cop ain't easy. I can vouch for that."

Taggart watched as one of the ambulances pulled away from the trailer and headed for the city.

"Started as a beat cop in Philly. Let me tell you, that's one tough town. The scum you arrest assume you're a racist pig or a fascist, and the people you vowed to protect don't give a shit about you until something happens to them. Then they just blame you for not being there to stop it." He stared down into his drink. "And the pay's not worth squat. You know that."

Lester nodded.

"And I got stuck. Didn't have what it took to make detective. My super hated me because he hated my old man. Guess I turned out to be a chip off the old block. Had an incident in Philly, so I joined the state troopers' office. Thought that would be a better way to go."

He really wanted to drink his vodka.

"Same mess, different uniform?" Lester asked, half smiling.

Taggart looked at him for a second, then back to his drink.

"My wife wanted more out of life than to be married to a cop. Sometimes I think she prays that I get taken down in the line of duty. She gets a payout and off the hook with one bullet."

Lester nodded. "The badge is a bit sexier before the vows."

"Got that right. Everything seemed to go sideways on me after I got married."

"I'd say that marriage is a tougher job than law enforcement. The good with the bad. Wouldn't trade a day of it, though."

"I want out." Taggart's words just hung there. He closed his eyes and clenched his jaw. "I did the right thing back there." It was more of a question than a statement. He opened his eyes and glanced over at the sheriff.

Lester reached into his breast pocket and pulled out the pack of Salems. He offered one to Taggart, and they both lit up.

"Son, you saw a situation and reacted. A man you didn't know had a rifle aimed point-blank at me. I knew Johnny Knolls. If you hadn't shown up, I'd be one more body getting zipped up in a black bag out there." Lester took off his hat and rubbed his head. "Let me ask you: If you had to do it over again, would you pull that trigger?"

Taggart thought about this for a moment. He tried digging deep inside himself. He wasn't ever very comfortable sharing with the AA crowd, but the sheriff had him dead to rights.

"If you can't trust your gut, you got nothing," Lester said, and handed Taggart back his hat. "So?"

Taggart took the hat and put it on. "I'd do it again."

Lester nodded. "Then I owe you my life."

"Thank you, Sheriff."

"Got one last question for you, then. What do you plan on doing with that drink in your hand?" Lester motioned to the cup gripped in Taggart's fist.

Taggart glanced down at the cup. "'One day at a time' is what they say."

"Sounds about right. Rome wasn't built in a day," Lester offered.

Taggart smiled at the comment. He cracked open the door and tossed out his drink.

"I ain't done needing your help, Officer Taggart. I got a deputy with a hair trigger, and the two Knolls brothers are more than likely gonna want to take matters into their own hands. We need to find the Bedford boy before there's more blood spilled."

Taggart shook his head. "I don't know if I can."

"Officer Taggart, if you didn't make a mistake out there earlier, don't make one now."

Lester stepped out of the patrol car, still sucking on his cigarette. Through the frosted windshield, Taggart watched him talk to the detectives, then looked down at his lifeline. He shoved the flask back under the seat and stepped out of his car.

Danny

Virgin snow blanketed the forest floor in a thick layer of brilliant white frozen crystals. The wind blew softly, causing the ancient trees to sway and creak rhythmically in the bitter-cold air. The snow had stopped, replaced by a skyful of blue, and made the forest deceptively peaceful.

Various breeds of birds—crows, bluebirds, and sparrows—were up with the sun, their chatter lively as they sprang from tree to tree, looking for bark beetles, gypsy moth larvae, hemlock woolly adelgids, or any other insects that made their home in the wood.

Danny felt the cold all around him, every bit of him shivering. He thought for a moment he had left his bedroom window open. Lots of times he slept with the window cracked open, even in the dead of winter. He liked the feel of fresh air on his face to wake to in the morning.

A stroke of sunlight tickled at his face, and he basked in its warmth for a few seconds. His eyes were still closed as he listened to the quick chirping song of birds. He took a deep breath and could feel a heaviness weighing on top of him. It felt comforting. Safe. He started to smile but was stopped short by a searing jolt of pain twisting in his jaw. He gasped, sending an even more painful shock wave through the rest of his body.

His eyes shot open, and his body lurched upright. A few inches of powdery snow tumbled off his chest and collected in his lap. His eyes squinted from the blinding glare of white all around him. So intense that it poked at his brain, and it took him a few moments to fully open his eyes and get his bearings. He licked at his lips, cracked open and bleeding, and tried to swallow, but his tongue still felt like a mass of marshmallows in his mouth.

Danny wasn't sure where he was. Then shapes slowly formed, outlines of the forest coming into view. For a moment the sheer brightness made him wonder if he was in heaven, but the dull thud of pain in his head made him know different—he was still in the place he'd always been. Still Wyalusing. Still dumb and fat Danny Bedford.

He tried to remember everything that had happened—Mindy bloody and dead; Sokowski promising to help, then kicking and hurting him; Carl talking of his kids and not wanting to go to jail—but all the thinking made his head feel fuzzy and funny, and he wanted it to go away. His fingers ran along his jaw. It was soft and swollen. Tender to the touch.

Danny sat there in the pile of snow and let things come into slow focus around him. He peered over the edge of the platform and saw that he was high off the ground—higher than any building he'd ever been in. He leaned back against the old pine and rubbed at a funny feeling on his scalp. A layer of snow and ice had frozen on his head—it felt like he was wearing a bathing cap. He wondered if part of his brain was frozen, too, but he didn't know if that was even possible.

As all his senses came back to him, he could smell the fresh sap from the pine—sweet and bitter at the same time. He wiggled his toes in his boots, slow at first, then got some feeling back. He didn't want to lose his toes to frostbite. Uncle Brett had told him a story about a man he called a "dumb-ass." Uncle Brett said the dumb-ass was from New Jersey and that he had no place hunting in these mountains. Danny remembered that the dumb-ass got lost and spent the night out in the woods, all alone, until hunters found him the next day. The dumb-ass hadn't been wearing good boots and had gotten frostbite on his toes. Two of them turned black, and a doctor had to cut them off. Danny didn't think Doc Pete was the doctor who did that, but he couldn't remember. What he did know for sure was that he didn't want to have any of his toes turn black and get cut off. He wasn't sure how he would be able to walk without all his toes.

His tongue clicked in his throat, stuck to the roof of his mouth like peanut butter, so Danny scooped up some snow and dropped it over his throbbing lips. He couldn't chew it, so he let it melt instead. A few drops trickled down his throat, and his stomach grumbled angrily, wanting more than just water. Eggs and bacon sure sounded good right about now.

Danny crawled to the edge of the deer stand and peered down again. His footprints were covered up by all the snow that had fallen during the night, and he couldn't tell which direction he had come from.

Uncle Brett had tried to teach him north, south, east, and west by looking up at the sun, but it was too hard for Danny to remember. Something about where moss grows or using the shadow of the sun on a stick or tree, but that didn't make any sense to him if there were no numbers to tell the time. Uncle Brett had gotten mad at Danny and slapped him hard on the back of the head.

How many times I got to tell you? Sun sets in the west, shithead.

Danny had nodded like he would remember next time, but he never did.

Now Danny gripped the edge of the platform and lowered his boots to the top rung of the ladder. He held on to each plank of wood real tight and worked his way down the side of the tree, slow and easy. Ice was frozen on the planks, and Danny didn't want to slip and knock his face against the tree. It took a few minutes to climb down—he was a lot slower than a squirrel running down a tree. When he reached the bottom, he leaned against the old pine and his breath rattled in his chest.

He looked around him at the woods. It all looked the same. Nothing but trees as far as the eye could see. Part of him wanted to climb back up into the deer stand and wait. Wait for someone to come and help him. Tell him what to do. Tell him that everything was gonna be okay.

But Danny knew that wasn't going to happen. Folks like the sheriff and Doc Pete thought he was the one who'd hurt Mindy, and they would want to put him in jail and lock him up forever. Even if he told the truth, that Mindy was already dead when he got there, everybody thought that he was dumb, and who would believe someone who was so dumb? Plus, deputies were supposed to protect people, not hurt them, so no one would believe that Deputy Sokowski had done anything bad.

Jail scared Danny. It was a place full of bad people who hurt other people. He sure didn't want to go there. Danny forgot all about the notion of jail when he saw something flicker in the woods up ahead of him. Maybe it was the voice in his head. Maybe it was back to help him.

A shape moved behind the trees. It was moving real peculiar. Jerking up and down like the Easter Bunny. But whatever it might be, it was much bigger than a rabbit. Besides, Uncle Brett said that there was no such thing as the Easter Bunny.

The shape kept moving right toward him. Danny pressed up against the tree and stayed right where he was. Maybe it was the sheriff or the deputy. He figured that they would be out looking for him by now. The shape stopped every now and again before continuing on. It jerked up and down and came closer. It moved behind a clump of large pines and disappeared for a second. When it stepped out, Danny could finally see what it was.

It was a white-tailed doe. Danny didn't see any antlers, so he knew it wasn't a buck. The deer had its snout up in the air and was searching for either food or signs of danger. It would stop, twitch its ears a few times, and then move on.

When it got closer, Danny could see why it was hopping like a bunny the doe had only three legs. Danny kept real still and watched the deer as it hobbled along. After it got to where Danny could see its eyes, he saw the reason why it only had three legs. A hunter's arrow was stuck in the flesh around its shoulder, over the left front leg. Or where its left front leg used to be. The shaft of the arrow was splintered off and stuck out a few inches. The doe had lost most of its fur around the arrow, and the skin was dark green and oozing pus and blood.

Danny had never seen anything like it before. He figured that the poor deer's leg must have fallen off somehow, and now it was forced to hop around on just three.

The doe stuck its snout in the snow and searched for some leaves or berries to eat. She was pretty skinny, ribs sticking out like a wash-board under her brown fur. She limped up not ten feet from Danny and the tree. Then the wind turned, and the doe finally caught Danny's scent. She froze and looked right at him. Uncle Brett said that deer were color-blind and couldn't see people if they stood real still. But the doe could smell him.

Danny stood motionless and observed every move the doe made—ears twitching, tail snapping. The deer's black eyes watched him closely right back. She snorted at him, trying to spook him.

Danny steadied his breath and licked at his lips. "I ain't gonna hurt you," he whispered softly. His swollen tongue made it sound thick and slurred. *Ah ain' gon' hurr ya.*

The doe's ears pressed back against her skull, then twitched a few more times. She fidgeted uneasily as Danny reached out toward her. He held his palms out and spoke softly again. "I ain't gonna hurt you."

The doe's ears went back up, and she limped toward him a foot or so.

Danny still had his hands out in front of him. "I don't know where to go."

The doe gave him a final sniff and began to limp past him and move deeper into the woods. She looked back at him one last time before hobbling on—almost like she was waiting for him. Danny watched her for a second and then began to follow after the doe.

Carl

arl looked over at Sokowski in the driver's seat of the truck. He
hated the motherfucker. He knew that Sokowski thought he
was stupid. Always treated him like some kind of moron or something, ever since high school. But over the years whatever Sokowski
wanted him to do, Carl would end up doing it. Carl didn't know why
exactly. Maybe it was because he was tired of being a wallflower. Or
maybe it was because he was short and fat and didn't really fit in, and
Sokowski let him into his circle of friends. That's all Carl really ever
wanted, he guessed. To fit in, no matter the cost or humiliation.

He'd jumped his dirt bike over Sokowski's Chevy truck in the
tenth grade. They had built a makeshift ramp out of flimsy plywood
and milk crates. Sokowski had invited over a bunch of the FFA
guys—wearing their blue corduroy Future Farmers of America jackets that they never seemed to take off, even in the summertime
when it was eighty degrees out. They bought a half keg with Carl's

money, and got good and drunk so that they could watch Carl make
an ass out of himself. Carl got good and drunk himself and played
right along. On his first and last jump, his back tire clipped the hood
of Sokowski's truck and flipped him up and over the handlebars.
Carl broke three ribs, fractured his left wrist, and tore most of the
skin off his legs, stomach, and face. To make matters worse, he had
been wearing only tighty whities, because Sokowski thought that
would be even funnier to watch. As Carl sat in a pool of his own
blood, Sokowski and the other burnouts laughed their asses off.

Carl always soaked up the attention that his stunts brought him.
He did stupid shit at the drop of a hat, because it was the only way
that the other guys would give him the time of day.

And he did a *bunch* of stupid shit. Usually at the expense of others. Mainly girls. Girls were easy targets. They fell for almost anything and couldn't kick Carl's ass. The meanest joke he ever played
on a girl still bothered him to this day. Years of guilt ate him up
inside. Sokowski had put him up to banging the fattest, ugliest chick
in their class. Susan Ross. Carl's cruel joke earned her the name
"Sexy Sue."

Sue was an outcast who never spoke to the other kids, ate by
herself in the cafeteria, and didn't participate in any gym classes
because she didn't want to change her clothes in the girls' locker
room. She was the unfortunate wallflower that Carl used to be and
was both fat and poor to boot. Because of that she had a big red target on her back.

The senior class was having a party down at the river toward the
end of the school year, and kids like the band freaks and bookworms
knew better than to go to that kind of party—it would be nothing
but trouble for them. But Sue fell victim to false hope. At Sokowski's

prompting, Carl invited her to the party to have a few beers and hang out. Sue was exactly like Carl—she just wanted to fit in.

Sue showed up that night wearing the same tight-fitting clothes she always wore, clothes that showed all her rolls of fat in all the wrong places. Long, greasy hair hung over her eyes, and she smelled like her father's barn, where she worked every day before and after school. With Sokowski and the other guys looking on, Carl fed her cup after cup of punch spiked with Everclear. She wasn't used to drinking and got buzzed pretty quickly. Carl gave her attention that she never received before. Asked her questions and made her laugh a few times. Sue never had anyone hit on her before.

It didn't take long to get her in the back of Carl's truck. She told him that she had never been with a boy before, and Carl just nodded at the confession. Carl had her clothes off quickly and took her from behind. He didn't want to see her face. He couldn't bear having her look him in the eyes while he performed his act. She was on all fours, and Sue's fat cheeks pressed into the vinyl seats as Carl grunted and thrust into her. The sound of sweaty skin slapping sweaty skin could be heard over the perky lyrics of Brian Hyland's "Itsy Bitsy Teenie Weenie Yellow Polka Dot Bikini" blasting from the car stereo. At the time Carl found it funny that he was having sex to this song. He knew that Sokowski and the guys would find it hilarious as well.

It was over pretty fast. Carl was drunk, but not drunk enough to come inside her. He pulled out and ejaculated onto her massive ass. She rolled over so that she could look at Carl, but he turned away and quickly threw his clothes back on. He told her he had to take a piss. As planned, he grabbed her large cotton panties on the way out.

Carl went and joined the boys. They drank and laughed and slapped Carl on the back like he was some kind of hero. They all watched and waited for Sue to get out of the truck. The fun wasn't over. Not by a long shot. It had to be at least fifteen minutes before Sue got up the courage to get out of Carl's truck when it was clear he wasn't returning.

Finally she stumbled out of the cab. Her hair was messed up more than it usually was, and her shirt was twisted and untucked. By this time everyone at the party was in on the joke. They were waiting for her grand exit from the truck.

A roar of laughter erupted as she spotted her audience of class-mates. A couple dozen kids stood around the bonfire, bent over laughing and pointing at her. A chant arose, initiated by Sokowski. Sue's head buzzed from the punch, but it only took a moment for her to understand what everybody was saying.

"Sexy Sue! Sexy Sue! Ain't no virgin and smells like poo!"

As the kids chanted, they all looked up at a tree beside the bon-fire and howled even louder. Sue peered at what they were pointing at and laughing about. Someone had hoisted her extra-large panties into the air, and they hung like a soiled flag from a tree limb.

"Sexy Sue! Sexy Sue! Ain't no virgin and smells like poo!"

Everybody was drunk, and they cackled and chanted over and over again for so long that it seemed surreal. But Sue stood para-lyzed, unable to move her fat legs. She took in the mocking faces of her classmates, most of whom she had known since kindergarten. And it wasn't just the boys who were laughing at her expense—girls were laughing at her, too.

Unable to contain herself anymore, she burst into tears and ran from the bonfire. Still drunk and uncoordinated, she tripped over her own feet and fell to the ground. She rolled in the dirt, which only made things worse. A new wave of laughter erupted around the party.

Carl stood in the middle of the delighted crowd beside Sokowski and remembered that Sokowski even had his arm around his shoulders. When Carl saw Sue on all fours on the ground, covered with dirt and grass, her face stained with tears, his smile faded a little.

A few weeks later, on graduation day, word spread around school about Sue's suicide. That morning she had hanged herself in her father's cattle barn. Carl knew why she did it. It didn't take a brain surgeon to figure it out. She didn't want to face her classmates on graduation night. It was just too much.

Carl and Sokowski never spoke about Sue or the suicide. Life went on.

Now Carl looked over at Sokowski again. Sokowski gripped the steering wheel and squinted to focus his drunken eyes on the road. They pulled in to Doc Pete's driveway and parked the truck. Sokowski grabbed two rifles from the gun rack and handed one to Carl. Sokowski's lousy grin was back.

Carl looked down at the rifle and said nothing. The same shit was happening again. People were dying because of them.

Scott & Skeeter Knolls

S cott was born three minutes before his brother, and he never let Skeeter forget who was older. Besides having a few minutes between them, the brothers had pretty similar personalities. They were both quiet men who didn't have a whole lot to say. Always had been. They both liked to fish and hunt and work with their hands. That's why they ended up opening their own auto-repair business. Cars and trucks didn't talk, didn't gossip about who was sleeping with who, didn't nag them about what they were wearing, didn't say boo. A good day was working under the hood of a Ford Mustang and fixing what needed to be fixed.

They were identical twins, and most folks around town had a hard time telling them apart, especially back in high school when they both wore blue jeans and red flannel shirts. Both stood an inch over six feet. Both weighed exactly one hundred and ninety-five pounds. Full heads of black hair, parted down the middle and feathered off to the sides, hadn't turned gray yet. Neither one of them smiled much, looking like they were perpetually pissed off about something. Seemed like the only time you could catch them smiling was when they were off by themselves and feeling the easy comfort of being in each other's company. Partly because they got tired of being mistaken for each other, Scott grew a mustache that had a hint of red in it, especially out in the sun. Skeeter opted for the full beard and kept it trimmed nice and short, using a pair of clippers every other day or so.

Neither one of them took to drinking either. They could thank their old man for that. Son of a bitch was a lousy drunk and a lousy father. When their mother told them what had happened out at Mindy's trailer, they both knew he probably had it coming. He would have killed the sheriff and then turned the gun on the state trooper. Scott and Skeeter didn't have to discuss this fact. They knew that's what the other one was thinking. Twins were that way.

Mindy, on the other hand, didn't deserve what she got. Sure, she was a bit too wild and too old to not be married and settled down, and she ran around with the wrong kind of men and partied a little more than she should. Pretty harmless stuff, but if she did what a sensible young woman was supposed to, she'd be taking care of a home and raising kids, not living alone in a shitty trailer. Neither one of them much cared for the deputy— he was bad news. Always had an edge to him. He was the kind of guy who would screw around on his wife. They thought Mindy could do better than him and told her as much, but for some reason she was drawn to the man and probably would have ended up marrying him. But Sokowski didn't turn out to be the problem—that turned out to be Danny Bedford.

Scott pulled his truck up in front of the Wash 'N Dry and left the motor running. They got out and walked up to the front door, their stride and body language exactly the same. Both of them wore green work coveralls stained with car and truck grease, oval name patches above the breast that specified who was Scott and who was Skeeter.

"Think it's open?" Skeeter said out loud.

Scott didn't answer. He pushed on the glass door, and it swung open. They looked down Main Street to see if anybody else was around. It was a little before seven, and none of the businesses were open yet. Just a handful of cars were parked on the street, but it was all pretty quiet.

They stepped into the laundromat and moved toward the steps in the back that led upstairs. Neither one of them had ever been inside the laundromat before, but everybody knew that Danny lived upstairs. They took the steps two at a time, Scott taking the lead, and pushed open the door to Danny's room. The bed was unmade, and the room was pretty sparse and depressing.

Skeeter looked around the room at all of Danny's stuff. He noticed all the wooden figurines on the dresser and picked one up. A green turtle with a little smiley face. It looked like a collection of kids' knickknacks. Being in here was tougher than he thought it would be. Seeing where his sister's killer had lived and slept and planned her murder made him feel like throwing up his breakfast. Skeeter's hands trembled as he turned the wooden turtle over in his palm.

Son of a bitch. Mindy was the only one around here who was nice to you, and you go and kill her.

"Don't mess with that crap. We ain't here for that." Scott avoided looking at Skeeter but knew that his brother was close to tears. He wanted to stay focused. There would be time for tears later. Not right now.

Skeeter nodded and returned the turtle to Danny's dresser, then opened up the drawers one at a time. A couple pair of mismatched socks, a pair of undershorts, and that was about it. He checked the closet next. A few shirts hung off hangers. He gazed over at his brother and shook his head.

"All his shit looks washed and clean. Ain't gonna help us none."

Scott fiddled with his mustache for a second as he glanced around the room until he found what he was looking for. He walked over to Danny's bed and picked up a pillow. He shook out the pillow and held on to the stained and threadbare pillowcase. He clutched it in his fist and looked to Skeeter.

"This'll do. Let's get the dogs," Scott said quietly.

Skeeter nodded. He took one final glance at the green turtle on the dresser, then followed his brother out of the room.

Taggart

Taggart rarely spent time in the woods—out in the middle of nowhere. He didn't get the attraction. If it wasn't hotter than hell, with the gnats and mosquitoes going after your face, sweat rolling in your eyes, pollen, and God knows what else being sucked into your lungs, it was cold and too damn quiet. Quiet was the worst. Nothing to block out the constant tug-of-war between guilt and cravings that waged in his head every single day. Noise and chaos helped keep it at bay.

Taggart was a city guy. Maybe Towanda wasn't exactly a big city like Philly, but it was big enough, and Binghamton was only an hour away and had more going on. Give him the traffic, the aggressive drivers, the steady drone of horns and music, and people screaming any day of the week. The call of ambulance sirens and helicopters was white noise to him and made him sleep like a baby. He'd gone camping with his father when he was ten and hated every second of it. Cooking hot dogs over the fire and sleeping in a tent didn't hold any charm for him. The incessant call of the katydids filling his ears was memorable, as was the sound of his father snoring a few inches away from his sleeping bag that smelled like a raccoon had taken a crap in it. Taggart had never been in such close physical proximity to his father for so long before. His father's breath stank of beer and cheap hot dogs. It was awful. And those memories were what now represented the great outdoors for him—nothing great about it. That was the last time he was deep in the woods. He had hoped it would be his last.

But now, here again, surrounded by nothing except trees and snow up to his ass, Taggart was reminded of the horrible silence. A few birds were singing, but even they didn't sound all that happy to be there. God, he really hated the quiet.

If I weren't drunk, I wouldn't have pulled the trigger. I would have con-fronted the man. Looked him in the eye to see if he was a real threat.

Taggart glanced to his right and caught a glimpse of the sheriff working his way through the trees fifty yards off. The sheriff had instructed him to make sure to maintain visual contact. If they got separated, the sheriff said that he would have to send out another search party just to find Taggart. He imagined the sheriff got a little thrill out of demonstrating his prowess in all things woods.

He and the sheriff had driven a few miles out of town to a spot where the sheriff thought they might find the suspect. The sheriff had *said* it was only a few miles away, but it took them twenty min-utes of riding in uncomfortable silence up and down so many rambling dirt roads that Taggart had no clue where in the hell they were.

Taggart checked his watch again. It was a little after seven and they had only been out here for an hour, but it felt like it had been at least eight. He had sweated out a lot of the alcohol from his system and was feeling slightly more clearheaded.

You killed him, Bill. His daughter was murdered, and you made the poor man's wife a widow.

Sobriety was letting the raw truth filter in more, and Taggart could hardly stand it. The truth about his entire fucked-up life started seeping out of his brain that he had worked so hard to numb and silence. He hadn't felt anything in a long time except self-loathing. And there was plenty of that nowadays. He was a piece of shit, exactly like his old man told him he was.

Okay. Just take a breath, Bill. It's going to be okay. This mess will sort itself out somehow.

He wiped a thin layer of sticky sweat from his forehead and rubbed it between his fingers. He felt like hell and wanted to crawl out of his skin.

You stupid idiot. You stupid goddamn idiot. You're never going to change. You're going to keep screwing it up and bring Shannon and the girls down with you.

He couldn't take it anymore. Being in between drunk and sober was the worst. He couldn't shut off his inner voice. It came in loud and clear and bared the naked truth that was just too brutal to handle.

Screw it.

He reached into his pocket and grabbed both of the flasks he knew he would eventually be going for. Starsky and Hutch. What a team they made. Starsky felt about half full. Hutch was running low to empty. A little bit swished around inside. That should do the trick for now. Starsky would be for later. Should be plenty to get him out of this day.

Taggart looked back toward the sheriff and saw the old man moving through the trees at a pretty good clip. Taggart ducked behind a large tree, uncapped the flask, and took a hard pull. The instant burn in his stomach was a welcome friend.

He took another pull.

Okay. Just stabilize. You'll get through this.

And another pull.

Think about it. The sheriff said so himself. You did the right thing. You saw a situation with an officer in jeopardy and you reacted. That is what you were trained to do.

His stomach glowed, and his brain anxiously waited its turn.

Stay the course here. Track down this son of a bitch and get the hell out of this cow pasture of a town.

Taggart found himself smiling a little. His buzz was coming back.

There we go. One more nip for good measure.

He drank a little more and screwed the cap back onto the flask. He stepped out from behind the tree and took a deep inhale of the country air.

Not so bad after all. Let's do this thing.

He looked to his right but didn't see the sheriff. The forest was both still and quiet.

A moment of fear crept up from his stomach.

Shit.

He could feel his buzz intensify. He had a good one coming on. He looked to where he thought the sheriff was last walking.

Screw it.

He started walking. Not knowing where the sheriff was or whether he himself was going in the right direction. And not really caring. He felt something growing deep inside him. A growing anger, a growing rage toward Danny Bedford. It was all because of this Danny Bedford that he was in hot water. Danny Bedford was responsible for this—not him. Rage was burning. Rage he could deal with. He fed off it, in fact. Taggart was going to make the guy pay for the shit he was causing. He was going to make him pay in full.

Danny

He hadn't seen the three legged deer in a while. Danny figured she must have gone off to be with her family or something. Maybe she had a baby to tend to or was looking for something to eat. Or maybe the deer knew that Danny was nothing but trouble and the best thing for her would be to leave him lost in the woods to fend for himself. Seemed like everything he was around ended up getting hurt or worse. His folks. Uncle Brett. Now Mindy. He didn't mean for people to get hurt, but trouble always seemed to follow him around. If he could take it all back and be the one who drowned in the pond that day instead of his parents, he would do it in a second.

Danny wished that the doe were still with him but understood why she wasn't. Besides, how could a deer really help him? A deer was just an animal that was even dumber than him. An animal couldn't help him figure out what to do.

But the doe did help him with something—she made him realize that he couldn't fend for himself out in the woods alone and that he needed to find someone he could trust. Someone who was nice to him and would believe that he didn't do nothing wrong. He felt bad for Carl and his kids and all, but he didn't want to get in trouble for something he didn't do. Aside from Mindy, Mr. Bennett had been nothing but good and honest with him for a long time. Mr. Bennett would know that Danny wouldn't hurt no one.

Mr. and Mrs. Bennett had Danny over for dinner one time a few years back. Mrs. Bennett had made a meat loaf with mashed potatoes, buttermilk biscuits, and fresh wax beans. He had never smelled or tasted anything so good in his whole life. Danny had three helpings and could have had a fourth, but he saw the way they were looking at him and he figured he should stop. Then Mrs. Bennett brought out a deep dish of peach cobbler, and Danny thought that he had died and gone to heaven. If that was what heaven was like, Danny wouldn't mind so much going there.

Danny remembered that they just let him eat his dinner and didn't ask him a bunch of questions or make him feel dumb or anything. Mrs. Bennett thanked him for coming, said it was an honor having him as a dinner guest, and gave him a big hug before Mr. Bennett took him back to the laundromat. That was the first hug he'd had since his mama and papa went away. That was one of the best nights in Danny's life for sure.

Danny noticed that his head was starting to feel funny. He put his fingers to his forehead—it was all slick with sweat and hot to the touch. That didn't make sense to Danny. It was real, real cold outside, so how could his head be hot? His jaw still hurt a little, but his feet and hands felt far away from the rest of his body, like they weren't even connected to him anymore. Maybe he had a fever. He remembered once when he was little, he had felt the same way. Kinda dizzy and light-headed. Uncle Brett made him go to school anyway, because he didn't want Danny at home with him. Danny went to school and felt real sleepy the whole time. He had trouble keeping his eyes open at his desk, his head snapping back and forth when sleep would take him for a second. He sat at the rear of the classroom where Miss Bradley made him sit. She didn't call on him like she did the other kids. She didn't even make him take tests. She told him to color on a piece of scrap paper or look at a picture book while the rest of the kids took the test. Miss Bradley said that he wasn't smart enough to take tests or do homework, so she acted like he wasn't even there. She wasn't mean or anything, but Danny could tell that Miss Bradley wished he weren't in her classroom with all the normal kids. But on that day when he was feeling sick, he remembered that she put her soft palm that smelled like lotion on his forehead and gave him a look that he had never seen her give him before. She sent him to see Doc Pete straightaway, and after that he stayed at home for over a week. Doc Pete said that his fever was real high and he shouldn't be around the other kids. Said he could be contagious. Danny remembered that big word because it rhymed with "outrageous." Uncle Brett got real mad, because Danny was supposed to be in bed and not go to school, so Danny stayed in his room and tried not to bother him. He ate Cap'n Crunch cereal for a week, because Uncle Brett didn't make him soup like his mama used to make for him when he was feeling sick.

Maybe Mrs. Bennett would have medicine or something for him. When you got sick, you were supposed to drink bad-tasting medicine to make you feel better.

Danny came to a place where the trees thinned out a bit and he could see a lot more daylight. He kept moving and stopped in front of an old road at the edge of the woods. He was pretty sure that this was the road that led up to the Bennetts' house.

He decided to stay in the cover of trees just in case someone was driving around looking for him, and he moved in the same direction as the road. He walked for a ways, not really thinking about much or paying attention to where he was going.

After a while he got to thinking about the doe again. He didn't understand why folks like his Uncle Brett enjoyed hunting and killing deer. Uncle Brett made him eat venison for many dinners even though he never much cared for the taste. Uncle Brett sure enjoyed it, but Danny thought it was too chewy, and the fat stuck to the roof of his mouth. But even the thought of a food that he didn't like all that much still made him feel hungry. The last meal he'd had seemed like days ago. He wondered if he would ever get to drink hot chocolate and have a batch of scrambled eggs at the Friedenshutten again. Probably not.

He caught a whiff of smoke in the air. He thought maybe he was imagining the smell because he was hungry and liked to eat food cooked over a fire, but then he took another sniff and could definitely smell the smoke of burning wood. Probably from a chimney or something. And if it came from a chimney, that meant he was close to someone's house. Danny sure hoped that it was Mr. and Mrs. Bennett's house.

He looked up into the blue sky and saw a cloud of black smoke drifting in the wind. He felt tired and wanted to go back to sleep but knew that he should keep going. Mr. Bennett would know what to do.

The smell of burning wood grew stronger, and Danny kept moving his feet forward. That faraway feeling in his body was getting worse. If he was dreaming, he sure wished he would wake up.

Over the last few hours, his walking had turned more into a stagger, feet barely lifting off the ground. He moved up a slope and stopped at the crest of a hill. There in front of him was a small house, painted blue like a robin's egg. Mr. Bennett's Jeep was parked in the driveway and had about a foot of snow piled on top of it. A small porch ran along the front of the house, and two rocking chairs were partially hidden under a heap of snow and ice. Icicles hung from the rain gutter like crystal daggers—sharp and glistening wet.

Danny wanted to smile at the sight but knew that it would hurt his jaw. He made his way down the slope and walked across the front lawn, where a birdbath and a few colorfully painted birdhouses were hanging from the limbs of birch trees.

He climbed the steps to the porch and stopped in front of the door. It had a doorbell, but Danny decided to knock instead.

Carl

They were Danny's footprints in the snow. No doubt about it. Carl watched Sokowski stop at the base of the tree and peer up toward the deer stand that was built on the side of the large pine. Sokowski was winded from the long hike up the hill, chest rising and falling as he tried to get his breath back. The whiskers below his nose and down on the tip of his beard were frozen with snot. He knelt into the snow and took a closer look at the footprints. They were pretty fucking fresh.

"Those his?" Carl asked. He already knew that they were.

Sokowski nodded. "Must have slept up there. Retard's smarter than I thought he was. I was hoping that the dumb bastard would have frozen to death during the night. Would have saved us the trouble." He stood and looked out into the woods, rubbed at his bad ear to warm it up a little. "He can't be far. Should be able to find him pretty quick."

Sokowski reached into his jacket and pulled out a Baggie of weed and rolling papers. Carl watched silently while Sokowski rolled a fat joint as easily as buttering a slice of toast, then put it between his lips and fired it up. He took a couple of tokes, held it and offered the joint to Carl. Carl shook his head and looked away.

"Don't be such a pussy. This shit's almost done."

Carl shivered even though he had on a thick layer of clothing and was sweating a little. He got to thinking about Kelly, probably at home, all pissed off that he hadn't even called. Probably thinking that he'd hooked up with some skank. Carl wished that she just missed him, wanted him at home so they could spend some time together. But Carl knew she wouldn't be thinking something like that—that part of their relationship had ended long ago.

"It ain't right," Carl mumbled quietly.

"What ain't?"

Carl cleared his throat. "All this. It wasn't supposed to happen. I think we should stop."

Sokowski took another hit and looked at Carl with a crooked smile. "Just stop and go home? Eat a pizza, watch some TV, and pretend it didn't happen? Kinda late for that, ain't it?"

"That ain't what I'm saying."

"Yeah? Well, what exactly *are* you saying, Carl?"

Carl looked at him. Wished that Sokowski wasn't so damned bullheaded, but he knew that he would never change. Never.

"Nothing."

"That's what I figured. Fuck, you're thick." Sokowski took another hit of the joint and pinched off the tip and put the roach into his pocket. He slung his rifle to the other shoulder and started following Danny's footprints deeper into the woods. Carl looked up at the deer stand, then followed after Sokowski like a beaten pup.

Scott Knolls

The two amped-up coonhounds paced back and forth in the bed of the pickup truck—they were wound up and ready for a hunt, something they were born to do. Their black nails clicked on the metal floor of the pickup, and their tails snapped feverishly in pure excitement. The younger of the two lifted her head and let out a low howl, while the older hound poked her snout up into the air and watched the passing countryside with her chocolate brown eyes. The truck scared up a few grouse hiding in the brush, and their wings snapped rapid-fire as they darted across the road. Both coonhounds tracked the birds' flight, whining and quivering at the sight of them.

The pickup slowed and pulled off to the side of Brewer Hollow Road. As soon as the engine cut off, both dogs leaped out of the back of the truck and ran to the cab, wagging and waiting for their master.

Scott stepped out first and patted both dogs fondly. They were his dogs. Loved them like children. Skeeter and his wife had three healthy children, two boys and a girl. Scott and Paula had one. Tammy. Poor little Tammy.

Scott and Paula had had a whole lot of trouble conceiving. After getting married they tried for five or six years, and it proved to be an agonizing process. Scott wasn't sure if the problem was with him or Paula. They didn't discuss that or go to a doctor to see which one of their bodies didn't want to cooperate. They kept trying, kept failing. They never discussed adoption either. Folks around Wyalusing just didn't do that kind of thing. Adoption seemed like something that weak people resorted to. It got to the point of being embarrassing that Scott didn't have any young'uns running around—like he wasn't man enough to have children. All his friends had three or four kids, and Scott didn't even have one. He didn't like visiting friends because he didn't like watching what he didn't have.

Just when they were ready to give up, lo and behold, Paula finally got pregnant. They were thrilled beyond words. Relieved that at last they had been blessed by God and were able to start a family. Paula had a pretty easy pregnancy, and Tammy was born near to the day that she was expected. But when she was born, there was something different about her, something a little off. She had all her toes and fingers and weighed over eight pounds, but her face was unusually round. Her brown eyes were almond-shaped, and her tiny tongue was perpetually sticking out of her tiny mouth. Scott and Paula both knew what her condition was when the doctor sat them down and explained the situation—they had seen babies like Tammy before when they took a trip to Wilkes-Barre to do some Christmas shopping or to look at a new truck in all the dealerships they had down that way. Tammy had Down's syndrome. And to make matters worse, she had a bad heart. The doctor said it was a common condition in children with Down's syndrome. Tammy had a congenital heart defect. The doctor advised them of the life expectancy of children afflicted with the disorder. Many children could grow up to be adults and live a healthy and productive life. Many lived well into their forties. But the doctor also warned them that raising a child with Down's syndrome would take a lot of care and a lot of patience and a whole lot of love due to her special needs.

Scott and Paula took Tammy home to where her room had been carefully painted yellow and outfitted with a slew of stuffed animals and baby gear. They had the changing table, a stroller, crib, baby clothes, and a ton of diapers at the ready. They had planned carefully for their daughter's arrival, but the addition to the family fell far short of their expectations.

Tammy cried and fussed a lot. It didn't matter if she was held or swaddled up nice and tight. Paula tried breast-feeding a few times but gave up quickly and instead switched to bottle-feeding. A few days went by, and Scott watched how Paula handled the baby. She changed Tammy when she needed a new diaper, fed her, burped her, gave her all the necessary care that babies need, but his wife never looked at Tammy. Never looked her in the eyes. Scott had imagined that the two of them would always be fighting over who gets to hold the baby, who gets to put her down for a nap, but that never happened. Scott never admitted it to his wife, but he didn't like holding his own child. She was different from what she was supposed to be. When he looked at his daughter, he didn't feel pride or joy. He could never put words to it, but he didn't feel connected to the child. It didn't feel like she was his own blood.

He came home from work one night after Tammy had been home for a few weeks, and the house was filled with the constant hoarse cry of the baby. He found Tammy in her crib, wet with pee and smelling of poop, red-faced and bawling, left all alone in her room. Paula was on the back porch, swinging side to side on the hammock, smoking a cigarette. She had a vacant look about her. Scott sat beside her until she finally gazed at him like he was a stranger. Then she started to cry. Scott cried along with her. The three of them cried together but separate.

The next day Scott called the county and went about starting the process of giving up Tammy for adoption. They were interviewed by a half dozen different county workers who asked them a lot of questions and made them feel guilty for what they were planning to do. Paula lost twenty pounds over the next month and was put on an antidepressant, but it didn't help matters much. Scott was angry at how the county was treating them. Angry with Paula for letting this happen to his baby. Angry with God for ruining his life. Angry with himself that he couldn't even bear to look at his own flesh and blood. But he couldn't do it. He couldn't raise a child like that. It wasn't the way it was supposed to be.

The day that they bundled up Tammy for the last time and drove her down to Wilkes-Barre, Scott and Paula didn't talk. Tammy cried the whole way there in the baby seat that had been barely used. For over an hour, the baby bawled and neither her mother nor father tried to soothe her. They didn't talk when they walked her into the county hospital and handed over their baby. They didn't talk when they got back home and Scott broke down the crib and packed away all the baby stuff. He and Paula didn't talk other than saying the token "Good morning" and "Good night" for over a month. The house felt dead and empty even after every remnant of Tammy was thrown away. They couldn't box up and throw away their memories. They had coexisted in the house over the last few years, but little joy was shared between them.

Scott was a supportive and doting uncle to Skeeter's kids, but watching them grow up made his grief even worse. The two hounds, Queenie and Charlotte, didn't sleep in coops like most hunting dogs. They slept at the foot of Scott's bed, which was in Tammy's old room now, and they followed him near everywhere in the house. They were the closest things to kids he would ever have.

"Okay, girls. You ready?" Charlotte let out an antsy yelp, her tail whipping a mile a minute. Scott reached inside the cab and removed Danny's pillowcase. He held it out for the two hounds. They shoved their noses into the fabric and took a good long sniff. Low growls worked up from their bellies, and their hindquarters quivered with anticipation.

"All right. Go on!" Both dogs lowered their heads toward the snow and bounded into the forest, yelping and barking as they began the search for their prey.

Skeeter handed Scott his rifle, and the two brothers followed after the hounds. They stepped over a barbed-wire fence that ran alongside the ditch and moved into the woods. They heard Charlotte and Queenie ahead of them and marched along in silence for a while.

Scott looked at his younger brother and was the first to speak. "Let me do it."

Skeeter regarded him, not exactly sure what he was getting at.

"Let me take him down. No sense in both of us going to jail."

Skeeter blew some snot out of his nose before saying anything. "I don't know. I thought we were in this together. One for all and all for one, kind of thing."

Scott tried to smile but wasn't really able to. He didn't think he was gonna be able to smile for a good long time. "You got Betty and the kids."

Skeeter thought about this. "Maybe we should just take him in. Ma's already lost one kid today."

Now it was Scott's turn to mull over the idea. "Maybe. But I just don't think I'm gonna be able to let him walk away from this. If we find him first, I don't think I'll be able to do that. Not after what he did."

Skeeter knew that his brother was right. They walked in silence again, arms and legs moving at the same exact tempo, listening to the hounds' calls ahead of them. Scott put a pinch of chew in his mouth and handed the pouch to his brother. They both walked along, spitting brown juice into the snow as they went.

"You replace the alternator in Murphy's Chevy yet?" Scott asked.

Skeeter shook his head. "Part's supposed to come in tomorrow."

Scott nodded and spit again. "Yesterday was Mindy's birthday, you know?"

Skeeter looked ahead of him and nodded. "Yup. It was."

Mr. & Mrs. Bennett

After Danny had shown up on their doorstep, covered in blood, face all swollen and black on one side, and every inch of him shivering from the cold, he nearly collapsed inside their house. Mr. Bennett had managed to get the overgrown man-child to the sofa to warm up before the fire—and the boy hadn't moved from the spot for the last fifteen minutes.

Mr. Bennett crouched in front of the fireplace, gripped a fire iron in a fist twisted up by arthritis, and poked at the logs to keep them burning. Droopy jowls quivered and shook with every prod of the fire iron. He still had a full crop of gray hair, but unsightly hairs sprouted up all over the rest of his head as well—on the ears, on the tip of a bulbous nose, patches of it creeping out from his nostrils. And while most of him seemed to be shrinking, his earlobes just seemed to be getting bigger. He wore thick-rimmed glasses—the same pair he'd worn for the last twenty-some years.

He glanced over at Danny, who savored the warmth from the roaring flames in the fireplace, liking the way it made his face feel and how the heat soothed his throbbing jaw. Danny sat mesmerized, watching red embers hiss and spit off the logs. The embers glowed for a few moments in a pile of ash before they slowly faded to a dull gray. Danny held a mug of hot tea in his hands and tried to sip it, but his mouth hung open and most of the warm liquid ran down his neck.

Mr. Bennett set the fire iron on the stone hearth, struggled to his feet, then took a seat beside Danny on the sofa. Before speaking he watched his wife skitter around the house looking for a blanket and some rubbing alcohol to clean up some of Danny's wounds.

Mr. Bennett clasped his leathery palms together and wore a heavy expression on his face and jowls. "Danny, if you didn't do nothing wrong, then you got nothing to be worried about. You just need to tell the sheriff the truth about what happened. Nobody's gonna put you in jail for something you didn't do."

Danny's head still felt funny, and Mr. Bennett's voice sounded far away, like he was speaking through a tunnel or something. Danny looked at Mr. Bennett's kind face and shrugged his shoulders, then took another sip of tea and grimaced as he swallowed. He began to speak, saying the words slowly and as clear as he could, and tried his best not to move his jaw too much. "But they think I hurt Mindy. I wouldn't do no such thing, Mr. Bennett. She was my friend. Besides—" A flare of pain shot through his jaw and stopped him short. His whole body jerked and he waited for the sharp ache to ease up some before continuing on. "Mindy was dead when the deputy and Carl came out of the trailer."

Mrs. Bennett hustled back into the living room, her face flushed red with worry. Her gray hair was pulled into a bun, and her hands trembled a little as she put a warm blanket over Danny's lap. She might be a little thick around the middle, but she moved with a lively spring in her step. A hardy woman with strong country hands used to digging in the garden, chopping firewood along with her husband, and plucking the feathers from a chicken when they were in the mood to fry one up for dinner. She gave her husband a look, and they spoke without saying anything.

Mr. Bennett nodded and turned back to Danny. "Okay, Danny. Just drink your tea up, and we'll get things sorted out." He gave Danny's knee a quick pat, and then he stood and hobbled into the kitchen on arthritic knees.

Mrs. Bennett was right at his heels. Her hands were cupped around the folds in her neck and her fingers twisted around an old mother-of-pearl necklace she favored wearing.

"You better call Lester and get him up here," she whispered, sneaking a peek back toward Danny in the living room. "That deputy of his is nothing but trouble. I bet *he* did something to that Knolls girl."

"Hold on, now. Danny's not exactly the best source for reliable truth. You know how he is. Maybe he *did* do something by accident and is getting the facts all mixed up in his head."

"You really think so, Sherman?" Mrs. Bennett asked.

Mr. Bennett didn't really believe that Danny would hurt anybody. Especially Mindy. "Well, no, I don't know for sure, but we'll just have to let Lester figure all that out."

Mrs. Bennett nodded reluctantly and watched her husband pick up the phone. He dialed a number and waited while the phone rang and rang on the other end. After ten rings he put the phone back in its cradle.

"Not in the office. Must be out looking for him. I'll take Danny back to town after a bit. Let him drink that tea and get back a little strength."

Mrs. Bennett's eyes widened with a worrisome thought. She gave Danny another look before saying anything. "You don't really think Danny would have done anything to that poor girl, do you?"

Mr. Bennett didn't answer right away. He poured himself a cup of coffee and blew on it for a minute. "Danny's always been quiet and kept to himself, and to be honest, I just don't know what he might be capable of doing. He's been carrying a world of hurt and pain around for a long time now. Can't be easy to live that kind of life."

Mrs. Bennett wanted to disagree with him, but she wasn't absolutely sure. "You think you should take him to town? I don't think he did anything to that girl, but I don't know if I want you alone with him."

Mr. Bennett tugged on his jowls, thinking on that for a second. "Can't let him stay here. Besides, his jaw is a mess. Looks to be broken pretty bad, and I think he's got a fever, which probably means he's got an infection, too. The boy needs to see a doctor."

His wife nodded. "Guess you're right."

They both nearly jumped out of their skin at a violent thudding on the front door. Three heavy knocks. They gave each other a look as whoever it was pounded on the door once again— harder this time.

"Probably the sheriff now." Mr. Bennett shuffled back into the living room and toward the door. As he passed by the couch, he noticed that Danny sat upright and rigid. The man's eyes were glued to the door, and he had an uneasy look about him.

"It's all right, Danny."

Danny shook his head. "I don't know, Mr. Bennett."

"You got nothing to worry about. You'll see." Mr. Bennett swung the door open, and Sokowski's wide shoulders were framed by the entranceway. A few paces behind him, Carl stood with weak shoulders bent south. Both men had rifles slung over their backs.

"Got us some police matters here, Sherman," Sokowski said.

Mr. Bennett took a quick step back. "I was thinking that you were the sheriff."

"Nope. I ain't." Sokowski glared past Mr. and Mrs. Bennett toward Danny, who sank a little deeper into the sofa. "We're here for Danny." Sokowski's eyes were a mess of bloodshot, and he breathed out a strong wave of booze. He never took his eyes off Danny as he bumped up against Mr. Bennett and stepped inside the room.

Lester

Lester hadn't seen the statie in a while. He'd been crystal clear with the big fella to stay in plain view. These woods were pretty unforgiving if you hadn't spent the better part of your life in them.

He decided to backtrack and see if he could find the man. Officer Taggart was a city slicker, and it seemed pretty clear the man was out of his element around here. Plus, Lester had a bad feeling in his gut about Taggart. It was plain as day that the man had a lot of anger knocking around that head of his. Taggart was a lost soul who thought the bottle would get him out of his life's worries, and Lester knew that that was a losing battle. Seen it too many times before.

Lester didn't want to lose much time in tracking Danny, but something told him that there was more to this situation than met the eye. He reached into his pocket for his pack of smokes and felt the robin figurine. He pulled it out and gave it another look. Had to admit, it was a fine piece of work.

The boy had shown up at her trailer to give her a present, then went and killed her? Still didn't make much sense. Maybe another rejection from her was too much. Living a life with nothing but limitations and ridicule would be a tough thing to bear. It would be understandable for someone like him to snap and do something awful. Understandable, but out of character for sure.

He saw some movement in a thicket of woods ahead of him, so Lester dropped the carving into his pocket and headed toward it. Lester's lower back had tightened up pretty bad, his legs not faring much better. He pushed on anyway. The sun had started to warm up a bit, making the snow soft and slightly more difficult to walk through. He moved past a grouping of pine trees that had trunks the size of his waist and saw Taggart trudging his way through the woods. It was pretty evident that the man wasn't paying much attention to where he was going—he just tromped along in the snow like a lost child.

Lester approached him and knew immediately he'd been drinking again. Slack face, glazed eyes, uncoordinated movement. "Son, you finish that bottle yet?"

Taggart didn't look at him. He kept plodding forward, so Lester stepped beside him and matched his stride.

"I've been straight with you, Mr. Taggart. I expect the same."

Taggart finally looked at him. "No. Still got a few drinks left."

"Look, son—"

Taggart stopped. "Save it, Sheriff. The last thing I need is a morality lesson from you. There's going to be an investigation into what happened, and I *will* go down. I'll lose my badge, my family. Everything. And when that happens, I'm going to implode. It's been a long time coming, so I can't think of any reason to stop drinking. Not one."

Lester nodded. "Fair enough. So where does that leave *us*?"

Taggart thought about this for a few seconds before giving the man an answer. "Let me just play this out with you."

"Ain't a game. Two bodies to prove that."

Taggart's own body tensed up, fighting back a growing rage. "I'll follow your lead. Won't do anything you tell me not to."

Lester took off his hat and rubbed at his head. "Just tell me why in the hell you want to keep on with this?"

"Because it's the right thing to do. It's still my job to bring in a guilty man."

"And you think you're in the right condition to do that? To help me?"

Taggart swayed a bit on his feet. "Yeah, I do."

Lester sized him up, considering.

"Just let me do one right thing today. Got enough regrets already."

Lester gave the man a sad look. "A little late to be self-aware now, son. I gave you a second chance already, and you didn't take it." Lester returned his hat to its proper place. "I'm sorry for your situation, but I'm sorrier for folks that I have known a helluva long time who are gonna be burying loved ones in the next few days."

Taggart's face reddened, but Lester continued. "I don't trust your judgment. You're impaired. God knows how much booze you got in your belly. You're a danger not only to me and my deputy but to yourself. I'll take it from here." Lester pointed behind him. "You head in that direction for a mile or so. Try not to drink any more until you get out of these woods. And try to think about your family if you don't care about yourself. Drinking is a selfish man's game."

With that said, Lester turned and walked away. He didn't look back at Taggart. Not once.

Sokowski

The fire had nearly gone out. A few coals still glowed, but it would only be a few minutes before they burned through and turned to ash.

The house was quiet except for the constant ticking of a six-foot-tall grandfather clock that stood guard in the corner of the living room—a little after ten A.M. Sokowski gave the clock a quick glance before turning back to Danny.

"Up on your feet, boy. It's time to answer for what you've done."

Sokowski noticed how Mrs. Bennett clung to the side of her husband—the poor old bitch looked scared enough to drop dead of a heart attack.

Mr. Bennett held his wife's hand tight and cleared his throat. "Just a minute, Deputy. Where's the sheriff?"

Sokowski turned his cold eyes on him. "Out looking for this

killer, I imagine." Sokowski lifted his rifle off his shoulder and tapped the barrel into Danny's chest. "On your feet, I said."

Mrs. Bennett let out a low moan as she watched Danny struggle to his feet.

"I didn't hurt Mindy," Danny managed in a soft whisper.

"Shut the fuck up. I saw what you did."

"Hold on there. Maybe it's best for Danny to wait until the sheriff gets here," Mr. Bennett tried again.

Sokowski kept the barrel of the rifle pressed to the center of Danny's chest. "I didn't ask what you thought, Sherman. Danny here is a threat, and you're pushing my patience. This is police business. I don't tell you how to run *your* business, and I would suggest that you don't tell me how to run mine."

Mr. Bennett stood his ground. "You've been drinking, Deputy. That much is clear. I think it best to wait for Lester."

Sokowski's reactions were a bit sluggish. His body pivoted like he was moving in slow motion toward Mr. Bennett and glared at the old man with utter disgust. "You had a killer sitting on your couch. You're lucky we showed up before he did the same to you and your wife as he did to Mindy."

Sokowski watched Mr. Bennett's face shift—a seed of doubt creeping in. Mr. Bennett took a slight step away from Danny, and Sokowski took note. "You're goddamn lucky." Sokowski grabbed Danny by the shoulder and shoved him forward.

Danny looked over to the Bennetts, eyes pleading, and struggled to speak with each word causing a world of hurt. "They were in the trailer when I got there. They told me to stay there."

Sokowski jerked Danny's thick, flabby arm to shut him up. "Save it, Danny. No one is gonna believe your lies."

Mr. Bennett took a breath and stepped in front of the door. Shook his head. "Sorry, Deputy. Can't let you boys take him. Something doesn't feel right."

"Goddamn it, old man, I ain't gonna tell you again."

Carl finally spoke up behind him. "Maybe he's right, Mike. Maybe we should just wait here."

"Christ. Why don't all of you just shut the fuck up? I'm handling the situation." Sokowski took a moment to level a look at all of them. "I'm the one with the badge. Am I making myself clear?"

Not one of them said another word.

Sokowski moved to pull Danny forward again, but Danny stood firm, not budging his near three hundred pounds.

"Don't get smart on me, Danny, or I'll be happy to put another hurting on you."

Danny looked Sokowski straight in the eye and took a breath. "This here is wrong. It was you and Carl."

Again the room filled with uncomfortable silence. Just the steady ticking of the old grandfather clock. Danny's words hung out there like big stained sheets on a clothesline for all to see.

"You're wrong about that, retard. You're dumber than shit, you know that? I know what you are. You act all quiet and meek as a mouse, but you ain't fooling me none."

Mrs. Bennett looked over to Carl, who stared down at the floor and couldn't keep her scrutiny. Her eyes went back to Sokowski and to the scratches on his face and cauliflower ear.

"What the hell you staring at, woman?" Sokowski snapped. His hand went up and pulled his stringy hair over the disfigured ear.

Mr. Bennett spoke up beside her. "Look here, Deputy. We've known Danny for a long time and can't see him doing something like this."

Sokowski felt all the judging eyes on him. He knew what they were thinking. "Yeah, but sometimes you don't always know people as well as you think." He noticed Mr. Bennett's eyes go to the telephone that hung on the wall between the living room and the kitchen.

"I think we need to call Lester," Mr. Bennett said, trying for steely resolve, but it fell far short of that.

"I don't think you folks are listening. I'm not here asking for your opinions."

"Whatever Danny may have done, he's in no condition to do more harm. You can see that, can't you?" Mr. Bennett asked.

Face flushing with anger, Sokowski didn't give him an answer. He had had enough. He walked over to the telephone and ripped it straight off the wall. He tossed it to the floor, where it made a dull, weak clang as the ringers knocked against each other inside the housing.

"There. You got me good and pissed off. You happy now?" Sokowski looked over at Mr. Bennett. "Christ. You got a liquor cabinet? Could use a drink of whiskey right about now." Mr. Bennett didn't say anything. "Well. Do you? A little drink, and then we'll be on our way."

Mr. Bennett shot a glance toward his wife before turning and shuffling into the kitchen for a minute.

Sokowski kept his position in front of Danny but looked to Mrs. Bennett, who had turned about as white as a bag of flour. He tried again. Kept his voice level and calm-sounding. Even forced a smile. "Ma'am, you got nothing to be scared of. Danny here did what I said he did. He's got the brain of a six-year-old. Probably didn't mean to do what he did. Confused, is all."

Mrs. Bennett nodded, then looked past Sokowski, and her face went even whiter. She tried to speak, but nothing came out of her mouth. Sokowski glanced back toward the kitchen, and his shit-eating smile faded right away.

Mr. Bennett strode back into the living room holding a rifle. He held it firmly, with the confidence of a man who was used to carrying a gun and not afraid to use it.

"All right, you listen up, Deputy. This here is my home, and no one marches in here telling me this or that. Danny is staying put. I'm only gonna tell you once to get the hell out." He lifted his rifle and held it on Sokowski.

Sokowski didn't move. His eyes squinted into narrow slits as he sized up Mr. Bennett—the old man didn't appear to be fucking around.

"Well, shit. Didn't see this coming from you, Sherman. You've been watching too many Clint Eastwood movies." He chuckled, but Mr. Bennett kept the rifle pointed right at him. "I guess I ain't getting that drink of whiskey, am I?"

Mr. Bennett tightened his grip on his rifle. "Nope. Not my whiskey, you aren't."

Sokowski nodded and looked back to Carl. "All right, then." Sokowski made for the front door in slow, easy steps. Then he stopped, and his shoulders dropped a little. "Shit." He spun back around and turned his gun on Mr. Bennett. Whether he was drunk or not, his reflexes were smooth and fast. He squeezed the trigger and fired a shot. Mr. Bennett's hand jerked as he flew back into the grandfather clock, shattering the glass panel into a hundred jagged bits, his own rifle discharging and sending a bullet up and into the ceiling. A hole the size of a fist was left in his chest from the bullet that tore through him, and blood and tattered pieces of flesh splattered into the fireplace, spitting and sizzling on the embers. The old man's heart stopped pumping before he even slumped onto the floor like an empty set of clothing.

Mrs. Bennett stared down at her husband for a moment as her brain tried to register what she was seeing. She watched as the blood poured from the gaping wound in his chest, and her mouth fell open, exposing her dentures and pink tongue. She let out a small breath, and her tongue began to undulate like a waking snake. Then she began to scream. Loud and shrill.

The piercing sound went right through Sokowski.

He had crossed the line, and there was no turning back—not now. He swung his rifle in Mrs. Bennett's direction and hissed at her, "Shut up, you old bitch." He started to squeeze the trigger when a shot rang out from behind him. Sokowski lurched forward as a bullet chewed through his side, but he still managed to pull the trigger. His aim was deflected, the slug going up and to the left, right through Mrs. Bennett's shoulder—she flew back and dropped onto the sofa in a heap.

The room filled with the smell of gunpowder, and the shots still rang in Danny's head. He looked to Carl, who stood by the doorway holding his rifle—a wisp of smoke dancing out of the tip of the barrel. Carl kept the gun directed at Sokowski's back as the deputy went down on both knees, gripping at a wound that spouted blood from his side.

Taggart

Taggart watched the sheriff grow smaller in the woods until he finally disappeared into a curtain of pine and maple trees. He sat down on a frozen chunk of wood, the cold seeping through his pants.

All he could taste was the vodka on his tongue. Vision blurred, the snow glowing white in front of him.

I just can't get out of this shit.

He reached into his jacket and took out both flasks—his constant companions. He shook one, and it was done for. He tossed it to the ground and checked the other—still felt about half full. A weary sigh slipped out from deep inside him, and he uncapped the flask and held it out in front of him as if in a toast.

Just one day. One goddamned sober day. That's all I'm asking.

But he knew better than that. He couldn't make it one day, could barely make it through an eight-hour shift. He'd never get sober.

This thing's hooks had him by the throat, sunk in too deep to shake loose.

He thought about his girls. His wife. If he couldn't get sober for himself, why couldn't he do it for them? They were the real victims in all this.

He stared at the flask, its contents too strong for him to resist. He wouldn't stop until the liquid was all gone, until every drop went down his throat. As he'd done a hundred times before, he brought the old flask next to his lips, ready to layer on a stronger drunk. He started to tilt the flask back when a sound in the woods snapped him loose from his sole focus, his singular intent of taking another sip.

He stared out into the trees. Hundreds of them.

"Hello?"

Nobody answered back. The wind blew, knocking down clumps of snow from the limbs up above, landing with wet thumps on the frozen ground.

Maybe the sheriff had changed his mind. Maybe he was coming back. Maybe the sheriff needed his help after all. Taggart stood up on two unsteady feet and squinted at the woods that surrounded him on all sides. "Sheriff?"

A rustling commotion stirred up the quiet. Twigs breaking. Something moving against the brush. The sound of some kind of footsteps.

With the flask gripped tight in his left hand, the right one went down to the stock of his service pistol. The wooden handle felt smooth and cold to the touch, and he took a cautious step forward, craned his neck in the direction of the disturbance. The liquor had his ears buzzing, but something was out there. Something or someone.

He took another step, and his left foot went out from under him. He went down hard, landing right on the tailbone. The impact made him bite his tongue, drawing some blood, and the flask tumbled from his grip and dipped into a drift of snow. Taggart let out a sound—half growl, half moan—and dragged himself across the frozen surface on his belly, hands reaching out for his precious flask. Snow slipped down the front of his shirt, into the cuffs, packed below his belt, but he kept crawling toward his faithful companion.

The sounds of footsteps got louder, even closer, but Taggart couldn't hear any of that. His eyes stayed on the prize—the flask, sticking in the snow at a crooked angle. He finally dragged himself close enough and seized the flask—a few drops of clear liquid leaked out from the tip, the snow around the flask wet and soft and melting away.

Taggart shook the flask, confirming what he already feared—it was empty, his fix soaking into the earth. He shook it again, then rolled over onto his back, clutching the empty flask to his chest like a child's stuffed animal. He stared up at the umbrella of trees over him, white snow and blue sky, maybe a thing of beauty to some.

Footsteps scurried closer, distinct under the call of birds and the swishing of tree limbs. Then the crunching of snow stopped and he could feel something nearby. Something watching him. He sat up, still clinging to the flask and refusing to let go.

Vision blurred or not, he saw the coyote staring over at him, head crouched down low, its ears pressed back, black nose twitching at his scent. The animal's grayish brown winter coat stood thick on its wiry frame, a buff of white on its throat and chest. The coyote stared right at Taggart with dull yellow eyes. It stood three feet in height off the ground, and had to weigh over sixty pounds. Its stance shifted and widened, either ready to pounce or take off running—Taggart wasn't sure which one.

He sat still as a rock, waiting to see what the animal would do.

Deep in his belly, he felt the fear creep up and twist at his insides. Over the years of being in the field, he had faced many dangerous men, staring down at the tip of a pistol directed right at his gut. But seeing those yellow eyes probe every inch of him, watching the hair stand up straight on the animal's haunches, Taggart had never felt fear like this. And as the bubbling terror grew and adrenaline kicked in, a semblance of forced sobriety returned in its place.

The coyote took another step forward, measured and methodical, maybe twenty yards from him now. Taggart began to tremble, slow at first, but soon every part of him twitched and jerked. He wondered how long it would take for an animal like that to bring him down. What it would feel like to have viselike jaws and razor-sharp fangs rip into his throat, tear open his throat. Even with the visions in his head of dying in such a manner, the irony of going out like that didn't escape him—a cop being mauled and pulled to pieces by a damn coyote.

He felt both his hands around the flask, the metal growing colder. He glanced down at his lifeline for a moment, knowing that there was nothing it could do for him now, even if it were filled up to the top.

Then his eyes settled down at his right hip—on his .357 Magnum Ruger, with its four-inch stainless-steel barrel. He had fired only one shot today—plenty of ammo left in the cylinder. Taggart looked back toward the coyote, still poised and ready to attack. He eased the flask down to the snow with his left hand while the right hand slid down onto the stock of the pistol. He kept his eyes on the animal as he unsnapped the strap with a slight flick of his finger— the coyote flinched at the sound of the click.

Easy, now.

The gun slipped out of its leather casing, and Taggart held the

Ruger low at his side. The coyote barely blinked those yellow eyes, watching him the whole time. He brought the pistol to the middle of his chest and gripped it with both trembling hands. His finger curled around the trigger, he took a breath, and then the coyote made its move. It sprang forward, paws digging into the snow, then cut to the right. A blur of dirty brown fur leaped up over a fallen tree, then disappeared behind a blanket of snow. In a matter of two or three seconds, the coyote was gone, almost like it had never been there.

Taggart kept the Ruger right where it was while he watched the trees to see if the animal would circle back. His heart worked overtime, pumping blood throughout his quivering mass. He stayed sitting in the snow for a minute, maybe it was five, then finally lowered the pistol and struggled back to his feet. He stared into all those trees, knowing that he'd faced death and death had just run off into the forest.

He holstered the gun and tried to slow his ragged breath. He couldn't feel the cold that snapped at his face—couldn't feel much, in fact. He took one more good look around the woods, then removed his state-issued hat, then the jacket, and tossed them both into the snow next to the empty flask. He stared down at the three things that had been a part of him for so long, then started to walk.

Carl

"You fuck," Sokowski snarled, wincing from the tattered hole in his side. He pressed a hand over the wound, but blood seeped through his fingers and streamed down his leg.

Carl held his rifle on him for a moment, then started to moan. "I didn't want none of this." He shook his head at Sokowski. "You fucker. All my life I did what you said. Did all those things because I thought you would like me more. I let you do all the thinking, but I'm done with that now."

"Like you? Jesus Christ, Carl. I just put up with your shit. Fucking *like* you?"

Carl tried not to but started to cry anyway. He hated Sokowski. Hated every part of him. The anger, the selfishness, the pure mean that spewed out of his mouth. But Carl hated himself even more for letting Sokowski bully and taunt him all these years. What kind of man lets himself get pushed around like a damn coward?

Sokowski glared up at him from all fours. "You better pull that trigger right now if you're gonna do it, Carl."

The rifle trembled in Carl's hands. Tears flowed as he tried to pull the trigger and end all this. He wanted to pull the trigger. Wanted to watch Sokowski die. The bastard didn't deserve anything better.

"You don't got what it takes, Carl. You ain't nothing but a gutless piece of shit."

Carl gazed over at Mr. Bennett, all blown to hell. Then he looked at Mrs. Bennett, slumped on the couch and leaking blood. Carl knew if he didn't pull the trigger, Sokowski would finish what he'd started—killing Danny, then probably even Mrs. Bennett. After all the years of wrongs he did with Sokowski, this was his chance to redeem himself, to finally do the right thing.

He stared back at Sokowski, and the man panted like a rabid dog. Carl knew he'd be going to jail anyhow. No way around that now. Kelly and the kids would be left to fend for themselves. Maybe they'd be better off without him. He was a lousy husband, and a crummy father. With him still in the picture, little Ben would probably end up doing all the same stupid shit that Carl did.

"What's the matter, Carl? Don't have the balls to do it?"

Carl's finger trembled over the trigger. Just an ounce of pressure and it would all end. He prayed to a God he didn't believe in to give him the courage.

Carl finally lowered the rifle. He couldn't kill anybody else—not even Sokowski. "You're right, Mike. I am a gutless piece of shit." He kept his eyes locked on Sokowski's and stuck the barrel of the rifle under his own chin. "And we're both gonna rot in hell." Carl pulled the trigger, and the back of his head was obliterated with a sharp boom.

Carl dropped to the floor in a heap, his life over in one split second. His rifle clacked to the hardwood boards and settled between the man's feet.

Sokowski stood on quivering legs and tried to stop the blood from vacating his body. "You stupid fuck."

He looked at Danny, laughed once, then fell forward into the glass coffee table. He went through the sheet of glass, slicing open his face and neck, and was finally still.

Lester

The shots had echoed through the forest from somewhere in front of him, deflecting off rocks and trees, the noise carrying down the side of the mountain. From the sounds of the pops, they appeared to be about a mile away. Lester had counted five shots, and he had a pretty good ear for the sound of different rifles. If he wasn't mistaken, they were discharged from three separate guns.

Strange.

The last day of hunting season was yesterday, but that didn't always mean that folks around here weren't out shooting at something. He usually turned the other cheek when he knew that a local was hunting off-season, especially only a day or two after regular season. That really didn't fall under his watch anyway. That fell to the game commission. Those fellas could be a bunch of tight-asses who liked nothing better than to give a hunter a hard time. Near as he could tell, most from Wyalusing respected the land and the game in the woods. You ate what you shot. Plain and simple. There were a few knuckleheads and some gun-happy teenage boys shooting at something they weren't supposed to, but it wasn't worth getting your panties in a bunch about.

Maybe he had heard wrong and it was only two rifles. Maybe his deputy and Carl had finally caught up with Danny and decided to do what he was afraid of. Sokowski had a history with the girl, which probably would make him act and react with even more emotion than he usually did.

Hell. Shouldn't have let him go out on his own.

But Sokowski had convinced him and Taggart that two search parties were better than one. He was right. They were, in theory.

Lester moved in the direction of the gunfire. He knew that the source of the shots could have been the Knolls boys, too. He knew that they were probably out here somewhere and that they wouldn't hesitate in taking Danny down either. As good as those boys were—hardworking, honest, upstanding folks—you put a murdered younger sister in the mix and all bets were off. And maybe they didn't care for and respect their father all that much, but Johnny was their old man and happened to be dead as a direct result of this whole mess. Blood would always be thicker than water. Especially around here.

He walked at a pretty good clip, and his heart was letting him know that fact. It thudded fast in his chest, and he was having a hard time catching his breath. He knew it was nonsense to even let the thought seep into his head, but he was getting too damn old for this bullshit. He'd be turning seventy in a few years and hoped to see that milestone. He should be enjoying Social Security and his pension from the county, doing some fishing, and tinkering around the house instead of traipsing through the woods on some damned wild-goose chase with his heart banging like a drum. The missus knew better than to ask him to hang it up, but he could tell by the look on her face when he was slipping on his boots in the morning that that was what she was thinking. Bonnie was a good woman and didn't deserve to have him dropping dead somewhere in the middle of the woods. She coped with the loneliness of not having little ones running around, but he didn't think she'd fare so well without having him in the mix. He was a pain in her backside at times, but their marriage worked nonetheless.

Lester slowed in his tracks when he heard the baying of dogs coming from the east of him. The low, bassie yelp of two coonhounds was pretty faint but growing a little louder. The boys must have heard the gunshots as well. They would be heading toward the source, but with the added advantage of having the dogs to lead the way.

Get a move on, old man.

He tried to ignore the pounding in his chest and sped up his pace. If Danny wasn't dead already, he soon would be. Lester knew that to be a fact.

Danny

Danny's knees trembled and knocked and wanted to buckle under him. He was covered in a warm spray of fresh blood from all the gunfire—Mr. and Mrs. Bennett's, Carl's, the deputy's. He'd never liked the sight of blood, and now it seemed to cover every inch of him. He looked at the mess in front of him—folks he'd known for as long as he could remember. His brain wanted to shut down and make it all go away.

Then Mrs. Bennett let out a small cough on the sofa. Blood leaked from the hole in her shoulder. It seemed to be bleeding pretty bad, coming out in spurts. He didn't know nothing about gunshot wounds, but at least she was still breathing. That had to be good.

He picked her up easily even though she weighed more than a hundred and fifty pounds. Her eyes flickered open for a second, stared up at Danny but didn't really seem to be looking at him, then closed again. Her chest rose and fell slowly, something gurgling from inside her, but she was still alive. Danny walked up the steps to the second floor and laid her down on a bed in the big bedroom at the top of the stairs. The wallpaper had prints of purple flowers, and the bed was made up all nice and neat. Next to the bed, the nightstand had a vase sitting beside a Bible with a leather cover and a bookmark stuck in the middle of the pages.

Danny covered her up with a blanket and stared down at her. She looked older than usual. "I'll be back with help, Mrs. Bennett. I promise. You're gonna be okay." His eyes fell on the open wound in her shoulder, and he could see ripped-up flesh and some white bone sticking out. He wondered if it hurt real bad. She coughed again. More gurgling.

"Be back as quick as I can, Mrs. Bennett."

Danny plodded downstairs and took another look at all the killing. He had never seen so much blood. He walked toward the front door and had to step over Carl's body—the entire back of his head missing. Even though Carl had always been mean to him, Danny felt bad for the man—Carl seemed to be sorry for what he had done to Mindy.

Danny stared at Carl's rifle for a second. Then, without really thinking, he reached down and picked it up. The barrel still felt a little warm and was heavy in his thick hands.

Danny stepped out the door and closed it behind him.

The room was quiet, the grandfather clock finally silent after a hundred years. Then Sokowski shifted from under the pile of glass and wood.

Scott Knolls

Charlotte and Queenie had been hard on the scent trail, barking with the excitement of the hunt, but after the shots had sounded, their howling had increased and the boys knew that they were going to be moving faster. Danny couldn't be far off.

Scott and Skeeter hadn't spoken much in the last hour or so because there wasn't much left to say. They had decided on what they intended to do, and there wasn't any turning back.

But Scott was having doubts, thoughts creeping out from where they were supposed to stay hidden. All the quiet had him rehashing ancient history. Tammy would be turning seven years old next month. Every year on her birthday, Scott would end up thinking about the party they should be having for his daughter, watching her tearing open presents, blowing out candles on a big birthday cake, running around with other young'uns. Seven years old. Hard to believe that his own flesh and blood was out there somewhere, living with a family that wasn't her own or in some kind of institution. He wondered what she looked like now. He wondered what kind of girl she was growing up to be. Probably losing her baby teeth and playing with dolls and pretending she was a princess or some other make-believe character. She was a kid now. A kid who didn't know who her real mother and father were. Although he and his wife didn't ever talk about Tammy—never, not a single word—they were both saddled with the guilt of what they had done.

I abandoned my own baby.

How do you live with something like that? You don't. Not really. He and Paula had just been going through the motions for the last six years.

As one year led to the next, Scott thought about Tammy less and less, but now the thing with Danny got him to thinking about her again. Danny and his daughter were similar in many ways—both had mental limitations, and both were unwanted and treated differently from everybody else. Wasn't their fault they turned out the way they did. Scott never paid Danny much attention around town, but the fact was, Danny lived on his own, and even though he might be quiet and kept to himself, he seemed happy enough. The question that popped into Scott's head while he was hiking through the woods with his brother was the one that he couldn't find an answer to: Were they so different?

I'm so sorry, sweetheart. I wish I could take it back.

Scott looked over at Skeeter and wanted to speak up about something else that nagged at him—that maybe Danny didn't do it. Scott didn't get the chance.

Skeeter saw it first. He saw someone loping along in the woods. Staggering, really. A big figure stumbling through the brush.

"On your left," Skeeter whispered to his brother.

Scott looked in the direction his brother was motioning and saw someone large and hulking lurching among the trees. They both moved in the same direction with their rifles brought up on the ready. They worked their way through some thick brush, trying their best to make as little noise as possible. When they got within a hundred feet, they saw a large man from the back, partially obscured by low-hanging limbs covered with snow. The man stumbled forward, dropped to the ground, then struggled back to his feet.

Scott shouldered his rifle, got the target in his scope, right in the middle of the broad shoulders. His finger wrapped around the trigger's cold steel.

"I got 'im," Scott whispered to his brother.

Danny

The sun had slid behind the clouds, and the temperature dropped fast. It was spitting snow again, and by the looks of the darkening sky it was going to snow for a while.

Danny trudged along in the woods but kept sight of the road to his left. He wanted to keep it in view, knowing that the road would bring him back to town. His arms hung loose at his sides. The stock of the gun was cold as ice, but Danny kept it gripped tightly in his fist. Something told him to. His vision had started to blur before it began to snow, but it was even worse now. The sky, the trees, even his own feet were fuzzy shapes. It was like he was staring through a fogged-up window.

He hurt all over. His fingers and toes were throbbing from frostbite. His head pounding. Every heartbeat sent a shot of pain into his brain. It felt as if his head might split open like an egg dropped onto the floor. He had given up trying to keep his tongue in his mouth. He let it hang out like a panting dog's on a hot August day. His eyes were heavy. His lids wanted to close and stay closed.

Danny had never felt so tired. The kind of tired that made your body ache everywhere. Maybe he was dying and this is what it felt like. He had always been scared of dying. Of just going away and never coming back. Of having his body being buried under the ground, where the worms and bugs would get to it. He knew that when he died, according to the churchgoing folks in town, he would see his mama and papa again. That would be nice. They were up there with God, but Danny wasn't so sure about God. He was supposed to be the one that made everything and brought everybody up to heaven when they died, but nobody Danny knew had ever actually seen heaven or God. And it seemed like everybody who went to church was afraid of dying, too. That just didn't make sense to Danny. If heaven was so special and God so great, why was everybody afraid of dying?

Danny knew that if he stopped to rest, he might not get back up again. And Mrs. Bennett needed him. If he didn't get help, she might die, and maybe she wasn't ready to go to heaven either. Besides, enough folks had died already because of him, and he didn't want someone else dying because he was too tired or too scared. Mrs. Bennett was nothing but good and kind to him, and he was determined not to let her down.

The sky was getting darker. Danny looked up and hoped that he would make it back to town before dark.

Come this way, Danny.

Danny stopped and looked deeper into the woods. The blurry outline of the three-legged deer stood in between some trees. Its tail twitched, and Danny was pretty sure she was staring at him.

"I don't want to get lost in the woods. The road leads back to town."

It'll take too long that way, Danny. Besides, there's someone in the woods who can help you.

"Who?"

I'll take you to him.

"Are you sure?"

The three-legged deer didn't answer. She turned and limped deeper into the woods. Danny watched her fuzzy shape disappear behind the trees and wasn't sure what to do. He looked down at his fist that gripped the rifle—it was white-knuckled from holding it for so long and so tight. He switched hands, then began to follow after the deer.

Danny sure hoped that the three-legged deer was right.

It is the right thing, Danny. You know that. Follow the deer. She knows the way.

For the first time, Danny thought the voice in his head kinda sounded like his own.

Taggart

His shirt was pretty well soaked through with sweat, and the wind had him shivering without his jacket. It wasn't just the cold that had him shaking—his body wanted another fix as well. He kept plodding forward, one step at a time. His legs and feet were ready to give out from under him—he'd put some serious mileage on his body for the last few hours. Taggart stared down at his watch—an old Sector watch that the wife had given him on their tenth wedding anniversary. Almost five o'clock. Seven hours without a drink. He knew. He'd been counting the hours.

All he could see were trees in every direction. He swatted at a low-hanging tree limb, and a blanket of snow powder shook off and fell onto his face and neck. As the cold touched his skin, he found that he didn't feel the anger or any form of loathing against the wilderness he stood in anymore. All that hostility got swept away with the wind that just wouldn't let up.

Part of him wanted to sit down and rest; the other part of him wanted to keep walking. With every new step, he felt a little more clarity seeping in. He had probably been walking in circles for the last seven hours. Just like his life for the last twenty years—walking in circles. But all this—the lack of sleep, the hours of hiking, and the absence of booze—had brought with it a distorted sense of lucidity.

The coyote had not only spared his life but had given him something as well. A simple, primitive message. He didn't want to die. Didn't want to give up on this life just yet. Maybe it could be fixed. Others had done it before him, and others would do it after.

He stopped in his tracks as his movement scared up a white-tailed jackrabbit, and the animal bounded up and over drifts of snow and fallen trees with easy grace and little effort. He heard its paws thumping on the snow, and the sound grew softer as the jackrabbit slipped deeper into the trees.

When he started walking again, his boots got tangled up with each other. He stumbled, almost fell, but caught himself against a tree that was as big around as he was. His body craved rest, his mind some sleep, but if he stopped now, he'd never get himself moving again. Can't fall asleep out here. He'd end up sleeping through the night and freezing to death.

Muscles burning and bones aching, Taggart kept forward momentum.

From all his reading over the years, Taggart knew a little bit about Native American vision quests and Inuit peoples participating in sensory-deprivation rituals—long periods of walking in mountainous areas with no food or water, the body needing some sleep. He knew that he still had booze coursing through his system and that his spirituality paled in comparison to most, but somehow he seemed to be inching his way out from the dark cloud he'd been walking under for far too long.

If he could somehow find his way out of these woods, he convinced himself that he could find his way out of his addiction.

Get me out of these woods and I'll change. I swear I'll change. Just get me out.

Scott Knolls

S cott held his breath, tried to check his heart rate. One eye pressed closed, the other shoved to the scope of the rifle. The figure in the snow moved in the opposite direction, getting smaller but still within range. He adjusted his shot, just slightly. Moved the cross-hairs right below the man's left shoulder blade—a direct path to the heart.

He heard Skeeter breathing beside him. Smelled the chewing tobacco on his breath.

Snow dropped down more heavily from the gray sky, danger-ously close to obscuring the target.

"Want me to take the shot?" Skeeter whispered.

Scott tensed up at the question. His brother didn't mean for it to sound threatening, but Scott knew he had only a few seconds before he lost his shot. He grunted a no and gripped the rifle a little tighter.

His finger tried to ease back the trigger, just like he'd done it a thousand times before—before when he was firing at game.

"Gonna lose him," Skeeter whispered again.

Scott heard the strap of Skeeter's rifle rattle and knew that his brother was lining up a shot. If he didn't take the shot, Skeeter would do what he couldn't. A few inches lay between fatal and nonfatal. Just a few inches of skin separated vital organs from a flesh wound. He didn't care so much about the ramifications with the law in killing Danny—murder was murder. It was other ramifications he just couldn't wrap his head around—taking a man down.

Skeeter's breath quickened. Scott had only a few seconds to decide.

His extended arm that clutched the forestock of the rifle dipped down an inch or so, and he squeezed the trigger.

Taggart

He heard a *pop,* then felt a sharp sting chew at his side. The force of impact spun him around like a dancer. Blood sprayed against the perfect white, decorating the snow in a perfect circle. Taggart clutched at the wound, felt the warmth spread from inside him, then sank to his knees in the snow and fell face-first onto the ground. The cold felt strangely refreshing on his skin.

The sound of running footsteps drew near. Taggart applied pressure to the hole in his side and waited—waited for help to finally arrive.

Sokowski

The old bastard had a bunch of liquor after all, and Sokowski found it in the cabinet above the stove. They didn't drink whiskey, but that was okay. They had a bottle of vodka, one of rum, couple bottles of wine, but Sokowski went straight for the bottle of tequila. Virgin bottle of Jose Cuervo Gold. Still sealed. Sokowski put an end to that.

He drank nearly a quarter of it while standing in the middle of the kitchen. It tasted pretty sweet going down, but the violent urge to vomit hit him fast. He leaned over and retched out the contents of his stomach onto the kitchen floor in three violent heaves. After he spit out the last of the chunks from his mouth, he decided to drink some milk from the refrigerator. He gulped some of that down to coat his stomach, then tried a few more pulls on the tequila bottle. He waited to see if his stomach would reject it again, but it appeared that the booze would stay down this time.

The burn in his side from the bullet wound throbbed red hot. It felt like his skin was on fire. Sokowski glanced down at the damage—blood gurgled from the hole in his flesh, dark and thick, and spilled down his shirt and ran halfway down his denim jeans.

Gotta stop the bleeding some. Stupid fucking Carl.

Sokowski reached back into the liquor cabinet and grabbed the bottle of vodka. He didn't want to waste any more tequila. He spun off the cap and poured it onto the gaping wound.

It stung like a son of a bitch. Like a hundred fucking bee stings. He bent over and clutched at his side, dropping the vodka bottle to the floor, where it popped and shattered. Sokowski took a moment to let the pain ease off. He leaned against the kitchen counter and waited for the tequila to get to his brain—not fast enough—so he reached for the Jose Cuervo and sucked on the bottle again. After an agonizing minute, the pain began to slowly drift away.

He looked around at the Bennetts' perfect little kitchen. Glass canisters of flour, sugar, and ground coffee lined up nice and neat on the counter, a toaster polished up like it had never been used, a bread box and a cookie jar. Sokowski stared at the drapes hung over the window above the sink, then at the tablecloth that covered a small kitchen table—they had matching patterns of pheasants in flight with hunters crouched behind a tree, aiming a gun at the birds.

"Goddamn."

Sokowski staggered back into the living room on feet that felt like cinder blocks. The old bitch was gone. If the retard took her with him, they wouldn't be too hard to find. He wanted to finish this—had to finish it. A few loose ends to deal with first, and then he would hop in his truck and never look back at this shithole of a town. Head up to Canada and start over. The border was about a four-hour drive. He'd be across it and free of this shit before Lester or the cops knew he was even out of town. Sokowski would have no problem smoking with and selling weed to the Canucks—that would be just fine by him.

He glanced over at Carl's body and took another pull on the tequila, then spit down on his corpse.

Stupid asshole.

The overwhelming urge to shit hit him like a boot to the stomach. He didn't know where the bathroom was and didn't really care. He just unbuckled his pants, squatted down, and emptied himself onto the carpet and didn't bother to wipe. Blood leaked from the puckered hole in his side and rolled down his naked ass and puddled onto the carpet next to his pile of waste.

Christ. My fingerprints are everywhere. The thought made him laugh out loud, sounding like the caw of a damn crow.

He stood back up and buckled his pants, then retrieved his rifle. He noticed the old man's rifle and picked that one up as well. He limped to the front door and peered back at the room one last time.

"Adios, motherfuckers."

And he staggered out of the house.

Lester

Lester dreamed that he was having breakfast with Bonnie. She had whipped up a whole stack of buttermilk pancakes with fresh blueberries, a pile of bacon, and homemade hash browns. The house smelled like a taste of heaven. The kitchen looked different but kinda the same. The table and chairs were the same—made of hickory wood from a shop down in Dushore. Same stove and refrigerator. The same cookie jar perched on the edge of the counter that he visited a few times a day. But there were no pictures or calendars of cats. No cat figurines. No cat magnets on the fridge. No four-legged critters winding between his legs, purring and screeching out their high-pitched meow. Not a single cat in the whole goddamned house.

Lester knew he must be dreaming.

Bonnie poured him a fresh cup of coffee and smiled down at him. She looked the same but was prettier than ever. Younger, too. She looked like she did when Lester still had a full head of hair.

He didn't say anything. Just smiled back at her. Sometimes saying nothing was a whole lot better than saying something that didn't mean nothing. The sound of children's laughter came from somewhere outside the house. Lester looked out the kitchen window, and it wasn't snowing one bit. The sun was shining in all its glory, and it looked to be a beautiful day.

Bonnie put two more breakfast plates down. She filled two juice glasses with fresh-squeezed OJ—nice and pulpy the way he liked it—and glanced toward the back door. She opened her mouth and called out, but no sound came from her mouth. Her lips moved, and she was definitely saying something, except Lester couldn't hear anything but the sound of a strong-blowing wind. He hadn't noticed the steady howl of wind till now.

Bonnie smiled as the back door swung open, and the kitchen was immediately bathed with bright, intense sunlight. Lester had to shield his eyes from the blinding light and he squinted at two silhouettes of small children framed in the doorway. As the children ran toward him and leaped onto his lap, the wind picked up and stung at his face. Then Lester woke up.

His eyes fluttered open. The wind was snapping at his face and neck. His back and head felt cold. Above him the sky was a checkerboard of black and white cumulus clouds. He still remembered learning that word, "cumulus," back in the tenth grade. Always stuck with him. His tenth-grade science teacher, Mr. Salsman, would be proud.

A major storm front was moving in. Lester stared up at the sky and watched the clouds fold into one another and move along at a snail's pace as the remnants of his dream still tickled at his brain. He noticed the snow-covered tree limbs that hung above and knew that he wasn't dreaming anymore, and he sure wasn't at home.

He tried to sit up, but the whole left side of his body felt numb. Lester knew that it wasn't the cold or frostbite. He knew what it was.

"Hell." He rested his head back on the ground again. He stayed there and didn't panic—wasn't exactly the panicking type. He needed to figure out how bad his condition was. If he got himself all worked up, it would just make matters that much worse.

He tried to lift both arms toward the sky. The right side moved up just as his brain had ordered, but the left side went up a little ways, a few inches off the ground, and that was about the extent of it.

He smacked and licked at his lips to get the feel of them. "All right, Lester, just what are you gonna do now?" It felt mighty strange to talk to himself, especially out loud, but his voice sounded clear and he didn't slur any. That was a good sign at least.

Once again he tried to sit up. He hadn't attempted a sit-up since he was growing the short and curly ones down below his belt buckle in the seventh grade. He managed to get his right hand under him and push himself to a sitting position after a few attempts. It was a long struggle that took well over a minute or two, but he managed. He sat in the snow and tried to catch his breath.

The forest stood quiet around him. The call of the coonhounds was gone. The wind blew steadily, causing creaks and groans from the trees. Dead brown leaves that stubbornly hung on to branches flapped and rattled like tiny dancers above him. Large snowflakes floated down, ending their long journey from the storm clouds. It was peaceful. So damn peaceful.

Lester didn't know why, but he smiled. Maybe that's what folks do right before they're taken to their Maker. He wondered whether he had done all the things he'd set out to do as a young man. He felt pretty confident that he had. He never had the yearning to move away from the place where he was born and raised. He had wanted kids, sure, but that wasn't in the cards. And that was okay with him. He fished and hunted and watched football and baseball. Played cards once a month or so. Those things made him happy. He knew of many men who constantly wanted more out of life. Wanted more money, a bigger house, a younger wife, a job that wasn't real work. More stuff parked out in the driveway. Those men made themselves crazy. Pacing and grumbling and hating everyone and everything they weren't.

Lester pretty much accepted what he got and didn't complain. He loved his wife and liked his job. His friends who were still living treated him well and were there for him if he needed to bend their ear. He had done good with his life.

He found himself getting a little misty and shook away all the sappy thoughts. "Hell, old man, you ain't in the grave just yet." He reached down into the snow and grabbed hold of a fallen branch and set it in the ground beside him. He readied himself and pushed up. His knees popped and his lower back ached, but he managed to right himself.

He waited a bit before trying to walk. While his body played catch-up with his brain, he looked around to get his bearings. Footprints trailed off to the left of him—the direction he'd come from. He looked at the sky again and figured he hadn't been out for very long. Maybe twenty minutes or so, but darkness wasn't far off.

He put his right foot forward, but his left wasn't so accommodating. He dug his makeshift cane deeper into the frozen ground and pushed himself ahead, dragging his left foot and leg behind him like a gimp.

He laughed at himself again and kept hauling himself forward. He was in sad shape, but he intended to take care of the unfinished business at hand. He pictured Danny in his head. Poor, big, slow Danny. Just an overgrown kid with his crew cut and clean-shaven face. Then it hit him. Just like that.

Clean-shaven. That boy doesn't wear a beard. Never has. Mindy's face was all scuffed up by a man's facial hair. Those marks weren't from the carpet. Hell.

Then he got to thinking about Mike's face and neck when he first saw him out at Mindy's trailer. The deputy said he got into a scuffle at some party in Towanda.

Lester pushed himself to limp faster, but his weary bones would only move so fast. *Hell, old man.*

Danny

Danny hoped that the voice in his head was right. It hadn't told him who was out there in the woods who would be able to help him. It hadn't said anything else to him since he started to follow the deer. Hopefully the voice would lead him to the sheriff—Lester would have to believe Danny now.

But if the voice in his head was wrong, and there was no one out there, Danny knew he would get lost. And, if he got lost, he sure was worried that Mrs. Bennett wouldn't get the help she needed. So many people had been hurt and worse.

The deputy was a bad man. Kinda like his Uncle Brett, but a whole lot worse. Maybe Uncle Brett would drink too much and hit Danny when he was a little kid, but Danny knew that Uncle Brett was just real sad about losing his brother and having to take care of him. Uncle Brett used to blame Danny for him not being able to marry a young woman and told him as much. Uncle Brett used to blame Danny for lots of things, like having to spend too much money on him for food and clothes and visits to Doc Pete—money he didn't have, he told Danny. Maybe if Danny wasn't around, Uncle Brett would have gotten married and finally been happy. Maybe, just maybe. That's why after Uncle Brett went away to heaven, Danny knew he should live on his own and take care of himself. If he wasn't anybody else's problem, then he couldn't make anybody else sad or mad and he couldn't get anyone hurt again.

He watched the three-legged deer hopping ahead of him. He had been following her for a while now, but she never let him get too close. Danny guessed that he scared her a little. Especially now with his face looking like some kind of monster's face and the fact that he was carrying a gun. Hunters carry guns and bows and arrows. A hunter is who hurt her and made her walk funny.

Maybe he should drop the gun in the snow and bury it so it couldn't hurt no one else. All guns did was hurt folks.

Keep the gun, Danny.

He looked toward the doe. She was standing still and staring back at him with big black eyes.

Keep the gun for a little while longer.

Danny nodded and kept walking toward her. The doe stayed put where she was and watched him approach. He got real close to her. Could see the deer breathing and the crystals of snow frozen around her mouth. If he reached out, he would be able to touch her soft fur now and pet the doe like a dog. He didn't do that, though.

The doe stuck her nose close to the snow and sniffed around for something. It was gonna be dark soon, so Danny didn't understand why they were staying put.

"I'm hungry, too, but I think we should keep going."

The doe looked up from the ground. Her nose was wet and had a clump of snow stuck to the end of it.

It's almost time.

Her ears twitched, then snapped straight up in the air. She looked forward and stared into the forest ahead of them. Danny stared in the same direction. He saw something move between the trees. Something big. And it was moving straight toward them.

The three-legged deer kept her watch and waited, and Danny stood beside the doe and waited right along with her.

Lester

His left leg had stiffened up like a son of a bitch. Lester thought that maybe it would loosen up or get some feeling back once he was on his feet and moving again, but the paralysis—he hoped to God it was only temporary—was getting progressively worse with time. The cold wasn't helping matters—the temperature dipping down in the low teens.

He felt like old man Moses wandering the wild with his staff in hand. Except he had no flock and he sure the hell wasn't headed toward the promised land—not yet at least. But he had put his faith in the Lord's hands back before he got married to Bonnie, at both her urging and insistence, and he had kept it there ever since.

His progress had been slow going. It took him three times as much energy to walk three times slower.

Keep moving, old man. More than your backside at stake here.

His stomach churned and rumbled in his belly. He hadn't eaten anything since dinner the night before, and he had smoked his last menthol cigarette a few hours ago. If God was hell-bent on testing him, he sure was doing a bang-up job of it. If Lester actually got through this mess, maybe he'd even give up smoking.

"Ha." The laugh shot out of him, and the sound of it surprised him. Maybe he was delirious after all.

Up ahead of him was a small clearing. The trees gave way to a snow-covered area that for whatever reason didn't have foliage of any kind. It was about twenty yards by twenty yards. He entered the clearing, dragging his useless leg and pulling himself along.

Midway through the clearing, he noticed them. It took him a second to register what exactly he was seeing, then another few seconds to convince himself that he wasn't dreaming again.

It was Danny Bedford, or what was left of him, sitting in the snow at the other end of the clearing. He had what appeared to be dried blood on his jacket and pants and caked on his face and neck— blood all over him, in fact. Lester had seen plenty of men on the losing end of a bar fight. Their eyes blackened, a bloodied nose, a gash upside the head delivered by a cue stick or a beer bottle. He thought he had seen it all till he glimpsed Danny. The boy appeared much worse off since Lester had seen him at Doc Pete's earlier in the day. The boy's head seemed enormous. His jaw hung open like the bottom half of a rotted Halloween pumpkin. Danny's eyes were swollen up like the rest of him, but they seemed pretty clear.

Or sane, which is what Lester was hoping for.

But to make the sight before him even more of a head scratcher, the boy he'd been searching for during the last fifteen hours and then some was in the middle of the forest, squatting next to a three-legged doe like it was his long-lost dog. The two of them weren't but twelve inches apart from each other, and they just stared at Lester like they'd been waiting on him for a lifetime.

Lester had never seen anything like it. A man and a wild deer keeping each other's company. Once he noticed the doe's stump, he knew that she was the victim of a bow hunter. The hunter's arrow had found its target but failed to make the kill. Lester had seen gangrene before. An animal that chewed off its own leg to free itself from a trap or deer that took a bullet or arrow but didn't lie down and die. Most deer didn't survive long after the infection had set in. The poison got into the bloodstream and killed them within ten days. This deer should be dead but apparently wasn't ready to die just yet.

When Danny stood up, Lester noticed the gun clutched in the boy's hands.

Lester took a few more steps toward the curious pair but was careful to move slow and easy. He kept his own rifle held down low in his left hand. The closer he got, the more the doe's tail snapped back and forth like a surrender flag caught up in a gust of wind.

"Hello, son. Been looking for you."

Danny nodded but stayed put. He watched the sheriff struggle to stay upright.

"You don't look so good, Sheriff. What happened to your leg?" Danny asked.

Lester stopped walking and pushed his cap back on his head a little. "I guess my body needed to remind me that I'm an old man."

"You gonna die?" Danny asked with no ill intent.

"I hope not. At least not today." Lester noticed the pained look in Danny's eyes. He figured that the boy must be in a world of hurt. He was surprised that he could even stand in the condition he was in.

"There's been more killing," Danny said. A simple statement of fact. "Up at the Bennett place."

"That so?" Lester tried to sound calm, but he clutched at his rifle a bit tighter.

"I didn't do nothing to Mindy, Sheriff." Danny's tone sounded hopeful, like he really needed the sheriff to believe him.

"Why don't you tell me about that, son?"

Danny looked to the doe for a moment before answering, like he had to check with her before continuing on. "I was just going to her place to give her a present. Yesterday was her birthday, you know?"

"That a fact?"

"Same day as mine. That's one reason she was my friend."

Lester nodded. "Mindy was a good gal."

"Yes, sir, she was. That's why I made a present for her. When I got there, the deputy and Carl were already there. They told me that Mindy had an accident. And when I went inside, she was already . . ." Danny choked up, unable to finish. Large tears flowed down red, chapped cheeks and glistened in the setting sun.

"I believe you, son. I really do."

Danny looked at the sheriff and seemed relieved. That brought on a new batch of tears.

"Danny, can you do me a favor and put that gun down?"

Danny looked down at the rifle he was holding and thought about it for a second, but he kept the gun right where it was. "He killed Mr. Bennett. And Mrs. Bennett is hurt real bad."

"The deputy and Carl did that?"

"Naw. Just your deputy. Carl used the gun on himself."

Lester was pretty sure he believed Danny but would feel a hell of a lot better if the boy would just drop his gun to the ground.

"Why'd the deputy do all these things, Danny?"

Danny gave him a strange look. "I don't know, Sheriff. I was hoping you would know that."

Lester nodded and gazed at the three-legged doe. He wished he had a good answer for that. "And what about the deputy? Where is he now?"

"Carl shot him. Before he put the gun under his chin. The deputy was gonna kill Mrs. Bennett. She's hurt real bad, but she ain't dead. I put her up in her bedroom. Told her I would go for help."

"I guess we should do that, but it sure would make me feel a whole lot better if you put that gun down. Those things can go off if you ain't careful."

Danny guessed that it was okay now if the sheriff wanted him to. He started to lower the rifle to the ground when a shot rang out, and the three-legged deer flinched. A splatter of blood exploded from her chest and she fell to the ground and twitched a few times before she stopped moving at all.

Danny and Lester ducked for cover with their hands held over their heads. They both watched wide-eyed as Sokowski stepped into the clearing with his rifle secure against his shoulder. He was swaying a little and struggled to maintain his balance. His right side was soaked with blood still flowing like a leaking bottle of maple syrup.

Sokowski looked at Lester with eyes so red that it was hard to see his pupils. "Guess we finally got our man, huh, Sheriff?" His speech came out slow and mumbled.

Lester stood upright and pulled his left leg under him and tried to stand tall. Sokowski noticed anyway.

"What's the matter with you? You look like shit."

Lester took a breath and was careful to speak nice and easy. "Been a long day, Mike. More walking than I'm used to. And my old bones don't like the cold so much, I guess."

Sokowski kept his ground, never taking his rifle off the sheriff. "The ticker, huh?"

Lester sighed his response. He had never seen his deputy in such sorry shape. Boozed up beyond repair, all the anger boiling to the surface. His gut told him that this wouldn't end well. Just like with Johnny Knolls.

"Why don't you go ahead and drop that rifle to the ground, Lester? You won't be needing it no more."

Lester kept the rifle clutched in his hand. "Now, listen here, Mike—"

"Go on. I ain't gonna tell you again."

Lester hated to do it, but he lowered the gun onto the snow and winced at the discomfort bending down caused him.

"Ain't so easy taking orders from other folks, is it, Lester?"

"No. Guess it ain't."

Sokowski had a strange smirk creasing his lips. "Things weren't supposed to turn out this way, Lester. All this killing, you know? But it's done and can't be undone."

"All right. That's a fact." Lester agreed.

A hard gust of wind swept through the clearing, whipping up sheets of powdery flakes all around the three men like they were standing in a snow globe.

"But I guess there's a few choices yet to be made. Danny here ain't nothing. You know that. No one really gives a shit about him." Sokowski looked at Danny for a second, then refocused his drunken gaze back on the sheriff.

"It's time to stop all this nonsense, Mike. No sense in going on with it. Enough bad has happened."

Sokowski lost his balance a bit but kept his rifle up.

"I don't want to kill you, Lester. Already going to hell for all that I've done today. But from the looks of you, I might not have to go and do that. You're a walking dead man unless you get some medical attention."

Lester nodded. "You're right about that, too. Been in better shape."

Sokowski spit and lowered his gun a little. Just a little. "I can walk away from all this. All that really stands in my way is you. Maybe it ain't right, but what choice do I got?"

Lester's heart pounded erratically in his chest. The big muscle felt like it was pulsing upward and might burst right out of his throat and drop into the snow. Sweat rolled from under his hat and down his neck and back.

"You got choices, Mike. You're right about not being able to undo what's happened, but there's still right and wrong here. Too many folks have died here today. No sense in any more."

Sokowski almost lost his balance. Squinted his eyes to block out the pain, then let go with a small laugh. "Right and wrong? Shit, Lester, when did I ever pay attention to the difference between right and wrong? You, maybe. You've always seemed to do the right thing in your life."

Lester wanted to keep Sokowski talking. If he got him talking long enough, maybe he could get some reason into him. If that didn't work, he needed to try to take the rifle away from him.

"Well, I try to do the right thing, Mike. Don't know if I always succeed, but I give it my best shot. Damned if I don't."

Sokowski shook his head at him. "What does doing the right thing get you here and now, Lester? Seems like it ain't gonna get you shit."

"It's not too late here, Mike. Just think about it for a moment."

Sokowski smiled at him and shook his head again. "Sorry, Sheriff. I've already thought about it, and I know what I gotta do." He turned the rifle toward Danny.

But Danny didn't flinch. Didn't cower or duck for cover. He just studied Sokowski with all the blood running down the side of him. Then he stared at Sokowski's messed-up ear, a brown, shrunken piece of flesh. He knew how mean kids could be and knew that something like that would be made fun of. He kept staring at the deputy's deformity, and for some reason he didn't quite understand, Danny didn't feel angry or scared of him anymore. He only felt sadness for the man.

"What you did to Mindy and the Bennetts was wrong, Mike."

Sokowski gave him a funny look, surprised that he would be talking right now. "Yeah? Is that right, Danny?"

"I guess what I mean to say is that you did something real bad, but maybe you couldn't help it. Like me, it's just who you are."

Sokowski's eyes narrowed, and his face twisted with confusion. "Christ. What the hell are you yammering about?"

Danny continued on. Determined and assured. "Some folks are dumb. Some are smart. Some good, some bad. It's just who we are."

Sokowski finally laughed, sharp and loud. "That's right, Danny. I was born one bad motherfucker." He grinned over at Lester. "Maybe your boy ain't so dumb after all. He knows I ain't gonna change. You should listen to the retard here."

"I forgive you, Mike," Danny said quietly.

Sokowski cringed at the words. Hating Danny for who he was. "What?" But he had heard him. Danny didn't need to repeat himself.

Lester took advantage of Sokowski's being distracted for a moment. He let his walking stick fall to the ground and reached for his holster. The pistol slipped into his right hand and came out by his waist in one smooth movement—he was quicker than his condition implied and had Sokowski dead in his sights.

"Let's not end it like this, Mike."

Sokowski kept his rifle on Danny. Grinned a little. "You ain't gonna shoot me, Lester. You ain't the kind."

"I'll do what's right, son. Trust me on that."

It was getting dark, but Lester could see Sokowski's smile fade. Sokowski started to lower his gun, then swung it toward Lester and squeezed the trigger. It was a wild shot, but it found Lester nonetheless. Lester felt a hot blast of pain as the bullet entered his leg right above the knee. The impact knocked him backward and laid him out onto the snow. His pistol dropped from his hand and sank into a few inches of snow.

Sokowski staggered toward the sheriff and stood over him. His eyes were wild but focused down on the man. "Damn, Lester."

Lester lay sprawled out on the ground like he was making snow angels and grasped for his pistol. He should've taken the shot. Sokowski was right. He wasn't the kind.

"You tried, Lester. You tried." He put the barrel of the rifle an inch from Lester's head and started to squeeze the trigger.

Another shot rang out, and Sokowski fell forward and thudded down beside Lester. He wasn't even able to put his arms out in front of him to slow his fall. His throat gurgled, arms and legs jerking and twitching.

Lester stared over at Sokowski and watched as blood pumped out in spurts from the dime-size hole in his neck. The deputy kept twisting in the snow, his boot heels digging little divots in the frozen earth. He clapped a hand over the wound, but the jugular vein had been severed and dumped blood like a water hose. Sokowski gurgled some more, arms and legs slowly losing their fight. The bleed-out took less than a minute, and then his body came to rest.

Lester squinted up toward Danny, and the boy wasn't holding the rifle on his shoulder like you were supposed to—it was down by his hips. It reminded Lester of how John Wayne held his rifle in some of his favorite classic Westerns.

Right before Lester blacked out, he saw Danny drop the rifle into the snow and kneel beside him. The boy wasn't crying anymore. There were no signs of fear or shock or dismay on his face. It was an expression Lester had never seen on the boy's face before. Danny appeared calm.

"We'll get you help, Sheriff. Don't you go and die on me," Danny said.

Past Danny's shoulder the sun was barely a sliver of light above the trees as night took over the day and Lester slipped away.

Danny

Danny woke up early like usual—before the sun had risen. He peered out his window and watched the snowfall in the orange dawn sky. The moon was full and partially hidden behind thick gray clouds.

The pain in his jaw had kept him up most of the night, and when he did sleep, Mindy was there, alive and well. Since all the bad things had happened, Danny thought he would have the scary kind of dreams. Dreams about what had happened and all the blood and about the man who made it all happen. But instead he dreamed about Mindy when she was a little girl. Dreams of sitting behind her in Miss Bradley's class and looking at her long pigtails—she always wore her hair in tight pigtails. Dreams of her on the playground, playing dodgeball with the boys. Dreams of Mindy sitting next to him in the lunchroom and sharing her tuna-fish sandwich and carrot sticks when no one else wanted to.

Danny shuffled to his dresser—he still had little aches and pains throughout his entire body—and picked up the bottle of pills that Doc Pete had given him. The bottle stood among the wood carvings of birds, snails, rabbits, squirrels, and the one lone turtle, Rudy. He opened the medicine bottle and shook out a pill. Just one. Doc Pete told him to take one every morning when he woke up to help with the pain. Most of the time it did.

He swallowed the small blue tablet without water and took a look at himself in the mirror. Most of the swelling in his face was gone, but his neck was still black and blue. He had tried to shave once since Mindy's accident, but the razor hurt his skin too much, so he let his beard grow out. He didn't like the way his whiskers looked. They made him look like all the rest of the men in town, and he didn't like that at all. And it was too itchy for his liking. He sure didn't understand why so many folks in town wore beards.

His tongue brushed along the pins in his mouth that the doctor had put in. The ambulance had taken him to a big hospital up in Towanda. It was the biggest and brightest building he'd ever been in, with nurses in blue uniforms bustling around, making him take medicine at all hours of the day and pee in a little plastic jug when he couldn't get out of bed. Danny couldn't remember the doctor's name, and he wasn't as nice as Doc Pete, but he was the one that fixed Danny's jaw and said that it would be as good as new in a few weeks.

Danny pulled on the same green pants that he always wore. Most of the blood had come out, but there were still a few dark stains on one of the pant legs. He had put it through the washer down in the laundromat three times and used extra laundry soap, but the stain was stubborn and wouldn't come out. He wasn't sure whose blood it was. There had been so much.

He opened his small closet, and behind his winter jacket hung a blue dress shirt. It was Uncle Brett's—the only thing that Danny had kept of his. Uncle Brett never went to church, but he had his one nice blue dress shirt that he would wear to weddings or fancy parties. It was the same blue shirt Uncle Brett wore to Danny's parents' funeral.

Danny slipped the shirt off the hanger and thought it would look nice at Mindy's funeral. He wanted to look real nice. It was important. He didn't remember his folks' funeral very well, but he remembered that Uncle Brett made him wear a nice shirt and a pair of pants with no stains on them.

He finished getting dressed and ate some applesauce on his bed. He couldn't chew nothing, but he could swallow okay. He finished the entire jar, then made his bed. After that he sat and looked at his wood figurines for a while. He wanted to start carving a new one but wasn't sure what animal to make. Whatever animal he decided on would be a gift for Mrs. Bennett. Maybe he would make a cardinal. She liked cardinals. Or maybe he would carve a doe. He had never tried carving a deer before.

The funeral wasn't for a while, so Danny decided to go downstairs and clean up the laundromat.

Mrs. Bennett wanted to keep the Wash 'N Dry open for business. She told Danny that it would be what Mr. Bennett would have wanted. She asked him if he was ready and willing to take care of it all by himself. It would be up to him to go and buy the sodas at the IGA and keep the machine stocked. Mrs. Bennett gave him the keys to all the machines, and he kept them in his dresser upstairs, safely hidden under his socks. He sure didn't want to lose them. She said that she would drive them to Towanda once a month or so to buy the little boxes of soap from the place that made those kinds. She knew that Danny couldn't drive, and it was too far to walk.

Danny flicked on the lights and went about sweeping and mopping. He checked all the machines for forgotten clothes and emptied the trash. The room was already pretty clean, but he knew he had extra time so he swept behind the washers and dryers, too.

It was still early, so he decided to go ahead and walk to the cemetery. He didn't want to be late and figured that he would visit his parents at the graveyard, since he was going there anyway.

He unlocked the front door and stepped out onto Main Street.

Sycamore and sweet birch trees surrounded the cemetery like tall, silent guardians. Hundreds of grave markers poked through the snow that blanketed the acres of burial grounds. Here and there dead flower arrangements leaned against old grave markers left behind by the left behind. Some of the larger headstones had bronze flower vases anchored to the side. Some had silk flower arrangements neatly placed inside the containers, but most of the vases had fresh-cut flowers, now brown and wilted, that hung forward as if reaching for the ground.

In the center of the large cemetery, a blue canopy had been erected over a newly dug opening in the ground. A John Deere backhoe was parked twenty feet away from the open grave next to a pile of dark brown dirt that had been covered up with a tarp, waiting to shoveled back into the hole. A funeral worker wearing green coveralls shoveled away some fresh snow to make room for stands of flower wreaths and sprays. After finishing with that chore, the man rearranged a dozen folding chairs and made them into nice, even rows. The worker took off an old cap, wiped the sweat from around his neck, then dug into his coveralls and pulled out a pack of Marlboros and lit one up. He looked up at the gray sky as if to check on the likelihood of snow before he made his way toward a single-story brick building.

The cemetery was quiet for a few minutes. The trees swayed in a slow-moving breeze, and a flock of blackbirds flew overhead, filling the air with the shrill sound of caws. The tranquillity was finally interrupted as a few cars and trucks started to trickle into the gravel parking lot, tires crunching on the small stones, and men and women dressed in black or dark colors exited somberly. Only a few wore dress clothes. Most were bundled up in flannel jackets and wore blue jeans. A few farmers still had on their work clothes, smeared with dirt and manure. None of them spoke. They kept to themselves but nodded to one another and made their way slowly into the brick building.

Danny hadn't been to the cemetery since his parents' funeral. He knew that this was the place that was supposed to be their final resting place, but they weren't under the ground in coffins like other folks. He hadn't seen their bodies at the funeral because there had been no coffins. Uncle Brett said that their bodies had been under the water for too long. After they fell through the ice, a current had sucked them under the black pond water and carried them deep. The ice was too thick and no one could find them. They sent a few volunteer firemen diving down into the pond, and they had looked and looked for his folks, but they never found them. They told Uncle Brett that the pond was too deep and that their bodies had probably gotten tangled up in waterweeds and tree branches.

Danny remembered that Uncle Brett had gotten a phone call in the springtime, when the ice had started to melt. Some kids had found Danny's papa when he finally floated to the surface. A few days later, they found his mama, too. Uncle Brett said what they found wasn't his folks anymore.

After they pulled his parents' bodies out of the pond, an ambulance took them away and they were burned up in a stove that made them into ashes. Uncle Brett took their ashes and buried them somewhere out in the woods up on Lime Hill. He never told Danny where he put them, and Danny never asked. When he wanted to talk to them, he would just go out to McGee Pond. That's the last place he had seen them at, and he thought that maybe part of them was still there somehow and that maybe they could hear him talking to them.

Danny had to walk around the cemetery for a long time, looking at hundreds of headstones until he found their grave site. Their headstones weren't as big as a lot of the other markers, and they didn't have any flowers or a fancy vase on them.

Danny stared down at the engraving on the pinkish gray granite but couldn't read all the words. He recognized his folks' names and the dates of birth and death, but that was about it—HANK BEDFORD, 1920–1949, and ELEANOR BEDFORD, 1922–1949. Danny wished he could read what else was written on their headstones, but now that Mindy was gone, he didn't have anybody else to come out here and read them to him. Maybe one day he'd ask the sheriff or Mrs. Bennett to come out to the cemetery and read him the headstones. Or maybe he'd teach himself to read at the library. That would be nice.

He was getting pretty cold, but Mindy's burial hadn't started yet. He shoved his hands into his pockets and tried to think of something to say to his parents.

"I'm real sorry for what happened. I should have listened to you, Mama. I shouldn't have gone so far out on the ice."

They didn't answer him.

"Mindy's coming to see you. Maybe she's already there. She's my friend, and I'm gonna miss her. She was always nice to me. I think you will like her a lot."

They still didn't say anything.

"I guess I'm gonna be in charge of the Wash 'N Dry now. It's a lot of work, but it's important. Mrs. Bennett says she's counting on me. I'm gonna work real hard and try not to let her down. I think she misses Mr. Bennett, because she cries a lot."

Danny noticed a few folks walking out of the brick building and moving toward the open grave. It was time. Danny smiled down at his folks' headstones one last time.

"I'm gonna be okay. Don't worry about me none."

Lester

The priest had finished with his eulogy and let the mourners stand alone with their thoughts and silent prayers. A few folks paying their respects had already moved back to their cars and trucks and would go about their day like it was any other—feeding and milking their cows, getting to their shift at Taylor's, making the necessary deliveries.

Scott and Skeeter were on either side of their mother. Sarah looked beat up pretty bad. She had insisted on having Mindy's funeral separate from her husband's. Johnny's was yesterday, and only the boys and Sarah and Lester had been at the ceremony. Johnny wasn't liked so much in town, and that was pretty apparent by the turnout.

Lester's leg was in a cast, and the meds that the doctor gave him weren't doing much for the pain. He fought back the urge to pull out his pack of Camels, but he knew that Bonnie would give him "the look," and he didn't need that grief right about now.

He saw Danny standing at the back of the group during the eulogy. There were plenty of empty chairs, but the boy stayed on his feet. He looked a little the worse for wear, but he'd been through a whole lot of misery in the last couple of days, and who could blame him?

Lester's memories of getting shot by the deputy were a bit muddy—like a pail full of pond water. He remembered going down, seeing Danny kneel next to him, and then he drifted off. He didn't remember a thing about the boy carrying him the three miles back to town. Lester didn't weigh much more than one-fifty, but that was a hell of a lot of pounds to be carrying off the mountain in the cold and snow and dark—especially in the condition Danny was in. Turned out that the cold did Lester a favor by slowing the bleeding a little. And how his ticker survived all that craziness—Lester knew that the man upstairs must have seen to that. He guessed that the big man must not be needing his services just yet.

Lester watched Scott and Skeeter help their mother to her feet. Then he saw how Sarah looked at Danny. She nodded at him, and Danny nodded back. They'd both lost someone special to them. It didn't make it any easier, but at least it was something.

Lester put his hand to Sarah's shoulder as she passed him by. "If I can do anything."

She nodded her thanks, and as the boys guided her frail form toward the parking lot, Scott whispered something to them and walked back over to Danny. Scott looked up at the sky that was slowly turning blue and thought for a minute about what he wanted to say. Danny waited for him to take his time. Finally Scott locked eyes with Danny.

"This whole thing. It's been real hard on my family. Especially Ma. She didn't have but one girl. And . . . well . . . I just wanted to say thank you, is all." Scott tried to hold back the tears, but they came anyway. "Mindy was lucky to have you as a friend, Danny."

Danny looked down at his feet and cleared his throat. "I was the lucky one. Mindy will always be my special friend."

Scott took a deep breath, tried to keep himself composed. "A lot of bad things happened out in those woods, Danny. To you, Lester, and that state-trooper fella." Scott looked toward Mindy's grave for a second. "We all had it wrong about you. All of us. And the state trooper . . . I guess he's gonna be okay. Thank God for that."

Danny nodded—he had heard about what happened to the state trooper from Towanda.

"I'm real sorry. I know things haven't been easy for you." Scott blew on his hands to warm them up a little. "If you had yourself a car, I'd offer to fix it up for you for free."

"That's nice of you. Maybe if one of my washers goes down," Danny said.

"Okay. That's a deal." Scott extended his hand to Danny, and Danny shook it. They looked at each other for another moment, and then Scott rejoined his mother and brother.

Lester glanced to his wife, and she knew his signals. Bonnie kissed him on the cheek, then stepped in front of Danny. She appeared especially small and vulnerable before Danny's wide mass, like a bear cub standing in front of its papa bear. Bonnie put an arthritic finger to Danny's cheek and stroked it gingerly.

"You're gonna heal up just fine, Danny. You're a strong boy. You take care, now." She gave Danny a wink, pulled her jacket around her neck to protect it from the wind, and left him at the grave site in silence.

Only Lester and Danny stayed behind. Lester limped over and stood beside him for a few moments. Not much left to say.

Lester found his pack of cigarettes and tapped one out. He lit up and inhaled deeply. "Hope you don't mind me smoking. The wife is on my case to quit, and I got to sneak 'em in when I can."

"Naw. I don't mind, Sheriff."

The sheriff nodded his appreciation. "How you feeling, son?"

"Okay, I guess."

Lester played with his cigarette a little and then remembered something. He reached into his jacket pocket and pulled out the small wooden robin figurine and held it toward Danny. Danny looked at it and smiled the best he could around the metal pins in his jaw.

"Been carrying this around for you. Nice piece of work. She would've liked it, I bet."

Danny accepted the robin from the sheriff and turned it over in his hands. He noticed that the bird's head and back had been gently sanded and repainted with a fresh coat of orange.

"Touched it up a little for you. The blood sanded right off. Hope you don't mind."

"It looks fine. Thank you." Danny limped up to the coffin and placed the figurine on top of the wooden box. The small bird seemed at home nestled in the flower wreath that was draped over the coffin.

"Happy birthday, Mindy. I'll see you soon," Danny said softly.

Lester flicked his cigarette into the snow and hobbled beside Danny as they made their way back toward the parking lot where Bonnie was waiting.

"Give you a ride, son?"

"Thank you, Sheriff, but I guess I'll walk."

"You sure? Colder than hell out here."

"I like the cold just fine."

"Okay, then. Be seeing you around. Take care of the Wash 'N Dry, you hear?"

Danny nodded that he would. Lester gave him a smile, patted him on the back, and climbed into the passenger seat of his truck. He watched Danny from the sideview mirror, standing all alone in the cold, feet set in the gravel, like he wasn't quite ready to leave the cemetery.

Epilogue

The snow was coming down pretty good. The radio said the storm was going to be around for a few days. Maybe even a week. They said to expect up to fifteen inches. Danny had shoveled away the snow in front of the Wash 'N Dry just like Mr. Bennett had taught him to do. He kept a bag of salt in the closet with the mop and brooms. Before heading to breakfast, he had sprinkled a few handfuls in front of the door so that no one would slip and fall on the way in.

Danny brushed off the powder from his shoulders and stamped his feet on the mat before stepping inside the Friedenshutten. This was the first time he'd been in since all that had happened. He hoped that his jaw wouldn't hurt too much for him to eat his breakfast.

The bell jingled above the door, and all the regulars looked up from their breakfast plates as Danny stepped inside. It got real quiet, and everyone stared at him. Everybody in town knew what had happened, of course, but not many had seen Danny out and about.

Danny felt the stares but didn't look down like he usually did. He nodded at the table of farmers, and they nodded back at him.

"Morning, Danny," one of them said.

"Morning," Danny answered back.

His usual stool at the end of the breakfast counter was empty. Danny made his way toward it when the big man that ran the meat counter at EB's Market patted the empty stool next to him. Danny couldn't remember his name. He didn't buy much fresh meat—it cost too much.

"Why don't you grab yourself a seat? Like to buy you breakfast," said the big man.

Danny nodded his thanks and sat down next to him.

"I'll tell you what. I'll be glad when it's springtime. Had about as much snow as I can take," the big man said, and sipped his coffee.

"Yeah. Springtime sounds nice," Danny answered.

The big man buttered his toast as Dotty walked up to Danny from behind the counter. Dotty had worked at the Friedenshutten for as long as he could remember, but she had never waited on him before. She smiled at Danny and took out her order pad. He figured she wouldn't know what he usually ordered.

"What's it gonna be, Danny? Want a stack of flapjacks?"

Danny thought about it for a second. He always got scrambled eggs with bacon and hash browns. He'd never tried the flapjacks before. "Flapjacks sound fine."

Dotty wrote it down, then took a mug from under the counter. She set it in front of him and gave him a wink.

"If I remember right, you like hot chocolate." She emptied a package of hot chocolate into his mug and filled it with hot water. "The hot chocolate is on me, hon."

"Thanks, Dotty. That's real good of you." Danny mixed the hot chocolate with his spoon and took a small sip. He noticed that Dotty had a daisy flower clipped to the lapel of her uniform. Danny liked daisies.

"That's a pretty flower, Dotty. Looks real nice."

Dotty flashed him a smile. "Watch it, now. I'm a married woman." She moved down the counter, refilling coffee mugs and clearing away plates.

Folks around him slowly went back to their own business. They talked over their breakfast, drank coffee, and exchanged stories about this and that. Everyone seemed to be chatting with a friend or a neighbor or Dotty as she delivered their eggs. Even the big man from the meat counter didn't say anything else to Danny. He was busy talking to a farmer sitting next to him about fly-fishing rods.

Danny listened to all the conversations around the diner that didn't include him. It was all the same folks that usually ate their breakfast first thing in the morning at the Friedenshutten. He knew all the faces and most of their names. Pat worked behind the grill, flipping eggs and making toast. Dotty hustled around doing every-thing now that Mindy was gone. Things seemed different, but kinda the same. Danny didn't sense all the stares and feel like someone who didn't belong there. He didn't feel like all the folks around him wanted him to go away and leave them alone. Didn't feel like they were talking about him and saying mean things. Danny watched all the folks he grew up around, and for the first time since the accident out on the pond he didn't think of himself as dumb and slow but just a little different from everybody else, and that was okay.

A dull ache started up in his jaw as he sipped his hot chocolate and waited for his flapjacks to arrive. He wished that Mindy would be the one delivering them but thought that something different for breakfast sure would be nice.

ACKNOWLEDGMENTS

Getting one's first book published can be a long and arduous journey. The following people made it less so.

Amy Schiffman, with Intellectual Property Group, was there from the beginning and saw something in my book that she insisted had to be shared—her persistence is to be admired and I thank her for that. I am extremely grateful to my agent, Natasha Alexis, and the Zachary Shuster Harmsworth Literary & Entertainment Agency for giving me a shot. I owe a tremendous debt of gratitude to my editor, Vanessa Kehren, and publisher, David Rosenthal, of Blue Rider Press for allowing a kid raised in the sticks the chance to tell a story.

Special thanks to fellow writers Brian Price and Jennifer Robinson-Arellano for giving candid feedback on an early version of this book, which helped shape and transform the story into something worth reading. Thank you to Corporal Scott Bennett, Field

Operations Bureau of the Maryland State Police, for his insight into state law enforcement.

I owe so much to my own personal team. To Ayn Carrillo Gailey, my wife, best friend, and confidante, who supports me in more ways than one. She inspires and edits every story I write before anyone else lays eyes on it. And, last, to my daughter, Gray. Though she be but little, she is fierce, and I draw strength from her every day.